"This book is by far one of the best books that I have ever read. It is beautifully and graphically written, with imagery and visions of Heaven beyond anything that I could have ever imagined. It is a true testament to the wonder-working power of our Creator and exposes the treacherous events that unfold around us constantly without our knowledge. There is a constant battle between the light and the dark and this book certainly brings it back to the forefront of our minds. It has everything you could possibly want in a book, joy, sadness, action, suspense, and beauty beyond belief! Be ready to put things on hold, because you won't be putting it down until the end!"

Jennifer Michiels, Author
Divine Instruction and *Outcry*
www.JenniferMichiels.com

"From the first page until the last; I could not put the book down. The author, Russell Martin, was able to capture my imagination drawing out multiple emotions of excitement, sadness, fear, peace and hopefulness. After reading this book, I absolutely want and desire to be a better Christian and hope that my actions on Earth will help lead others to have an opportunity to experience an eternity of bliss. What a wonderful and detailed description of what Heaven will be like. The book answers many questions and is a warning on demonic warfare. It is a true roadmap for believers and non-believers alike. I can only imagine what I will do or how I will react when the day comes that I go to Heaven. I just hope that everyone takes this opportunity to meet me there! This is a must read for sure."

James Schaefer, Chief Operating
Officer/ Co-Founder
www.DeliveryMaxx.com

"This book has it all... excitement, sadness, happiness, wittiness, love -lots of love- and beauty. Oh my, the perfect portrait of Heaven; I stand amazed! I couldn't turn the pages fast enough... brilliantly written and graphically perfect! The best book, second to the Bible, I've ever read! I loved it, and can't wait for next one in the series! I remember Summer ❤ and can't wait to see her again when I get to Heaven! Thank you for sharing this irreplaceable masterpiece!"

Wanda Harlan
Co-Owner, Office Supervisor & Accountant
Harlan Insurance Agency
www.HarlanInsurance.com

"I have always wondered what Heaven might be like. We all have ideas and most are probably far from the truth. My mother, about a week before she left this earth, said, 'I think I know why God doesn't tell us more about Heaven. If we knew how good it was, too many Christians would be in a hurry to get there!' This book opened my mind to possibilities I had never considered. Rusty is a wonderful story teller and I found myself caught up in his stories about his younger days, his family, and his work experiences. At times I was not able to stop reading as I laughed and cried. So many emotions are stirred by the different real and imagined happenings! I highly recommend *Scars of My Guardian Angel* to anyone who enjoys Christian fiction!"

Roselyn Nicewarner
Retired Computer Consultant and Teacher

More Praise For
Scars of My Guardian Angel

"From the first page to the last, I was captivated by Russell Marin's marvelous writing, feeling like I was right there with Chado through thick and thin. *'Scars'* drew raw emotion right out of my inner being – from hairs standing up on the back of my neck to tears welling in my eyes, from the rush of adrenaline to a calming sense of peace, and from gut-wrenching sorrow to pure elation. Every one of my senses, including my sixth, was tapped by such superb imagery in both the worldly and spiritual realms. And heaven – oh my – what a vivid portrayal of our Creator's true masterpiece! For a fictional novel, *'Scars'* possesses so much truth about the importance of our relationships with each other, our guardian angels, and our Lord and Savior, Jesus Christ. What a blessing it was to read."

Chris K. Moody
President
Osage Energy Group, LLC

Scars of
My Guardian Angel

Weep Not; They Are Just on the Other Side

The Portal Series

✝

A novel by

Russell L. Martin

Lift Up Solutions, LLC
Dry Prong, Louisiana

Scars of My Guardian Angel
Weep Not; They Are Just on the Other Side
The Portal Series

By Russell L. Martin

www.russellmartinauthor.com

Scripture used from the Spirit Filled Life Bible, New King James Version ®. Copyright © 1991, by Thomas Nelson
Novel written following the Gratis Use Guidelines

International Standard Book Number: 978-0-9998366-0-6

Library of Congress Control Number: 2018900741
Lift Up Solutions, LLC, Dry Prong, LA

Published by Lift Up Solutions, LLC
Printed in the United States of America

Cover design by Aaron Michiels

CONTENTS

Scars of
My Guardian Angel

Weep Not; They Are Just on the Other Side

Is

Dedicated to the memory of my beloved daughter,
Summer Allyce Martin
1986-2008

"Therefore you now have sorrow; but I will see you again and your heart will rejoice, and your joy no one will take from you."
John 16:22

From the author:
Some people label strange events in life as coincidence. I agree that some are; but then there are the ones I truly believe are divinely appointed. My daughter was born on the 16th and she was 22 years old when she made her heavenly journey. I was asked by her mother to find a scripture for her headstone. I sought the Lord in prayer to find the perfect verse.
When I opened my Bible, there was no searching;
He brought me directly to John 16:22.

FOREWORD

"Are Angels not all ministering spirits, sent out to serve for the sake of those who are to inherit eternal salvation? Therefore, we must pay closer attention to what we have heard..." (Hebrews 1:14 -2:1).

God's Word is replete with the mention of angels. We find them intervening in the affairs of nations, often executing judgment upon them. Angels are found to offer comfort, herald the Gospel, and guide the people of God. They are also shown to afford relief and protection for the people of God regardless of crisis. The latter are known as Guardian Angels.

Russell L. Martin is a multi-gifted brother in Christ. He is an exceptionally gifted storyteller. He is excited about sharing the Gospel and fleshing it out. Whether it be in his beloved song lyrics and music he composes for the body of Christ or in his writing of this book, Rusty loves glorifying God.

I first discovered Rusty Martin when I became his Worship Pastor at New Prospect Baptist Church in 2010. I could tell as I led worship that Rusty loved the Lord. His whole manner of worship was so reverent and respectful of God's presence among us. Not much time had passed when my wife, Sandy and I were invited to his home. He and his wife, Laura welcomed us with open arms. We quickly realized we were all kindred spirits. I soon appreciated that what you see is what you get with my friend Rusty. He is what you call the genuine article. He is a man of God. He loves his wife, family, and his horses. The deep southern "country" life suits him to a tee. Let me warn you now, don't let that "southern gentleman" nature fool you. Rusty has been around, he's had ups and downs in his life. He's seen a thing or two, because he's been involved with a thing or two. All of this is Rusty Martin and so much more. It forces him to create. It drives him to communicate. It motivates him to produce and fashion incredible stories about that which matters to him most, that which has saved his life, and gripped his heart...His God.

As much as I am astounded by the songwriter who is Rusty Martin. I am even more excited about the storyteller, Russell L Martin. When he first told me about writing this book, I had no doubt that he could. However, I marveled at the short period of time that it took him to write this book. The only explanation is the fullness of God in his life and therefore the prompting of the Spirit. I am convinced this book was written from a place of overflow; a place where the words flow like the water over the rocks of a southern creek.

I am an educated man; it has been my delight to read many books. There are a rare few novels that caused my soul to tremble and my mind's eye to see so vividly that which the author writes about. *"Scars of my Guardian Angel"* is such a rare book indeed.

I want to be in that throne room when God scolds Satan: *"Silence son of darkness. Have you wisdom so great that you now see into the mind of The Alpha and Omega? Were you there when I formed the springs of the deep, or when I breathed life into the nostrils of man?"*

I am transported to Heaven when one finds out about the athletic prowess of one John the Baptist and that we might find a baseball league there, when we read *"...when I first got to Tabula Rosa, he hinted around about playing baseball, Allayer and Nipper said he was a strikeout king."*

I rejoice at the visual imagery and heart capturing script that is the "Valley of the Children" *"God calls this the Valley of the Children because this is where we receive the aborted babies...Tears of joy fill my eyes as the ancestor pulls the aborted baby back through the portal..."* Wow, glory to God!!
This book is full of real life stories mixed with the possible spiritual activities of God we will find on the other side of death.

When I first picked this book up to read, I could not put it down. It is full of hope and mystery. One can find tears of sadness and joy in these pages. I can easily see Heaven and walk down her golden avenues and admire the various mansions. I am reminded of the wiles of the devil and to know my enemy. You can quickly realize an Angel's role in your life as a child of God. There is so much here to digest, and such an easy read.

Find yourself a quiet place and a couple hours. Be prepared to feel the brush of angel wings, the wrinkle of a gentle smile as it appears on your face, and then hear the gentle breeze through the trees and the laughter of aborted children as they run across your front lawn. You will struggle to walk away from the journey of Chado Cole. Do not be afraid to embrace the nearness of God.

Russell L. Martin knows he has a Guardian Angel. That knowledge has caused him to share this incredible tale of what it could be like to be in a personal relationship with your protecting Angel. Furthermore, and more importantly, to be in a relationship with a Savior that provides that Angel for you! It is my prayer that God will use this book to bring you great encouragement and joy in your journey.

Rev. Ronnie J. LaLande
CEO, GospelMaxx
www.gospelmaxx.com

1

Little Soul

A silence fell over the throne room as the Angels of Heaven watched closely when Lucifer came to present himself before the Lord.

The Lord God said to Satan, "Lucifer son of perdition; why are you walking with the Host of Heaven? What business do you have here? Where is it you have come from?"

Satan answered the Lord, "I have need of your mighty patience and that you would bend your ear to listen to my request as I humbly stand before you and the Host of Heaven. I have been walking upon the earth, roaming throughout, passing back and forth."

"Deceiver of man, you have my ear, I will hear your request."

"Oh God of Heaven and Earth, Designer of the stars, I seek the soul of a child. His bloodline has no purpose to you."

"What child do you seek, Prince of the air?"

"My servants informed me that the Christ has visited this Little Soul and allowed him to see into the Spiritual Realm. This child's bloodline has been cursed for six generations. His fathers before him have rejected the Holy Trinity. Allow me this request; he is of no value to you. God of Abraham, take away his hedge of protection, surely you have no need of this Little Soul."

"Silence son of darkness. Have you wisdom so great that you now see into the mind of the Alpha and Omega? Were you there when I formed the springs of the deep, or when I breathed life into the nostrils of man? Have you knowledge of how to create the birth of a galaxy? Son of perdition, I hear the reverent prayers of this Little Soul's mother, and her groaning from fasting cries out to me in the night. As she humbles herself before this throne, I shall break this generational curse with the father of this child you call, Little Soul."

* * *

Eight years earlier; it was August 25th 1960, when a proud father of his second son leans over, resting his head against the thick glass of a newborn nursery. Staring at this little 7lb, 8oz., bundle of joy, Mr. Travis breaks into a subtle smile, relieved that mom's ok and we seem to have all ten toes and fingers. He's got a bit of a cone head, but that's normal considering just making a journey through the birth canal.

Travis feels a slight tug on his pants leg; it's the three year old big brother, Gerald. "Hey there big man, you want to see your baby brother?" The dark eyed toddler stretches his arms out for a lift up. He settles in on the hip of his tall slender father as they both continue to stare at the only baby in the nursery of this small family clinic.

"Daddy, what his name is?"

Travis points to the name tag on the front of the clear plastic crib. "See right there, it says Chad Cole."

The toddler giggles, "Shadow, Shadow, Shadow."

"No big man, it's Chad Cole."

Gerald shakes his head, "Shadow, his name Shadow."

"Well big man, he will probably be your little shadow, so what if we give him a nickname and call him Chado? How's that?"

"Okay Daddy, Chado my brother's name."

Travis grins from ear to ear as he follows Gerald. The happy toddler bounces all the way back down the hall to Mom's room. "Chado, Chado, Chado' Momma, my brother's name is Chado."

Mrs. Mildred, very tired from just giving birth, looks over at Travis, "What's he saying, Shadow or Chado?"

"Well honey, usually folks wait awhile before they give their kid a nickname, baby brother has only been here a couple hours and Gerald just gave him one. He's saying Chado."

Nurse Louise comes in the room smiling, "Mrs. Mildred, are you ready to make that trip back home to Black Creek?"

"Yes Ma'am, I am ready!" Louise rolls her out to the parking lot and kindly helps a slow moving mom climb into an ole 1951 four door car. Travis drives out of the small town of Montgomery, Louisiana, making his way through the back-roads leading home.

* * *

We lived in a humble little wood frame house nestled in heavy timber country with a crystal clear creek within a rock throw from our house. We actually were blessed with an old pump that furnished my Granny's house and ours with water from that spring fed creek.

Our local church also used the swimming hole for baptisms. I missed out on getting dunked in our creek because I was saved in the wintertime. We used a sister church that had an indoor baptistery, thank God, because Black Creek was ice cold. Our community was named after that creek; it was our little piece of Heaven on Earth.

13

I guess I had a normal childhood, other than hovering at or around the poverty level, but we never seemed to want for anything. We lived almost entirely off the land with fresh vegetables from granny's garden, having an occasional hog killing, deer meat, fresh eggs and butter from the chickens and our milk cows. Granny had peach trees scattered all over the place, and a huge fig tree on each side of the barn. Man, my granny had a green thumb; everything she planted seemed to be blessed. It wasn't unusual for me or my older brother to have peach juice running down our chins or elbows from the biggest peaches you have ever seen.

There were several times when we had little or no money and my dad would work at a local gravel pit running a dragline. But this was a seasonal job; he was often laid off during the winter. My dad would set what we called drop hooks in a nearby lake to catch "mud cat" a type of catfish we had in our local waterways. They were a little less desirable than what you get in a restaurant. But in those days, folks would give Dad a few bucks for a few pounds.

Getting paid to fish might sound like easy work, but it was not. I remember Dad getting back from the lake after running his lines and hovering over the wood stove to warm up. He would often complain about having to break the ice to get to his lines. He had a big cage in the creek he would store his fish in to keep them alive. I don't think the fish sales were a big money maker but it did keep the lights on. You know, when I've found myself complaining about how rough my dad was on us, I remind myself that he really did all he could to provide for our family during those lean times.

We had an awesome mom who seemed to always lead us in the right direction, and one of those directions was straight to our local church. My brother and I knew better than trying to avoid going. If the doors were open at the church, she was herding us through. I thank God for my mom.

My brother was three years older than I was, and buddy, he reminded me of that regularly. I was either getting beat up or held down. Often when he held me down, he would drip spit over my face and then skillfully slurp it back up, just before the long gross spittle broke off landing on my forehead. You know - showing the brotherly love. There were times when I was able to make him retreat if I could get my hands on a weapon of some kind...a stick, ball bat, hatchet, or oh yeah, the BB gun.

Once, I was sneaking around the house and about to take aim at a defenseless red bird sitting on the power line connected to the house, when ole brother grabbed my BB gun. He snatched it so quickly the sight cut my hand. He took aim, killed my bird, turned back around and threw my cherished gun on the ground. He walked off, giggling all the way across the yard toward granny's house.

That was it; I slowly cocked my BB gun, took close aim and popped him on the back of the head. Yes, I was in trouble... my brother got carted off to the doctor to get a BB cut out of his head, and if memory serves me I got my heinie torn up. I regret popping him, but that day was a turning point in our relationship. From then on he used more caution when being hateful to his little brother.

During our woodsy secluded childhood we didn't get a lot of company and the highlight of our year was our family reunion. We would all gather down at the camp house located at the creek. Everyone that could play an instrument or sing would gather up and play together. The music, smiles, and laughter seemed to never end. Our swimming hole would be full of shivering blue-lipped cousins and floating chilled watermelons due to the ice cold spring fed creek. Even after all these years, I can still remember the sound of the guitars and mandolins echoing through the creek bottom. After all our kin would go home, sadness would come around. But it was slowly removed by our dad lining us out on chores or teaching us to throw a curve ball.

Thinking back over that part of my life I thank God for it and I wouldn't have traded it for anything.

As we got older, I learned a few things about my dad that made me understand more clearly why he was a bit rough around the edges. From all the stories we were told he had a wild childhood and trust me that side of him would occasionally show up. He was a day-light to dark hard worker and he expected us to walk the same road.

To say dad's childhood was rough is putting it mildly. One incident he told us about stands out in my mind. This particular day, dad's older brother...who was the oldest of nine kids was attempting to open, what was known in those days as an ice box. As he did, Grandma Green threw a butcher knife sticking my uncle in the calf of his leg, and hollered; "stay out of the ice box!"

My uncle left home at that point and moved to California. My dad and one other brother joined the military to get away from the ongoing family battle field.

Dad told me that sometimes for Christmas, he would get one apple and a box of shotgun shells. When he opened the shells, he was warned that he'd better not waste any on cans or bottles; they were to be used to bring in wild game.

All in all, my dad was well liked in the community. He loved his family the best way he knew how, and eventually came to know the Lord on his death bed.

We went to school in Dry Prong, a small hick town located a few miles south of Black Creek. At this point everything seemed to be normal until desegregation came in the picture. Some idiots in Washington decided to bus us way over to Colfax, Louisiana, to attend school, while having their kids in private schools. Go figure.

We were about to be attending school where the famous 1873 Colfax Massacre occurred. The democrats back in those early days were in bed with and running the KKK. This politically driven historic and horrible massacre resulted in the deaths of 60 to 80 black and white citizens of Grant Parish.

This was not a place where you would want to even have a school, much less throwing everyone in this chaotic soup bowl.

We were the test dummies of the seventies. I didn't have a problem with getting along with blacks, actually I have to hand it to my dad; our family wasn't anti-black at all. He had several black friends, as a matter of fact. I looked at blacks the same way I looked at everybody else. Well I was about to meet the city side of thinking.

On my first day of school, I was standing alone because I didn't know anyone. Some knot-headed black guy and his gang of twelve to fifteen friends walked up and the leader of the group smacked me on the side of the face. To his surprise, I didn't back down, I threw my books down and wore that dude out. He soon realized I was stronger than he thought...and that he'd picked the wrong kid to walk up and hit. I'd spend the summers peeling piling by scraping the bark off cypress poles used for power lines. This is very hard work and makes you stout.

Having an older brother to fight with also helped my ability to defend myself. Although I taught that gang leader a lesson that day, I was now labeled as a scrapper and ended up fighting regularly... so my grades tanked. I got suspended more times than I can remember. It was a struggle from there on to the twelfth grade, and I finally dropped out before I could finish my last year.

Through all the trouble in my school years that came from the deep rooted historical hate, in my heart I never held any animosity toward the black community from how I was treated. My beliefs were to love everyone.

2

Soggy Bottom of the Gulf

So, now that I missed the small boat of education, I entered into the school of hard knocks. I was a pipeliner for years working in or around the oil & gas industry when one day I was reading a magazine that had an article about the coolest job in the world. Deep Sea Diver, "Oh yeah, that's me." I got enrolled straight away down in Houston at a deep sea diver academy, and went through 18 weeks of rigorous training. Before I knew it, I was standing on the back of a pipeline lay barge, ready to jump with a deep sea helmet and garb on looking like a bad Jules Verne movie.

After gaining skills and becoming a pretty decent diver, I set my sights on getting in on the super deep stuff. That's where the real money was. But you didn't just get a degree, walk out on a barge and say "I'm here for saturation dives." I met a few divers that worked for years and never got the opportunity. In some cases this is due to dive politics - who you know - and in other cases some divers are simply just not cut out for the work. Well in short, saturation diving was my goal.

I had a long road ahead of me to reach my goal and to prove my capabilities. I worked hard and fast and got to the point that when it was my turn I would try to beat everyone's bottom time, and often did. The less time the lay barge was shut down for a dive the more the oil company and the barge captain liked it. That meant they wanted you in the lineup more often.

I was coming up from a pretty normal dive out of a couple hundred foot of water. As I was slowly making my way up what we called the "down line," going through the in water decompression stops... O yeah, let me explain a couple things.

The down line is a safety line tied to the jet sled that sits on the bottom. The jet sled is used as a huge ditching machine to cut a ditch up to ten feet deep on the ocean floor, and it's attached to the barge by huge cables called Popeye lines. These lines allow the barge to pull the jet sled along the bottom, cutting the ditch for the welded steel oil line to sink down into.

Okay, I'm coming up the line very slowly, talking with topside and he's directing me when to stop for decompression. Each stop would last a few minutes, following the Navy Dive Tables. At this point - around ninety feet deep - I was moving into the light from the barge illumination. Total darkness below, I could hardly see my feet and my upper body had penetrated the light. I was literally hanging on the edge of darkness. It was probably the coolest sight I had ever witnessed, unlike any other dive. The water was so clear, you'd think you could see forever, but at this depth, it was like the light said this is where I stop.

Let's talk about the biggest fish in the world. The guys on topside were asking me if I was seeing any fish. Well, I had just seen a small school of Amberjack that had passed by. They caught me off guard because they came from behind and were traveling at a high rate of fish speed and came within a couple of feet of my head.

I shared my little surprise, what I thought was funny. Funny then turned into, what the heck is that? When I had just settled in on a five minute decompression stop around eighty feet deep, I witnessed what looked to be a swimming RV camper. I don't know if it was a Whale Shark or something else; all I know is I noticed how small I was, in this huge ocean helplessly dangling on a line with this unknown whale of a fish, not moving away but circling me. I immediately asked topside how long I had left on this water stop and also let them know I had just seen the biggest fish in the world. Either it wasn't hungry, or it was just curious about this small wiggly thing suspended on a line with bubbles coming out of its mouth. I believe the latter, it moved on and I chalked it up as one of the most awesome dives of my career.

I had a buddy that I met back at Dive Academy who kind of adopted me as a big brother. Matt was from Illinois, and let me tell you, he was so funny and witty you couldn't help but really like the guy. Matt had a strong northern accent and didn't seem to have the skills of someone coming up with a strong work background. This might have been one of the reasons Matt took to me. He saw early on that I was comfortable with physical labor and maybe he felt he could learn from me. I had earned my work ethics from my dad, and it came in handy during our dive training.

We went through eighteen weeks of vigorous commercial dive training in Houston, Texas. We were trained in underwater welding, saturation dives, advanced physics, advanced physiology, dive medicine, rescue, advanced rigging and well, you name it; we went through it. Shortly after school, I found myself signing on with a deep sea dive company, and my little adopted brother Matt followed right along. We both worked for one of the global dive companies in south Louisiana. I soon found out I could do a little freelancing on the side with other dive companies when they were a little slow. And yes, Matt followed. I really got use to Matt being around. He turned out to be a pretty good and trusted friend.

3

When Things Go Wrong

We were working on a lay barge installing a 12" steel oil and gas pipeline on the bottom of the Gulf of Mexico. Our working depth was around one hundred seventy feet deep when we all learned just how easily things can go wrong.

The incident occurred sometime in the middle of the night, I'm not really sure on the time, at this point some worker came and woke me out of a deep sleep and stated, "hey bud, it's your turn to dive." I jumped out of the rack and tried to shake off the sleepy head syndrome. I slowly moseyed over to the galley and grabbed me a gallon of hot water that I could use to pour in my wet suit to keep me warm on the dive, and then headed out to do my chore.

When I got to the dive shack, the guy running the dive lined me out on what I actually already knew I needed to do. There were no special details involved, I was to go down while the whole pipe laying operation was on all stop, at least until the diver returned to the surface. This was a safety precaution we tried to follow. It was one safety rule we liked, we didn't want anything moving down there but the diver especially in total darkness.

On my dive, I was also to check all hydraulic lines and Popeye lines on our jet sled, then crawl down into the ditch that's below seabed level and walk down the ditch away from the barge checking depth of pipe and depth of ditch. The gas company wanted us to walk back at least three to four pipe joints away from the barge, checking depth of the ditch to insure proper cover so that nothing would harm the pipeline as it rested in this seven foot pipeline grave.

Each joint section was 40 feet long, so when you were 170 feet down to the bottom and 160 feet to the end of the last pipe joint and also an extra 100 feet of drag length behind the barge itself, you were pushing around 450 feet from the barge, give or take a few inches. If you were to get in trouble that far away from the barge you could be in a world of hurt.

After a bit of small talk with the tenders and a couple other divers, we hear over the intercom, "Jump diver." At this point, I pour my gallon of warm water inside my wet suit and my tender helps me get geared up with my dive helmet and checks everything out. He walks me over near the edge, then turns away to check my dive lines to make sure nothing is tangled in this carefully rolled up figure eight pile of 800 feet of dive line. While he was busy making sure everything was a go, I'm standing on the edge of the barge in position to jump and looking at the water. The sight of the twelve to fifteen foot seas had my heart racing with excitement, the adrenaline pumping, making every muscle in my body swell with overheated blood. As I gazed down at the sea, I'm thinking, what a wild ride this is and how with each jump, my life is in God's hands.

I feel the tender's hand hit me twice on the back, a signal letting me know that everything is a go. At that point I jump with a twelve foot drop to the water. I splash down and immediately descend, grabbing onto the down line that leads directly to the jet sled. As my speed picks up on the descent, it seems my ears pop every few feet as I continue to feel the minor shock from the decrease in water temperature as I swim through each atmosphere. The illumination from the barge lights fade as I pass through the light penetration level and then total darkness.

I finally reach my destination, the jet sled. On every dive, I would get a sense of comfort when I arrived at the sled. I really never understood that, but it was a sort of comfort and that's nice at any depth. After arriving at the sled, I immediately start working on this two story monster of a machine. I climb slowly around on it, inspecting several checkpoints and find everything in working order.

4

Trip Down the Ditch

Let me pause a second. You're probably wondering why this guy isn't using a light. We didn't use lights on most of our dives, because with the jet sled being shut down just before a dive, the bottom was so stirred and muddied, hand held lights were useless and just something else to carry. But to be able to accomplish my task, I had to close my eyes and concentrate on where to go, and feel. This was a trick I learned from an old diver, Dee Sautell. He told me if I wanted to get really good and fast underwater in total darkness to use this technique. He said, "when you're standing around on the barge before the jet sled is lowered in the water and it's sitting on the back of the barge, just start staring at it, then shut your eyes and try to remember where everything is at on the sled. Open, look and then close your eyes again and so on." I remembered what he taught me, and I stuck to this advice or should I say his wisdom, and it worked. Okay, back to the ditch.

I then climbed down and off the sled, and stood on the soggy, muddy ocean floor, while keeping a hand on the machine as I moved toward the back. I recognized each nut, bolt, and clamp with the touch of my hand, as if I had an old black and white photo etched in my memory. I know I'm near the edge of a seven foot drop off into the cut ditch, so I shuffle one foot ahead, hoping I'm on the mark. Suddenly, I'm there, I feel the edge, and I grab the knotted rope hanging off the back of the sled. We use this rope to get in and out of the excavation.

I rappel to the bottom of the ditch, turn and head away from the sled down the ditch line. I continue to communicate with the guys on the surface, letting them know where and what I'm doing. At this point I advise topside, "I'm ready to start checking depth." We used what was called a pneumo to check depth.

Let me explain how a pneumo works. It is simply an airline connected to a gauge that is used to measure depth. The crew on the surface would apply air pressure through the pneumo, forcing all the water out of the quarter-inch line connected to the diver's safety harness. I would then hold the line and wait until I felt bubbles and that the tip of the pneumo was on the point where they would document the depth. Our slang communication words were, "SHOOT THE PNEUMO." The guys logging info would let you know what they wanted and it was usually at the bottom of the ditch, top of pipe or natural bottom for our logged depth readings.

Okay, I was positioned on the bottom, below the sea bed in a seven foot excavation, when I began to have trouble concentrating. I closed my eyes in order to force myself to focus and try to fight against this first symptom of nitrogen narcosis.

This is a type of sickness you start experiencing around one hundred and fifty feet deep. The best way I could explain this reaction is you feel drunk or high and it could be very dangerous. Some divers have been known to freak out and try to take off their dive helmet or other sorts of crazy things, kind of like someone who's had way too much to drink, while others can control it or tolerate it better. At this depth we would depend on our dive supervisor, who would have to make a decision whether to start using mixed gas to offset this sickness or just monitor the diver and get by with normal breathing air supplied from the surface. I had built up a sort of tolerance or had just come to a point of controlling it, sort a like someone that could hold his liquor better than others.

I started moving down the pipeline ditch sliding my hand along the surface of the pipe, knowing each time I would feel a shrink sleeve located at each weld or pipe connection, that I had moved another forty feet away from getting back to the sled. Upon feeling each connection I would report back to the surface. They would in turn say at each joint section, "SHOOT PNEUMO".

On this particular dive, there was enough current after shutting down the jet sled, that the water cleared up midway through my dive. I had opened my eyes to the black darkness and to my surprise; I could see millions of particles of glowing phosphorus. Each one suspended, hanging in the darkness, glowing, giving off enough light together that I could almost see. This strange scene made me wonder how the silt had moved away from my area and the particles of phosphorus remained. All just suspended, looking like a distant galaxy within an arm's length away. The only way I could possibly try to explain what I was seeing would be to imagine standing in space with a million tiny stars surrounding you. It was beautiful.

As I continued making my way down the pipeline, almost to the last checkpoint, I noticed a change in the sound of my air coming out of the free flow valve. The free flow was a continuous flow of air in your helmet that worked together with your oral-nasal air supply. The free flow would force extra air into your helmet so you wouldn't over breath and deplete your breathing air when you were working fast and hard. The sound was like hearing an air tank that you had opened a valve on and it was slowing down losing pressure.

I had the thought that maybe I bumped the valve and it had turned down.

I immediately reached up on my helmet and started turning my free flow valve to the wide open position. But I had to really concentrate to do it, and was unsure that I was turning it the right way because my body was saturated with nitrogen, making me feel stoned.

My air started to smell of petroleum and I could even seem to taste it in my mouth and nostrils. I frantically told the guys top side, "Check my air."

A moment of silence, again I tell them, "I believe I'm running out, check my air, check my air!"

5

Chaos on Deck

Before my late night dive, midway through the project we had several break downs. The equipment we had brought was two separate 5120 diesel air compressors. They usually work very well, but this job seemed to be what I call snake bit... what some people would refer to as jinxed or cursed. After a few days of use, both the 5120's broke down, so we were relying on the two small electric compressors located down inside the barge in the decompression room. It's a very nice setup when everything is working. Later, we got word the night of my dive that one of the electric compressors went down, the cooling line blew and it was losing so much air it was no help. We should have shut all dives down until everything was replaced, but money and time were more important than the lives of our dive team. Go figure... a huge oil company and a major dive company in the Gulf watching out for a few humans, not a chance! I believe sometimes these huge companies don't realize their field supervisors are gambling with our lives.

So now we were relying on one small air compressor to supply around 200 psi and furnish the entire diving operation with breathable air. It takes that much pressure to supply one diver at 200 feet deep. And here we were using it to supply a diver and a chamber with bad seals. That's tough to stay up with, even for the 5120's.

Remember my adopted little brother Matt? He was in charge of running the decompression chamber that night. He usually did a good job, but I believe he was unaware of the air compressor issues.

29

Not only were we having trouble with compressors, we were also having problems with the seals on the chamber doors. Both needed changing, inner door and the outer door. The chamber had an inner area where you would have your diver lay back while you ran him through the Navy Dive Tables. Time spent in the chamber depended on how long your bottom time was. It usually took around an hour on a normal 200 foot dive. When you finished running a diver through and he was out of the chamber, you would then clean the chamber up a bit, wipe out the oxygen mask with a little vinegar and then blow the inner chamber back down to around 80 feet of depth pressure. Rule of thumb, you would always leave the outer door open. Now the chamber is ready for the next diver.

Leaving 80 foot of pressure on the inner chamber was a safety precaution, so that if your compressor was to break down and you had a diver in need of a chamber run, you would have enough pressure stored that you could put a guy in, close the outer door then release the stored pressure from the inner chamber and blow him down to a depth of forty feet.

On this particular night, Matt was in the process of attempting to blow the chamber back down to 80 feet. Actually, he was getting it ready for me. This was a chamber run that would never happen.

Matt and the diver that just got out of de-compression were having a hard time getting a seal on the inner door. Matt was throwing as much pressure at that inner door as he could, trying to get it to seal. He didn't realize that he was draining the whole system, or that he would be part of the events that would kill his buddy 600 feet away.

I don't blame Matt; he was doing all he could to work with the junky equipment we had. I'm pretty sure we were all to blame with this critical mistake we made to continue with the scheduled dives. The two old 5120 air compressors should have been taken out of service years ago. On top of crappy machinery, the rubber seals on the chamber doors should have been inspected and changed out before allowing any diver in the water. It's strange how things turn out.

6

"Check My Air, Check My Air!"

While I was waiting for topside to answer my distress call, what seemed like minutes was actually only a few seconds. These brief seconds I was continuing to twist and turn on my free flow valve, hoping I had only bumped it somehow and everything would be straightened out so that I could continue my work. This was wishful thinking. All of a sudden, an unfamiliar voice came over the com speaking loudly and I could hear the panic in his voice, shouting, "GET BACK TO THE JET SLED, GET BACK TO THE JET SLED" over and over.

I was standing down inside the excavation at the end of the fourth pipeline joint, some one hundred and sixty feet from the jet sled when I received that panicked message. As the message echoed in my head, my heart started racing when I realized the other sound I'm hearing is my air pressure slowly fading away. The intoxication of nitrogen narcosis had now saturated my system and I found it hard to make decisions. Standing in total darkness, I realized I didn't know for sure which direction the jet sled is in. I could tell from reaching down and touching the pipe with my hand it was either to the right or the left. This simple decision had to be made now. I was running out of precious seconds. I quickly turned to my right and started to run as fast as I could possibly go under water, wearing deep sea gear. The loud voice on the com had stopped and all I could hear now was the last bit of air pressure coming from an exhausted system. As I leaned into a forward direction heading for the sled, I had a horrible thought, what if I run into the back of the sled and break the glass in my helmet? I quickly

32

stuck my hands out in front to avoid slamming into this huge machine. By this time, I had to heave on the oral nasal for the last bit of air in the system. Even though I was in the best physical condition of my life, I suddenly had to make the hardest one hundred and sixty foot run in dive history.

On my arrival to the jet sled, the first thing I felt with my hands was the knotted rope hanging off the back that we used to climb in and out of the excavation. At this point, I felt that small sense of comfort I mentioned earlier on each visit to the bottom as I would reach the sled. But this time was a bit different, getting back to the sled didn't take away the fact I was almost totally out of air. Getting a good grip on the knotted rope, I started climbing and suddenly remembered I had a small bailout bottle on my back. This bottle held extra air in case of an emergency. I guess the excitement of this discovery and being drunk from the effects of nitrogen narcosis, along with a bit of panic, would be enough to confuse anyone.

I immediately reached up with one hand and started turning the valve on my bailout, while holding onto the rope with the other hand. Suspended still hanging over the ditch, I had another simple task. I was to turn the valve to the open position, *is it to the left or to the right?* Such a simple task...I keep turning the valve, but nothing is happening. *It can't be...*I believe when I first discovered my air problem and all the chaos started, I must have accidentally turned on my bailout bottle. This whole time, I was using up my emergency air. I had to face the fact that my last few pounds of air were about spent.

My energy was starting to fade, as I was struggling for each breath, trying hard to inhale the last bit of air remaining in the system. I continued to climb up this two story monster, thinking if I could just make it back to the top of the sled, somehow, some way, they would get my air back on. I was sure that by this time a standby diver was on his way down. As I climbed up the sled, suddenly I realized my dive line has snagged somewhere behind me. My heart sinks.

7

Killed My Best Friend

The loud speaker booming, "DIVER OUT OF AIR, DIVER OUT OF AIR, JUMP EMERGENCY DIVER!"

The standby diver is supposed to be sitting in a chair on the back of the barge, with all his gear on and his dive helmet in his lap, ready to be in the water and to the bottom within a few short minutes. Our Emergency Diver was sitting in the dive shack, hanging out in street clothes, shooting the breeze with the tenders.

The workers were gathering at the back of the barge, staring over the edge not saying much, some mumbling, "I wonder if he's still alive."

Two of the divers grabbed the dive line and started pulling as fast as possible, commanding some of the nearby riggers to join in.

"Hey you guys grab hold and y'all pull and pull hard, he's out, he's out of air."

Matt and a co-worker were still jacking with the chamber trying to get a seal on the inner door, and from the loud noise of the air blowing in the chamber, he could hear the intercom but couldn't make it out what they were saying. As he shut off the valve, Matt was griping, "This junky equipment, we need to let the air build back up, this electric compressor is a piece of crap, they should know one compressor can't keep up." The guy with him told Matt, "Hey hush up for a second, there's something going on upstairs, what are they saying on the com?"

As they walked away from the noisy struggling compressor, they could now hear the loud speaker, it was still repeating, "Jump diver, EMT to dive shack, diver out of air."

Matt suddenly realized, and shouted to the other diver, "That's my buddy; he's still on the bottom, Oh, no!" He then suddenly ran back to the compressor and looked at the gauge, and it had built back up to a lousy 43 psi. Matt started running toward the dive shack, saying over and over, "Oh my God, Oh my God, I've killed my best friend, Oh my God!"

When Matt reached the shack, in a frantic tone, "Is he ok? Is he ok?" At this point the dive supervisor, Captain Lee, was on the scene and had taken over the dive operation. Matt came in shouting, "Is he alive?"

Lee responded, "Be quiet! I can't hear!"

Jimmy, the guy that was running the dive, passed Matt on his way out. The look on his face told Matt without having to say anything, this was bad. Other workers were coming to the shack asking stupid questions. At this point Lee shouted, "Okay that's enough!" Turning to Matt he shouted "Get them out of here now!"

Lee had just told the guys on deck over the intercom to stop pulling him up. At about the same time a tender rushed in the shack and announced, "He's hung up! We can't pull him up!"

Lee turned to Matt and said, "If they had pulled him to the surface as fast as they were going it would kill him."

Lee stated, "What in the world is wrong with our compressors?"

Matt looked down at the floor and mumbled, "I didn't mean to."

Lee responded, "What in the hell are you talking about?"

Matt explained, "Captain, I unintentionally drained the system trying to get the chamber ready for the next run. We lost all of our air pressure trying to get that inner door to seal. I didn't realize..."

"Okay, ok I get the picture." Now Lee was mumbling, "I knew we should have shut this whole damned operation down until we got some decent equipment!"

"Captain, let's just hope he's got enough air in his bailout to hold him until the emergency diver gets down there."

"Hey Chado, can you hear me? Talk to me son. Hey bud, are you there? Talk to me, let me hear you. Are you ok?"

"I'm here. I'm here. It isn't good Captain. My bailout's gone."

"Roger that. We're about to jump an emergency diver now. Where are you?"

"The sled, I'm at the sled."

"Roger that. Stay calm. We're on our way."

Struggling, only a few feet from reaching the top of the sled, I suddenly realize I'm hung up. Somewhere behind me my dive line has fouled. I pull hard trying to free my line. It's no good, it's tangled somewhere below. At that point a deep sense of fear came over me as I knew I was beat. Suddenly out of nowhere a sort of peace started to push the fear away.

I decided to let go, and as I loosened my grip I started to fall backward and down and as I was falling, I said out loud, "God, I guess you've got me!"

The voice of Captain Lee on the com was starting to fade.

"Hey Chado, what did you say? Come back, please repeat. Come back, repeat."

When I landed on my back, it was a gentle touchdown on this soft muddy bottom. I was dizzy to the point of passing out and I could feel the cold water being slowly forced into my helmet from lack of pressure. I knew at this moment it was almost over. I then opened my eyes to this cold dark world and I guess you could call this my last surprise on Earth. I started to smile because I could still see the millions of phosphorus particles glowing against the darkness. At this moment I felt a peace beyond all understanding or comprehension. I closed my eyes for what seemed to be only a few seconds, and I felt a tug on my right arm and then the left. *Could this be two divers coming to rescue me?* When I opened my eyes expecting to see divers coming to pull me out of this dark tomb, it wasn't divers at all.

* * *

Matt, now standing at the back of the barge slumped over with what seem to be a half a can of snuff in his lip. Shaking his head as he looks over into the water wondering. *What the hell just happened?*

Captain Lee walks up and tells Matt, "Hey bud, the rescue diver is almost on bottom looking for Chado. Come on back to the shack and let's listen in." They walk in the shack and hear the chatter back and forth.

"Roger that, I'm almost to the sled."

"Okay, Nate; how's your visibility?"

"Vis is good, no muddy water here. All the silt has cleared away. Dang!"

"Nate, what's wrong?"

"Ah, it's my light blinking on and off."

"Roger that, just when you need them they take a crap," chuckle, "Roger that."

"Okay, I'm coming up on the sled."

"Roger, you see Chado?"

"Negative Sir. He's not on the sled."

"How's the current?"

"Moderate."

"Roger that. Is it enough to wash him away?"

"Maybe so sir; can't tell yet."

"Hey, Nate, this is Lee."

"Hey, Captain."

"Look, the last time I heard Chado on the com, he said he had made it to the sled."

"Roger that Captain."

"Nate."

"Yeah, Captain?"

"Nate, I believe I heard him talking to God."

"Captain Lee."

"Yeah, Nate go ahead."

"Ahhh, come back on that last transmission."

"I said he was talking to God."

"Roger that Captain. Hey, Captain Lee, you mind telling me what they were talking about?"

"Roger that, I think I heard him tell God, '*God, I guess you've got me.*' "

"Roger that Captain. Wait... I found his dive line!"

"We copy you Nate."

"Following his dive line."

"Roger that, Nate."

39

"Hey Captain, I see why the tenders couldn't pull him up."

"We copy; what's it hung on?"

"All the slack he had out when he was at the end of the last pipe joint looped around when he was on his way back and must have hung on the bottom of the sled."

"We read you bud; he's got to be close."

"Roger that Captain, I'm continuing to follow his line...Dang!"

"What's wrong Nate?"

"My light, it went out again and it's dark as a sack of black cats down here."

"We read you, don't waste time trying to fix it, follow his dive line."

"Wow, what the heck is that?"

"Come back Nate, we didn't read you, come back, what are you seeing?"

"I can't believe."

"We read you. Talk to us son. What are you seeing?"

"Ahhh, Captain I don't need a light anymore."

"Repeat last transmission, you say your light is back on?"

"Negative Sir, I don't need a light, I can see. Captain, you said Chado was talking to God?"

"Roger that."

"Well I believe God is down here right now."

"Come back Nate, what are you talking about?"

"Captain, you know the phosphorus that the jet sled stirs up out of the mud of the Gulf floor?"

"You bet; it's usually scattered all over the place!"

"Well, Captain it's not scattered, it's all in one place."

"Come back Nate, did you say it's in one place? Didn't you say you had moderate current?"

"Roger Captain, I don't see how this is possible."

"Okay Nate, just let me know what you're seeing."

"Captain, I'm looking at a mass of what looks to be, millions of glowing particles that seem to be hovering in one place. Oh, Captain?"

"Yeah, go ahead Nate."

"His dive line is leading me right to the glowing ball of phosphorus."

"Hey bud, nobody here in the dive shack has ever seen or heard of anything like you're describing. Proceed with caution."

"Roger that. Hey I found him Sir! I found him! He's lying flat on the bottom with these glowing particles all around him. This is freaky... Hey Captain; it doesn't look good. Y'all get ready on the pneumo."

"Roger, we are standing by on pneumo."

"I can see his face, his helmet's full of seawater. I'm sticking the pneumo underneath his neck dam now."

"Roger that, we're ready."

"Shoot the pneumo! Send it Captain, send it! Ok I'm getting air Sir, it's working. It's pushing out the water, almost there."

"Roger Nate, hook on to his harness."

"Yes Sir, hooking up. Okay, I've got it."

"Okay Nate it looks like the tenders have all the slack out; you should feel a tug at any second."

"I'm ready Captain Lee. Y'all pull like hell!"

The captain announces over the barge intercom, "Pull them up." He immediately turns and instructs two divers standing near the shack, "You guys get both chambers ready for emergency decompression. Blow the inner chambers down another 80 feet, and be ready to get Chado and Nate down to emergency depth at 160. Let's go boys, make it happen."

"You got it Captain, we're on it!"

"Boys at the rate we're bringing them up, they'll have an arterial embolism if we're not careful. Let's don't screw it up!"

"Yes Sir."

"Come in Nate."

"Go ahead Captain."

"Hold on, we've got several people pulling y'all up and it's going to be one hell of a ride. Nate?"

"Yes Sir."

"Blow out, try to keep your lungs as empty as possible."

"Captain they're dragging us along the bottom, hope we don't hit the sled."

"Roger Nate, you should miss it; the tenders are pulling y'all to the east side of the barge so the crane can reach you with the personnel basket."

"Okay, we just left the bottom, we are coming up. God let us survive this."

"What was that Nate?"

"Oh nothing sir, just saying a little prayer."

"Yes we could use God about right now."

"Okay Captain, looks like we are clear of the jet sled."

The barge intercom blast off again, "Bring them up! Let's go! Let's go!" The old man that operated the crane was still in his pajamas. He had gotten up because he knew his skills were needed; he had been down this road in past emergencies.

The old operator immediately fired up the diesel engine, causing black smoke to drift across the deck. He raised the boom of the crane up and over, dropping the headache ball directly over the personnel basket with exact precision. Captain Lee continued to direct the men on deck, shouting at a couple riggers, "Hey you guys! Hook that personnel basket up to the crane! Hurry up!"

"Nate, is he responding?"

"Negative Captain, he's pale Sir."

"Roger, keep forcing air in his helmet."

"Will do Captain."

* * *

They explode out of the water like a great white coming up after a seal. Two standby divers, already in the water, help roll Nate and Chado into the basket. The crane operator, not even waiting for a signal, starts picking them up and swinging the boom at the same time. With the crane operator moving so quickly, it causes the basket to start twisting and twirling around, almost out of control as he swings them over the deck. Several riggers tackle the basket to bring it back under control, and finally the crane operator gently sets the basket down right next to where the EMT's have a stretcher waiting.

Captain Lee starts yelling. "Go, go, go! Get them to the chamber before they have an embolism!"

As soon as Nate stands up and gets out of the personnel basket he collapses. A huge 6'4" tender immediately picks up Nate and starts heading for the chamber. Nate had already taken his helmet off but still had his dive lines attached to his harness. This big tender was dragging his helmet and hoses as he was attempting to get Nate to the chamber when he falls, because the dive line is snagged on a pipe roller. Someone quickly unhooks his harness, tosses it to the side and the same guy arms him back up and continues on to the chamber.

Matt and Lee watch from a short distance away when a diver takes Chado's helmet and neck dam off. He steps back a couple feet when the EMT's immediately start working on Chado Cole. Another diver steps back in and unhooks his weight belt and harness, while a greenhorn tender is trying to get his boots off. An EMT lady with a stern voice tells them both, "Get back! Don't worry about his boots." As she is pulling out a blade of some sort, ripping open his wet suit.

They have a defibrillator unit charged and ready, "CLEAR!" Bang they hit him several times and in between each charge they are doing CPR.

This is all taking place as they are walking beside his stretcher on the way to a secondary decompression chamber only a short distance across the deck.

All of a sudden, the EMTs look at each other. One of the ladies shakes her head and turns to the guys carrying the stretcher. "Hey guys, stop, set him down."

Someone in the crowd mumbles under his breath, "He's gone."

Matt stutters, "That's it. It's over."

Lee looks over at Matt and sees tears running down his cheeks. He reaches out with a rough calloused hand and gently places it on the side of Matt's face. With a soft voice, "Hey bud, I know y'all were like brothers. We all loved Chado. How could you not?"

Matt turns his head and looks down, and Lee continues speaking softly. "Let me tell you this, you can't live blaming yourself. We were all to blame. We shouldn't have allowed anyone to be in the water with all the crap that was screwed up on this project to begin with."

"Captain, if I had just paid more attention to the pressure."

"Matt, I said don't you go there."

With a few moments of silence both Matt and Lee now staring out across the Gulf of Mexico, Lee breaks the silence with a prayer: "God, we hope Chado Cole didn't suffer too much when you took him and we pray he's in a better place now, Amen."

Both Matt and Lee turn at the same time and watch as an EMT tucks one of his arms underneath the sheet while slowly covering his head.

Captain Lee with his voice quivering, "Hey bud, you want to know something?"

"Sure Captain."

"There is something I came to know about Chado. He loved God and didn't mind telling you about it. He's with God right now as we speak. He's seeing stuff we could only imagine. Chado talked about a daughter he lost several years back. I guarantee it won't take him long until he gets to see her. The Bible says that God numbers our days. This is just the day Chado Cole went home."

"Captain, you know Chado would talk about things in the Bible sometimes and compare stories in the Bible with things that would happen in our own lives. It was pretty interesting, but I never believed any of it. I believe he knew I didn't think any of it was real, but you know, he would always still talk about it and tell me, "Little buddy, you might want to get you a relationship with Jesus. The clock is ticking."

"I would laugh and then change the subject, and he would give me that funny look of his, and then grin from ear to ear. I guess, thinking back, he was just letting me know he cared. I wish he was standing here right now telling me one of his Bible stories."

"Roger that bud, Roger that. Matt, you know I believe in God too. I know, I know, I might drop a few curse words every now and then and I wasn't as open with my beliefs as Chado Cole, but when I'm home me and my wife go to church on Sunday. You know, it might be time to be a bit more open with my walk with God. This whole big screw up tonight makes you think... that could have been me."

"Captain Lee you're killing me. I don't really want to talk about walks with God and dying."

"Okay, ok Matt. I understand. Oh, by the way, the company has some kind of counseling program for this kind of event, if you think it might do you some good."

"Counseling... I don't need some pinhead telling me about my inner thoughts. I appreciate it Cap, but when I hit the shore after this hitch, I've been saving for a brand spanking new Harley Davidson, and a good cold beer will be all the counseling I'll need."

"Okay Matt, just keep me in mind if you ever need to talk, and Matt, you know God is always there if you ever want to talk to Him."

"Thanks Cap."

8

It Wasn't Divers At All

When I felt someone or something pulling on each arm, I opened my eyes to what had to be a dream. Yes, I'm sure this is a dream. I was seeing two small childlike Angels that had almost the same glow around them as the particles of phosphorus. *Was this real?*

They pull me up to a standing position and both let go of my arms. Suddenly, I realize I'm standing on the bottom of the Gulf of Mexico and I'm naked. Yep, this is a dream.

Then one of the Angels hands me what looks like my favorite pair of short pants with a T-shirt. The other one hands me a pair of sandals. Okay, at this point it's time to wake up in my bunk on the barge and tell Matt about this crazy dream. Now I am embarrassed and feeling a bit vulnerable with the two Angels standing right in front of me... not to mention all the other people that might be standing around down here in 200 feet of water seeing me naked... well, maybe a few fish are watching.

So I humble myself, turn away from my new friends and get dressed in my new duds. And while I'm turned in the other direction, I see a light blinking on and off and then finally it's out completely. Okay, I've got two childlike Angels standing behind me and someone else is walking around down here that's doing Morse code with a light.

There has to be an explanation, because I can't seem to remember anything past the last few seconds.

Whoever this is with the light is heading straight for me, maybe I can get some answers.

No way! I recognize this guy. He's wearing a Miller dive hat covered in graffiti. I would recognize that helmet anywhere. That's Nate. He looks like he's headed straight for that lit up mass of phosphorus. Wait till I tell Nate he was in my dream.

I start heading over to where he is; I see him kneel down, *what is that rascal up to?*

I feel both Angels grab my hands, I turn and look at the Angels and they are shaking their heads no.

"No? Wait a second; I want to see what Nate's doing."

I turn back around and I recognize another dive helmet, it's mine...*what's going on? Hey that's my wet suit. What the heck?* I pull away from the Angels and now I'm standing directly over Nate. About that time, his light comes back on, and I'm looking at a pale blue reflection of myself. *Could this be me, is this really happening?* I see Nate as he hooks to my harness and all of a sudden Nate and this lifeless corpse are being pulled away.

If that was me does this mean I'm a spirit, and I'm standing here dressed in shorts, T-shirt and sandals? And standing on the bottom of the ocean? Hmmm, okay, I guess it's really happening.

I look over at the two Angels and they are grinning shaking their heads yeah.

"*So, can you guys tell what I'm thinking? Wow, I heard y'all and your mouths didn't move. Can I tell what y'all are thinking? No? Just when y'all want me to? Well that's not fair.*"

Both Angels start laughing with a contagious laugh and I can't help myself, I start laughing too. I can't believe I'm laughing and just saw what looked like a dead me being pulled off and up toward the surface. This is so crazy!

"*So, what's next?*"

Each Angel takes one of my hands and starts pulling me upward at a pretty good clip. A short distance above us, I see a huge Angel with a wide wing spread and he's traveling in the same direction we are.

Suddenly our upward ascent is stopped; something has grabbed my left ankle. The two small Angels are struggling because we are being pulled back down. Then this mighty Angel above us circles back around and starts to unsheathe his sword, revealing only a couple inches of it. The sword creates such a brilliant bright light, it looks like it lights up the whole bottom of the Gulf. I turn to see what has my ankle, and fear grips me when I see what looks like some kind of demon right out of the pit of hell. When the light from the Angel's sword hits this demon, he lets go and with a flash he is gone.

Before the light faded from this mighty Angel's sword, I could see everything. The jet sled, the pipeline and all sorts of fish. *Could this be real? Could it be some fantastic dream with such detail, unlike any other dream I've ever had? This couldn't be a dream. I can hear what the two small Angels are thinking. They are allowing me in their conversation of thoughts. Am I losing my mind? I can hear their thoughts.* They were talking about that demon that grabbed my ankle. They were saying *"he was a bad one, and that he had great authority and dark power, and they were glad Chado Cole's Warrior Angel was with us."*

Wow, I have a Warrior Angel! I suddenly have a funny thought, *well that's always good to have a Warrior Angel along especially when you are being grabbed by a demon.* I look over at the little Angel on my left and he's laughing again, and I burst out laughing too.

I have a feeling of peace and protection with an overwhelming abundance of joy. We all three continue to laugh

49

as the light of the Warrior Angel's sword slowly fades, when he replaces it in its sheath.

Continuing upward, we suddenly break through the surface of the water. Our laughter stops as I can now see the lay barge with its bright lights and workers scrambling around on deck. I can even hear the loud speaker, with Captain Lee shouting, "Go, go, go! Get them up!"

All at once I could remember everything that happened. And this was, without a doubt, real. I had just died on the bottom of the Gulf of Mexico...

At the same time, both Angels squeezed my hands slightly and smiled to let me know, "*It's okay. We are on our way to Heaven.*"

9

The Spiritual Realm

I finally came to the point of accepting this unbelievable event and knowing I was truly on my way to Heaven. I started to wonder if we were about to go into hyper drive or maybe light speed or would I just blink my eyes and arrive at Heaven's gate?

"What's next?" I look over at one of the Angels and I see a big grin and he shakes his head no.

Well, I'm thinking, *Okay I'm just hitching a ride. You guys are in control. This is actually my first trip and I have no idea how to fly.*

Both Angels are laughing again. I forgot they can hear my thoughts. *Man this is so awesome! This is going to be a fun trip.*

On this exodus from Earth I had always imagined shooting straight up with a flash of light or instantly vanishing, but this wasn't the case. The two Angels were still holding my hands as we went up a few hundred feet above the water and started heading north. Yes, north. I can tell because at this height, I can see the glow of the rising sun due east. Yes, I'm certain we are heading north. I can now see in the distance the lights of what looks like New Orleans.

At this point we seem to be slowing down and getting a bit lower as we get closer to the city. It's like they want me to see something.

Out of nowhere, my Warrior Angel shows up and the sound of his mighty wings slowing him down to match the pace of the Angels transporting me, catches me off guard and startles me a bit. He's right beside us, and this is the first time we've

51

been this close. Wow, I can see his face as he looks over at me. He's not smiling like the two small Angels have been; he's got a stern, serious look on his face. I'm thinking, *Is something wrong?* He suddenly flies ahead of us just a few yards and then slows back down, maintaining our speed.

I can now see how big this Angel is, and the morning light peeping over the horizon makes his armor glisten. I can make out several different colors embedded in his armor and clothing. Oh my, that's not just color, that's sapphires and rubies and maybe even diamonds. This Angel must be something special in Heaven or has a high rank if there are ranks with Angels. Or are all Angels decked out like this one? My little Angels aren't dressed like him, I'm sure he's got to be special.

The outside of his wings looks like they are coated with steel, but they flex and move with the wind. He's carrying a shield strapped to his back, along with a huge sword. His shield looks like it's made out of some kind of odd looking metal. I can't make out the engraving in the shield. It looks like some sort of symbols and there are several words written on the shield that look like an old or strange language. I'm wishing I knew what it all means. Maybe I can ask him someday if he ever gives me the chance.

As we slow down over the city of New Orleans, my little Angels are letting me know they want me to look at something. As we drop down a bit more, I start seeing dark images all over the place, and as we get closer to the ground I can make out what those images are. They are just like the very same thing that grabbed my leg when we were coming up out of the Gulf: Demons... They are everywhere, thousands of them. I suddenly notice our Warrior Angel is gone; *where is he?* I start looking all around and finally look up; he is hovering just a few feet over us. I think he got a kick out of me getting spooked when I thought he was gone, because he actually dropped the Marine Corps stare for a second and grinned slightly. That minor grin sure helped me, because what I was seeing was a scary sight.

One of the little Angels lets me know I was now able to see into the Spiritual Realm.

The Spiritual Realm; I remember Dr. Forester teaching a Friday night Bible study about that. He said if you could see it with the human eye, it would probably scare you so bad you couldn't bear it. Well, he wasn't far off.

I could now see the people walking up and down the streets. I can hear the music and the laughter. Wow, it looks like Mardi Gras. Yes, I believe it's Mardi Gras, they are partying hard.

I'm thinking, *"Are all these dark spirits trying to get those people?"*

The little Angels let me know, *"The fallen angels are invading the hearts of the lost and controlling them with persuasion, some with oppression, and some with possession. Some have turned away from the light and some have never known the light."*

I can see several people scattered in the crowds that stand out as being different; they have a sort of glow around them.

And before I can ask, the little Angels let me know, *"They were a certain kind of Angels that are chosen by God to infiltrate the darkness and are trying to help some of the people that are being prayed for by their family or maybe friends. If they don't hear the still voice of God and run for His protection it will soon be too late."*

As we make our way across the city, I see a small church nestled in between two very tall buildings, and I notice two large Angels standing at the door, both dressed like the Warrior Angel that we have with us.

I ask the small Angels, *"What are they doing there? Surely there's no one there, this time of the morning."*

They replied, *"Yes there is someone there. It's an old preacher and his wife that have been there for sixty-three years. They have ministered to the lost in this city and have led thousands to God. Those demonic forces you've seen hate them and Lucifer wants them gone. So God has placed these two Warrior Angels here until they have completed their work and are called home."*

They also let me know, *"This same scene here is taking place all over the world, with legions of Angels that are fighting the fallen angels and the hordes of their satanic demons. They continue in constant battle for the souls of man. God has allowed this battle to go on from the beginning of time. It will only end at the unknown hour of God's return. The presence of darkness is now getting stronger than ever, and there's only a small remnant of people who truly show love to God. All the Angels of Heaven know that the hour grows near for the final battle that will take place in the valley of Megiddo. We all stand ready for the second coming of Christ and the command for the seven seals to be opened."*

When I heard how serious the two little Angels were when they explained this frightening scene, I was thinking *"If everyone could just see a small part or maybe even catch a glimpse of this Spiritual Realm and know this evil darkness is swarming around them, they would run to this little church and fall on their faces and cry out to God."*

I hear the two Angels' thoughts, and they let me know *"You've got a lot to learn about how and why God won't allow the natural man to see this."*

As we continue to head north, I'm thinking: *Why in the world are they showing me all this and explaining details about the end time stuff? I've read about most of it in the book of Revelation, studied about Jesus and the prophets, read the Bible through several times, heard a lot of preachers bang on the pulpit through the years trying to get us to understand time is short. 'Be ready, you could die at any minute or God might call us home at any time'; not to mention seeing into the Spiritual Realm. Why are they doing this? I figured we would be walking around in Heaven by now.*

So they burst out laughing again, and let me know. *"We are in the dark on this one too. We were instructed to pick you up from the bottom of the Gulf of Mexico and transport you across the United States through Canada on up to our exit point in Alaska. We were to travel at a moderate speed, having to show you several key cities along the way. You are instructed by God to remember everything you see, and you will also remember every detail of your life, death and adventure in Heaven."*

"What in the world are y'all talking about? It sounds like we are taking a vacation across North America, and by the way I'm no writer, I'm a diver, well I use to be a diver."

One of the little Angels smiled as he answered. *"We feel like God is up to something, His ways are not our ways. We just do what He tells us. We usually are there to comfort Christians when they pass over, and then we immediately bring them to Heaven. That's our job, well sometimes we get to bring messages, but our favorite is to comfort and transport."*

* * *

"Well, do you guys usually poke along? It seems it would take forever to get to Heaven at the speed we've been traveling."

With laughter; "Speed, you want speed? Just wait, we will show you speed!"

About the time we hit the Louisiana- Arkansas line, they caught another gear and with a couple blinks, we were hovering over the ghettos of Chicago.

"My God, that was awesome, was it light speed? I want to do it again." And suddenly, the thrill was gone and my laughter ceased as I looked around, realizing we were witnessing almost the exact same dark forces as we had seen in New Orleans.

From there, city to city to city, the darkness and the demonic forces were saturating the land like some kind of virus, *"How could this be?"*

I'm thinking, *"Do we have enough Angels to fight the final battle, or any battle? I've only seen a few Warrior Angels along the way, and legions of demons."*

The smaller of the two Angels let me know with a bit of expression, "We've got this. Well God's got this. The power of God is unmatched and the Warrior Angels have the power of God with them. You've read in the scripture about the Full Amor of God haven't you?"

"Yes, I have, Ephesians 6."

"Well, stop worrying about how many demons and fallen angels there are. We are telling you, God has everything under control. Have you noticed we haven't had any more attacks since that demon grabbed your leg when we were leaving

56

the bottom of the Gulf? Satan has a way of communicating with his crew. As soon as your Warrior Angel unsheathed his sword, the whole satanic army knew you were off limits."

"Wow. That is amazing."

"Now, He just wants you to keep making a mental note of what you see, and try to understand as much as you can. He has a plan, and His plans always work out, you'll see."

10

Angels' Names

I'm really getting used to hearing these little Angels' thoughts; it already feels natural to communicate like this. But, I noticed the few times I was near the Warrior Angel; I couldn't make out what he was thinking. *"Is he private with his thoughts? Or does he even like me?"*

"Hey, Chado, you've got to quit thinking like a mortal. Of course he likes you, he's your Guardian, and he's been with you since birth."

"What, since birth?"

"Yes he was assigned to watch over you, your entire life."

"Well, why didn't he save me from dying on the bottom of the ocean?"

"All I can tell you is God needed you for something. So don't blame your Angel. I guarantee he loves you. Communicating with your Warrior Angel is a bit different than with us. We comfort, they protect. Understand?"

"Well, no, maybe, I guess."

"Trust us. You will catch on." They start grinning again. I ask, *"What is so funny?"*

"You only have eternity to understand it all."

"Hey that's right, eternity, what a nice thought... eternity."

"Hey guys, I had a thought when you called me by my name. Wait, is that the first time you used my name? Well anyway, what the heck are your names? We've been together all the way across the US and part of Canada and I don't know your names, and what's my Warrior Angel's name?"

The smaller of the two, said with a loud voice, "My name is Nipper and his name is Allayer."

I grinned and said, "Well hello there and pleased to meet you, Nipper, and what a pleasure it is to make your acquaintance, Allayer."

They both giggled and lowered their heads with a short nod as we were continuing over a mountain range somewhere in northern Canada. As I thought more about their names, I had to ask, "Guys, I've never heard of anyone with the names Nipper or Allayer, can you tell me what they mean?"

"Yes, God gave us our names."

"Really, do you know what they mean?"

"Sure we do Chado. Do you know anything about a battle between Israel and the Philistines, when God allowed the Philistines to capture the Ark of Covenant?"

"I think so; I remember reading something in 1st Samuel about Israel getting the Ark taken away. I believe God was angry with his people or something like that."

"Yes, back in those days, some of the kings would allow their people to worship idols and they would build small statues of what they thought was a god and even place them in their homes. Some would go as far as building statues on top of the high places around the city. You could imagine, after God blessed His people repeatedly and showed them so many miracles, that He would certainly be angry about them building some stupid idol. Chado, He would give them multiple chances by sending prophets like Elijah, Jeremiah, and Samuel to warn them. But if they didn't heed God's warning, He would take away their protection. They had to face droughts, being killed or captured, and living in slavery for years... some even died as slaves.

Back to your question about our names, Nipper and I were living as mortals in the time when the Ark was taken away from Israel. We witnessed 34,000 soldiers die during the battle of Aphek. Shortly after the battle we lost our lives when the Philistines raided our village. The two idiot sons of Eli brought this whole catastrophe upon Israel, well anyway, that was a long time ago."

Nipper laughed as he stated, "As a matter of fact it was 1120 BC and Allayer; you need to let that go about Eli's two evil sons."

"I did let it go, they were just bad."

"Wow, you guys are old as dirt, well I mean y'all are pretty old. Ah - So, what do your names mean?"

Allayer looked over at me and said, "God told me my name means to comfort."

Nipper with a chuckle, "My name means abandoned child, you know like a street urchin."

"Why did he call you that?"

"Oh, I was an orphan back in my mortal years, so Nipper kind of fit. You know God has got a sense of humor, you'll see.

Ok Chado, we've told you how we got our names. Would you mind telling us how you got yours? It is a rather unusual name."

"Sure. My full name is Chad Cole. But, I have been called Chado all my life. My dad told me, my three year old brother gave me that nickname. They were standing in front of the newborn nursery when I was only a couple hours old. Dad was attempting to show big brother how to pronounce it and he kept repeating shadow over and over, so Dad compromised and I guess they met in the middle and settled on the name Chado.

It wasn't long everyone in the community was using it, so I guess it kind of stuck with me all these years."

As we continue on our journey, Nipper and Allayer start to explain about how time is different in this realm than it is on Earth. Nipper asks me, "Can you remember any Bible verses where God talks about time?"

"As a matter of fact, I do, I remember something in James 4:14 that says. *'For what is your life? It is even a vapor that appears for a little time and then vanishes away'.*"

"That's a great scripture verse and you're on the right track, but the one we were talking about comes from 2nd Peter 3:8, It says: *'Beloved, do not forget this one thing, that with the Lord one day is as a thousand years, and a thousand years as one day'.*"

"Yeah, yeah, I remember that! So what about time, can you explain it?"

Nipper turned and looked at me with a bold look on his face and said, "We hope you can comprehend the depth of time in the realm. You're understanding won't fully develop until you enter into Heaven."

"What? What do you mean?"

Allayer tells Nipper, "You shouldn't have told him that, at least not yet."

"Okay guys; tell me what's going on. Allayer, will you please explain, what the heck are y'all talking about?"

"Chado, here it is in short story. As you know, we usually transport someone that's just passed over, straight to Heaven. They don't have time to ask any questions, it's sort of like what you were thinking earlier about the flash of light and boom, you're in Heaven. After arriving in Heaven their minds are opened and their understanding of how things work is revealed.

61

So, with God's special orders and having to give you a tour of the Realm, I guess we can try and answer a few questions you might have."

Allayer starts to explain about the extra mind capacity. "Fully developed humans on Earth can only use around ten percent of their brain. God has allowed a selected few through the years with a bit higher capacity when He would bless the human race with inventions, art, music and things that would give comfort and happiness to His people. Some misused the blessing and led people down paths of destruction, and some gave God the Glory, and blessed the nations with their knowledge and wisdom."

Nipper jumps in, "Hey Chado, once you pass over into the Spiritual Realm your brain capacity increases fifteen to twenty percent. This allows you to easily tap into a section of the brain that opens your mind and heart so you can see into the Spiritual Realm, and your understanding of what's going on around you is a bit clearer."

Allayer states, "The additional percentage allows you to talk to us with your mind, and when you get to Heaven and receive the rest, you will be able to block someone from knowing all your thoughts. As your mission continues, this will come in handy if you ever go into battle or have to deal with anyone that stands against the Holy Trinity. You don't want demons to know your thoughts. That only makes them stronger, you'll see."

Allayer continues, "So when you enter into the Kingdom of Heaven, God allows you to have around seventy five to eighty percent, and you will love that. We've watched thousands of souls when they receive this gift and it's more fun each time. All the Angels get a kick out of it, watching someone go from a chatterbox asking so many questions about the silliest things, to complete silence... Then a super funny look on their faces and finally, and always a huge smile."

Nipper says, "and this process of receiving more understanding takes on average around an hour after entering into the Kingdom."

"Wow. That sounds so exciting. I've always wanted to be smarter."

"Just wait, that's only a small portion of the mysteries that will be revealed."

"Okay, what about the time thing?"

"We wish you would wait on the answer to that. But we will tell you this, there is no such thing as time in Heaven, or at least not like it is on Earth. Do you remember the word eternity and the true meaning?

Take a calendar for example or a clock, one after the other, days pass, tick after tick the seconds, the minutes, the hours, the days, the years. The sun rises and sets, the shadow of the seasons is ever present. In Heaven, freed from this measurement of time, you will be able to see the rapid decay of everything on Earth. Plants and animals will wither away in what seems like seconds. Rocks and even mountains will erode and crumble in a surprisingly brief amount of time. In God's Word He says time is but of a vapor. One day is to a thousand years and a thousand years is to a day.

Remember eternity is without measure, God's creation is without measure. Can you say it is this day or that year? Or the sun came up from the east and it set in the west? Where is the west? How then can you measure time?"

Nipper jumps in with a giggle. "If God wants you to know what time it is He'll tell you."

63

"I guess so Nipper, and thanks guys for brain capacity 101. I kind of understand most of that but the time lesson might need a little more tutoring."

They both laugh and Allayer tells me, "Just wait, your understanding of how it all works will clear up when you get to Heaven. Savvy?"

"Sure, I'm savvy".

* * *

As we arrive in Alaska, Nipper squeezes my hand and lets me know. "We have one final place God wants to show you before we leave Earth."

"Okay, that sounds great, is it more demonic forces, battles in the Spiritual Realm? I'm ready for anything, kind of getting use to the scary stuff."

Both Nipper and Allayer start their giggling again, "Okay guys, what are y'all up to?"

About that time, we slow down over what looks like the prettiest place on Earth. It is a gorgeous valley with a huge lake surrounded by mountains that has snow covered peaks glistening in the bright sunlight. I can see a small village near the lake, and a pretty good size clay and straw building in the middle of town. "Hey, I don't see any demons or any kind of darkness lurking."

Laughing, "You will never see any dark presence here. This is Holy Ground. "

"Holy ground?"

Nipper, chuckling, "Is there an echo around here? Yes Holy Ground. This place is off limits to any dark presence, they don't even know it's here."

"So what's so special about it?"

"We think it might be God's favorite place on Earth."

"God has a favorite place on Earth?"

"We're not for sure, but we believe so. He has special protection around this whole valley."

Allayer explains. "This tribe of Indians has lived here for over two thousand years in peace and harmony. They are taught the Word of God from birth with no influence or contact from the outside world. No mortal has ever witnessed what you're seeing. God has made this valley invisible to the rest of the world. Satan can't even see it, he has no idea it even exists."

Nipper chimes in, "The people here call God, the Great Spirit and some of the elders call Him, Jehovah-Jireh."

"Why did God want a village way out here separate from the world?"

"We don't know, I guess it was like His special project. All we know is he really loves this place and the people. Generation after generation and nothing changes, and you can see how happy they are."

"I know, this is so amazing, I can't believe I'm witnessing how they lived two thousand years ago."

"We believe God comes here sometimes to fish."

"What? Fish? God goes fishing?"

Nipper smiles, "You think God needs a license?"

"Well No, I just figured..."

"You figured what? Remember what we told you earlier, stop thinking like a mortal."

"Okay, okay. Hey guys, I like to fish too. You think God might let me go with Him? Or maybe even turn me on to some of His honey holes?"

Both Angels start laughing, with Nipper saying "I would probably not hit God up on His favorite fishing hole."

65

"Hey, I haven't seen our Warrior Angel since we got to this valley. Where is he? Or where did he go?"

Allayer lets me know, "He has probably already left."

"Left, what do you mean he left?"

"Well, he knows we're no longer in any danger here in God's Valley. We may not see him again until we enter Heaven's Gate."

"What if we are attacked again?"

Nipper grins and says, "Remember we are on holy ground."

"Oh, yeah, holy ground, God's favorite place on Earth. Yeah, total protection, I get it. What about our Warrior Angel's name? You guys never told me."

Nipper and Allayer seem to be having a minor disagreement, or maybe it's just a discussion they don't want me to hear.

"Hey do y'all mind letting me in on your thoughts? What's the big secret, guys? You can't tell me his name?"

Allayer tells Nipper to explain.

"Well Chado, Warrior Angels are very secret about their names. Some like Gabriel and Michael are known throughout history, but down the ranks of God's Warrior Angels they are very private. The name of each Angel is given straight from God and with each individual Angel's name, a unique power is given to them. This helps in the battle with the principalities of darkness. It's hard to understand, but it goes along with the power in God's spoken Word. In this case, the power in the names He gives.

You'll see. Well anyway, God's Angels know each name of the fallen. When the fallen angels were cast out of Heaven, over the centuries they have forgotten the names of all God's

Warrior Angel's. This is part of the curse that fell on Lucifer and his fallen during the Great Rebellion."

"Yeah, I read about that, when this happened, God kicked a third of the angels out of Heaven, right?"

Nipper tells Allayer to fill me in on details.

"Yeah guys, what happened?"

"Yes, there was a rebellion in Heaven, it was awful. Lucifer was one of the most beautiful angels and had awesome power. You've probably read about the five 'I wills' that Lucifer used to show everyone his awful Pride against The Almighty God."

"Hey guys, can you refresh my memory how Satan got into trouble with the five 'I wills?'"

Nipper says, "I'll tell him. God's Word is written from Isaiah 14:12: '*How you are fallen from Heaven,*

O Lucifer, son of the morning! How you are cut down to the ground.

You who weakened the nations!

For you have said in your heart;

I will ascend into Heaven.

I will exalt my throne above the stars of God;

I will also sit on the mount of the congregation on the farthest sides of the north;

I will ascend above the heights of the clouds,

I will be like the Most High.'

We believe this was the beginning of the war in Heaven and the creation of Hell. The casting down of Satan resulted from a great battle between the hosts of Heaven and the followers of Lucifer. In this battle, Heaven's Warriors forced Satan and his fallen angels, forever from the Heavenly realm.

The evil entities are those angels who rebelled with Lucifer and were cast out of Heaven with him. Their minds and understanding have been covered with the horrible darkness of deception, the same method Satan still uses to lead his victims astray."

Nipper asked me, "Chado, do you want to learn another mystery that the people of Earth have gotten wrong for years and are blind to a simple truth?"

"Sure, I love a mystery."

Nipper tells me, "The scientists, archeologists, and atheists have used the bones of what they think is prehistoric man to try to prove their theory of evolution is real, but they are so far off."

"What are you talking about, Nipper?"

"Allayer, you want to fill him in?"

"Chado, you're going to love this!"

"What? Let me have it with both barrels."

"All the schools are teaching kids their theory of evolution, and convincing the weak minded, well that's a bit strong... should we say the minds and hearts lacking of the Holy Spirit. They are truly convincing most everyone the opposite of the truth. This group of scientists fell right into one of the oldest tricks in Lucifer's handbook of lies."

"Okay, can you explain to someone with only fifteen percent brain capacity?"

Nipper starts laughing, "For a dead guy you're pretty funny. Okay, you remember in the history books when they dug up and discovered Neanderthal man, dinosaur bones and so on?"

"Sure, I've even seen some in the museums. What? Weren't they real?"

68

"Sure they were real, let me explain. When all this took place, I mean the war in Heaven, or should I say the royal butt kicking of Lucifer with a third of the fallen angels.

God had just formed the world and it was a violent place. The Earth went through what I guess you could call growing pains: Earthquakes, violent storms, hurricanes that would last for years, mountains literally rising up over night with the Earth constantly trembling and shaking, oceans forming and overflowing creating lakes, seas and huge rivers, and going through several ice ages, almost totally uninhabitable."

"Man, that wouldn't be a place to go on vacation."

"That's the point, Lucifer and his crew were cursed and cast down to Earth when all this was taking place. God was so upset, He not only stuck them on the most violent planet in all the galaxies; He took away their beauty. He distorted the bone structure of their faces, lengthened their arms, shortened their legs and covered their bodies with stiff hair like you would see on a wild boar. He also gave them teeth like a jackal to be able to eat raw meat. At this point in time, these fallen angels would now be called the dammed of the Earth."

"My God, that's incredible. Well I guess it was a sad time in Heaven."

"Yes, we think God was hurt. He loved all the angels, but He is a just God and He means business when it comes to rebellion or turning away."

"So what happened to all the fallen, that were cast down to Earth?"

"He gave them an allotted time to live, which was several hundred years and then they finally died and became demonic spirits and angels of hell. They have been roaming the Earth ever since, angry at God trying to help Lucifer steal as many hearts and souls as they can before the final battle. Lucifer has figured out a way to transform dark and lost souls into a type of demon. They aren't very strong but they do his bidding, and there are millions of them. Lucifer has a false hope of defeating God. We can tell you this, that's not going to happen. Hey Chado, you want to know one of Lucy's tricks?"

"Lucy? Who's Lucy? Oh I get it, Lucifer. You bet, let me hear it."

"Lucifer made sure, when each fallen angel died, he would place their bones where the scientists of your time would dig them up and have worldwide exposure in the news with the headlines...

(Neanderthal Man Discovered – Evolution Real)

The theory of evolution has sent millions down the road of deception. It's just a slick lie being forced down the throats of generations."

"Well what about the dinosaurs?"

"Oh yeah, that's the funny part. Whenever they first touched down on this violent, shaking Earth, God had a few surprises waiting for this prideful crew. Having all their angelic powers stripped from them, with no defense of any kind, they were immediately being chased by huge dinosaurs. This forced them into caves living like wild animals.

That wasn't all. God also took away their additional brain capacity and left them with a very low sense of thought. He gave them just enough to barely survive."

"Wow, that's amazing. So all these years this was a trick to fool millions?"

"Yes, I guess you could actually say that was the oldest trick in the book."

"Do you guys know when this all took place?"

"We think it was a couple million years before Adam and Eve came into the picture."

"You've got to be pulling my leg. How old is the Earth?"

"We don't know exactly, maybe you can find out when you get to Heaven."

"I reckon so. Come to think of it, I've got a lot of questions."

"When we get you there, you have eternity to ask whoever you feel the need to ask. But remember; when we enter into Heaven, your mind is free from mortal thoughts and open to a spiritual view of how things work, and you won't need to ask a lot of questions, you will just know. God blesses all who enter with knowledge."

11

Written In Stone

After hovering over this beautiful, ancient village, for what seemed like only a few seconds, I could tell Nipper and Allayer were ready to move on.

"Hey guys, are we about to leave God's Valley?"

"Yes, it's time to head out. Are you ready for more adventure?"

"I am. Well, is it Heaven bound? Or do you guys have more surprises waiting?"

Nipper laughs. "We always have more surprises, and you will love what we are about to show you."

They carry me across this gorgeous lake at a very slow speed, heading in the direction of a steep cliff facing back toward the village. As we near this beautiful rock formation, I could see chiseled writing from the top of the flat face, all the way back down to the bottom of this very tall mountain. The letters I think are in another language. "Hey guys, what language is that?"

Dead silence.

"Okay guys, a little help here?"

Nipper looks over at me with a huge smile and says, "Here's a small hint, Hebrew."

"Nipper you are too funny. And thanks, so it's Hebrew. Do the folks back at the village speak Hebrew?"

"Yes they do, and they also were taught every language known to man."

"What? That's impossible."

"Nothing is impossible with God. He blessed them with an abundance of knowledge, pretty much like he did Solomon

72

back in the day. Do you remember in God's Word when He asked Solomon what he desired? Solomon didn't ask for worldly treasures, he asked for knowledge, and God blessed him with knowledge, more than any other human that ever lived on Earth."

"So are they smarter than Solomon?"

"We don't think so, but they run a pretty close second. It all has to do with how much knowledge God blesses you with and when He feels the need to do it. Savvy?"

"Yep, I understand. I guess that additional knowledge hasn't happened to me yet. I still have a hard time with English."

Nipper and Allayer burst out laughing "Yes we can tell you were raised living next door to Einstein."

"Very funny guys. I can't help I was raised in the back woods. And I still for the life of me, oh yeah... the death of me... can't imagine why God would choose to show me all this."

"Yes, that is a mystery. He must see something in you."

Nipper chimes in, "Hey, God used an ass a couple times in the Bible to get His point across. He could use you!"

"Thanks a lot Nipper."

As we got closer to the face of the mountain, I could see numbers in front of each line and the letters had to be at least fifty, no, that's got to be seventy five or a hundred feet long, measuring vertically from top to bottom. How could anyone hang from ropes and chisel out something so perfect from this giant mountain?

As we get closer; my goodness the depth of this writing was four or five feet deep into the rock.

"Guys, did the people of that village do this? It had to have taken them the whole two thousand years they lived here to accomplish a task like this. Not to mention, how could it be humanly possible to chisel what looks like granite? I just can't believe anyone could do it, even with today's machinery and the best mountain climbers in the world. Now would you guys please tell me what the writing means, how and who did it?"

Nipper and Allayer start their giggling "We want to see if you can figure this one out. It's actually very simple. Just give it a little extra thought and while you're going through this minor struggle of figuring it out, we are going to show you another great wonder."

As I look over at these huge letters written in a foreign language, a bell goes off. I need to use our English numerals and count out the lines as we pass by. Duh.

"So, there are ten lines, what could the writing mean? Okay, this is God's favorite place on Earth. Ten lines, hey I've got it. It's got to be the Ten Commandments!"

"Hey, give the dead guy a couple angel wings. You got it!"

"Wow, so did He have the villagers chisel all this out?"

"Nope. Tell him Nipper."

"Okay, you bet. Alright Chado, you know how no one knows where the Arc of Covenant is located?"

"Right. Where is it?"

"God took it away from mankind and placed it in the mountain that you're looking at. Then the finger of God touched the face of that cliff, writing His law in the stone of this mountain for a reminder to this tribe, that He is the God of Abraham, Isaac and Jacob.

You're witnessing the fingerprints of God."

"I don't know what to say. I wish the whole world could see this."

Allayer tells me, "Through the centuries, God has shown His signs and wonders. He sent the prophets, He sent His son Jesus Christ to die on the cross of Calvary. His unchanging Word has been written in millions of Bibles scattered all over the world, and still man cries out, just show me a sign and I will believe. God has given man a free will and most have chosen the wide road to destruction and have turned away from God.

God still continues to bless man with miracles and the people that recognize these miracles are usually the ones that truly worship and adore Him. The unbelievers can't see it, and as long as they don't have the Holy Spirit, they will never see it. Just like this wonder you're looking at, the unbeliever would explain it away with some stupid theory. So, do you think He needs to reveal this? God has nothing to prove, just look around at His handiwork. Can anyone say there is no God?"

"I understand. Thinking of it all like that makes me sad for the millions that will perish and miss out, not only on eternity with a God that loves them so much, but an awesome life here on Earth. Right Nipper?"

"Yes, we try not to think about how many souls that won't make it to Heaven, but instead are transported to Hell. Allayer and myself are glad we don't have that job, we enjoy the opposite, seeing people enter the Gates of Heaven."

"Yes, let's change the subject. You guys were about to show me something else."

* * *

I feel a slight tug, and Allayer lets me know we are going to back off about a half mile from the cliff because he wants to see if I can make anything else out. So we move out over the lake and start hovering at a certain point.

"Well guys, I don't see anything other than the writings."

Allayer tells me, "Wait for it."

"Wait for what?"

"Patience Chado, keep watching the face of the mountain."

Just about the time I'm ready to give up, the sun peeks between two other mountains on the back side of the lake and the sun's rays bouncing off the water create a colorful barrage of golden rays shining on the Ten Commandments. Now I can see a silhouette, no, it's like a mural painting of Jesus. He is kneeling over a Lamb with a huge Lion sitting behind him looking down at Jesus and the Lamb. I ask Nipper, "What does this represent?"

"We think it represents the Holy Trinity, but like the other thousand questions you ask, God will reveal everything to you when we get to Heaven."

"Okay, okay. I get it, patience."

As the sun slowly rises behind us, each letter of the Commandments seems to come alive with gold pouring down from one line to the next, moving very slowly like lava from a volcano. But it's not pouring, it's gold shining when the sunlight hits inside the letters. This mountain must be made of pure gold with the limestone covering the face of this magnificent rock structure.

Nipper asks me, "How's that for a surprise?"

I am totally speechless.

Nipper giggling, "Hey, Chado, you can close your mouth now. Not saying anything with your mouth wide open makes you look funny."

Then, within a couple minutes, as the sun continues to rise, this beautiful scene disappears. Jesus, the Lamb and the Lion vanish, with only the Ten Commandments remaining.

Allayer tells Nipper "We need to be moving along."

They bring me up and sit me down on top of the very same mountain that God had placed the Ark inside. They both at the same time tell me to take off my sandals.

I immediately tell them, "Let me guess. We are standing on Holy ground." With kind smiles they shook their heads yes.

As I am sitting on a small rock taking off my shoes, I realize this is the first time I've stood on mother Earth since I was standing on the bottom of the Gulf of Mexico. I'm thinking what an awesome journey so far.

Allayer smiles, "This journey has only just begun. Come and walk with us. We have something very special to show you."

The top of this mountain looks to be a couple square miles wide, covered in wild flowers and ferns of all different colors, the beauty unending. We walk past several mountain goats feeding on the darkest green grass I've ever seen. There are soft trails leading in several different directions through the low hanging branches of white bark pine, spruce and foxtail pines. *"Wow. How did I know the names of all these trees way up here in the mountains? I'm from Louisiana, with no recollection of any such trees."*

Nipper laughs, "God is giving you a little touch of knowledge, just take it in, it's going to get better."

We walk out into a small opening with rocks sitting like benches circling the entire area. There are three different rock formations near the center of the circle, each shaped like a door.

Nipper and Allayer go and sit down on the stone bench, and ask me, "So, what do you make of this?"

"Well, I don't know. I can see it looks like three doors, but I can see right through each one. So they couldn't be doors. Is it the ruins of God's summer home?"

They both laugh, still keeping their secret, making me guess.

"Okay guys; is this another Stonehenge way up here on God's mountain?"

Allayer tells Nipper, "We need to get a move on, go ahead and fill him in."

"Chado, there are three portals, we know where two lead and the third remains a mystery."

"Portals... wow, is it a gateway to Heaven? "

"Yes, one of them leads straight to Heaven."

"Well, let's get in the wind. I can't wait to see Jesus, God, the rest of the Angels, my family that's passed on and especially my daughter Summer. Yeah, let's get going."

I start running toward the portals and Allayer stops me. "Hold up Chado! If you go through the wrong portal we may never find you!"

"Well, which one leads to Heaven?"

"That one over to your left, we don't know where it leads. It's forbidden to enter. The one in the center leads to Heaven."

I start walking toward the center portal and Nipper grabs my hand. "Chado Cole, you need to slow down. We have to explain something."

"What? All this way and I'm not allowed in Heaven?"

Allayer puts his hand on my back and tells me "Yes you're going to Heaven, just not right now."

"What do you mean, not right now?"

"We have another place God wants to show you, as part of your mission."

"You mean another place here on Earth?"

"No, it's through that portal to your right."

"Okay, where does it lead?"

Nipper tells Allayer, "Let's just go and we can explain on the way."

"Okay Chado, are you ready for a ride on God's highway?"

"You bet, let's do it."

"Hold our hands and let's all step through together."

12

The Vision

When I slowly walk through the doorway, it feels like my entire body was being submerged in warm wax, with the heat starting from my feet very slowly moving up over my entire body.

With this sensation, I am reminded of a time several years ago when I was at a Friday Night Bible Study. I had gone through a sad time in my life experiencing a terrible divorce and losing my family. I was a fool in those years. The most important people on Earth to me were my three kids and my wife, and they were suddenly stripped away in what seem like overnight.

I turned to God more in that time than ever before. I was a lump of clay in God's hands, poured out with nothing left in me.

One particular Bible study stands out in my memory. At the end of our meeting, Dr. Forester wanted to prepare us for spiritual warfare, because there were several people that needed special prayer, and we were about to go into battle for God. Before we stepped to the front line, he asked that we would pray for God to totally cleanse our hearts of any hidden sin.

As I was praying, I leaned over slumped with my elbows resting on my knees with my face buried in my hands. As I prayed, *God, please forgive me and cleanse my heart. Take away the pain of my failed life. Please Lord purify my soul, make me as white as snow.* Suddenly I started weeping heavily with tears pouring between my fingers and running down my arms. My heart moaned with a great depth of humility and sorrow. I felt like all my strength was poured out, totally gone; and out of nowhere, a vision appears.

I see a huge wooden cross standing in the darkness that suddenly catches fire. The bright white flame started at the bottom and moved up the cross very slowly, finally covering the entire cross. The bright white blaze didn't seem to harm the cross at all, and at times it even looked like the tips of the blaze were a light blue color. This vision lasted only a minute or two, and when Dr. Forester finished praying and started talking to the group, my vision had disappeared.

With this strange vision still fresh on my mind, I actually shook my head and asked myself, *What was that? Where did that come from?* I tried to dry my eyes without anyone noticing my moment of weakness.

Doc stated, "At this part of our Friday Night Bible Study, we are going to have special prayer for anyone who needs it."

With me being a full blown Baptist, I wasn't use to the laying on of hands, anointing with oil or praying over anyone. With my shyness, I stand in the background and watch how this will all unfold.

The first lady we all prayed for, you could tell by her countenance she was in a bad way. She looked very sad, so several of the folks there gathered around her to pray. Since I wanted to be involved, I placed my hand on a shoulder of one of the ladies that was standing on the outside ring of people. We all prayed with Doc leading and anointing her with oil.

To my surprise, after praying over this young lady, I could see an amazing difference in her countenance. She was smiling and looked totally healed of her problems, whatever they were. I'm thinking, *Okay, they must be about finished and ready to close.* But then, I hear someone in the group say; "A lady has come forward and asked for prayer and her friend says that she has a demon of adultery."

This catches me totally off guard. Okay, with my Baptist up-bringing, I'm thinking *this it a bit much, but I guess I'll hang in there....*

As we gather around this lady, I'm still standing on the outside of this circled-up band of prayer warriors. I have a clear view of the lady's face.

Doc and everyone else start praying and everything is going pretty good. With my eyes closed, I'm trying to pray for this lady when I hear her starting to slur with a type of hissing and then she was talking in another language that sounded just like an Arab dialect.

I couldn't help myself; I opened my eyes to see what the heck was going on. What I saw was an awful and scary site. This very nice looking lady's face had transformed right in front of me. Her facial features had changed into a horrible, distorted mask of what looked like something dead, fresh out of the grave. She continued to get louder and her face looked worse than ever, as everyone continued to pray.

I felt God telling me to grab her left hand and lift it as far up as I could. I actually was so scared; I started to argue in my mind with God. I told Him, "*I'm not touching her, that thing will get into me!*" Again and what I believe was the Holy Spirit, telling me, "*Grab her hand and lift it up.*" This time it was more of a command. I suddenly step closer in and grabbed her by her left wrist, closed my eyes, and at this point I wasn't even praying, just doing what I was told.

Suddenly, just like earlier during our special prayer time when God gave me a vision of the cross burning from the ground up; this same thing was now happening to me. It felt like my feet had caught on fire. No, it was more like being lowered in warm wax or some kind of thick, soothing hot liquid. This sensation beginning at my feet and very slowly moving up through my whole body, continuing up my arms and finally out through the tips of my fingers. All the while, I continued to hold on to this lady's wrist. I felt like I had super human strength and at that very moment I could have lifted her and the whole group off the floor!

Immediately after what I felt was an anointing of the Holy Spirit passing through my body, the lady stopped slurring and speaking in a demonic tongue. Her face was now normal and peaceful, with tears streaming down both cheeks.

In all my years of being a Christian, I had never experienced anything that even came close to that night when God allowed me to experience His touch of the Holy Spirit.

I was at one of the lowest points in my life...I had lost everything dear to me, I was sleeping in the bed of my truck, working away from home, trying to get back on my feet. In that moment, at that meeting, I was humbled before a Father that had reached down and delivered me out of the mire of my life. I truly believe God chose that moment to draw me even nearer to Him, to bless me with this supernatural experience.

I've only shared what happened that night with a few people, and these friends I felt were at a place in their walk with God that they would believe me, and would understand how real the ongoing war with the principalities of darkness is... and that it continues even now.

13

Portals & Planets

As I continue stepping through this doorway, the sensation of being submerged in warm liquid has spread to my entire body. I wonder if God is reminding me of my experience with the anointing of His Holy Spirit, or was this normal for travel after entering this portal to God knows where.

We suddenly are moving at what seems like light speed. After only a couple seconds, I turn and look back, thinking I'll get a good look at God's mountain as we are leaving Earth, and to my surprise the planet I lived on for so many years was now just a speck.

A bit of sadness came over me as I thought of leaving my family and friends behind. I knew I would probably never return, and that the next time I would see any of them would be if they accept Jesus as Lord and make it to Heaven. I wish I could go back and warn a few of my buddies that are straddling the fence, or as it says in God's Word, in Revelation 3:15-16, "*I know your works, that you are neither cold nor hot. I could wish you were cold or hot. So then, because you are lukewarm, and neither cold nor hot, I will vomit you out of My mouth.*" I believe Jesus was talking about being sold out to Him and not holding on to the worldly side of life.

I guess by this time, a bunch of my friends are probably standing around the funeral home, cracking jokes or telling 'remember when stories' about my foolish days.

Nipper tells me "Hey Chado, stop thinking about the past. Your mortal days are gone. You need to take in all the sights, just look around at this blanket of stars and God's creation of the Heavens."

I look back one last time, maybe to just catch one last glimpse of Earth, but no, it's gone, and even our sun looks like a distant star.

Allayer tells me, "We are now on the edge of what you call your galaxy, and about to enter another."

At our speed, each planet and star we pass by is just a blur. I try to focus ahead to see if I can make out what direction we are headed in. I see a cluster of several stars in the distance that looked like they were in our path. I ask Allayer, "Is that where we are going, that cluster of stars up ahead?"

"Nope, we have one more galaxy to pass through."

"Well guys, now that we're on the road again..."

Nipper butts in and starts laughing. "I guess he thinks he's a country and western singer."

Allayer mumbles under his breath; "I hear that."

"Nipper, what I meant to ask is if we aren't headed for Heaven, where in the world, I mean where in the universe, are we going?"

"We're bringing you to a planet that God designed strictly for a special purpose."

"Okay, what purpose would that be?"

"Can't tell you, you'll just have to wait and see."

"You guys are killing me with suspense." We enter a third and final galaxy, and we seem to be slowing down.

"Nipper, you want to show Chado which planet we are headed to?"

"Sure. Chado, you want to guess or do you want me to tell you?"

"Nipper, you are a card, just tell me already."

"Okay, can you see that bluish green one over there between those two moons?"

"Yes. Wow, it looks a lot like Earth."

"Yep. You can tell God really loves the Earth because it's almost exactly the same."

"So is it full of people like on Earth?"

"No, not exactly."

"What do you mean?"

"Just wait, you'll see."

As we continue to slow down and get a bit closer, I start seeing flashes of light coming to the planet and leaving the planet.

"Hey guys, what's with the flashes of light going and coming?"

"That would be souls of people."

"What? Souls of people, is it like a second Heaven?"

"Nope."

"Well, can you guys please let me in on what I'm seeing? No guessing games, just tell me."

"Nipper, go ahead and explain what this place is used for."

Nipper looks over at me with his funny little grin. "Okay Chado, this planet is called Tabula Rasa. Do you know what that means?"

"No I don't, I had a limited education; as a matter of fact I got most of my education at the school of hard knocks."

"Well Tabula Rasa means fresh start, clean slate or an opportunity to start over without prejudice."

"So does God send people here from Earth and give them another shot at Heaven?"

"Well it's sort of like that. Why don't you wait until we get there? Then you can look around and get a handle on God's handiwork."

"Okay, but I am totally confused at this point."

We drop down over a secluded forest, now hovering just a few feet above the trees. I could see a river that leads directly into a small town. Allayer tells me, "That's where we're going." He points in the direction of a large crowd standing near the shore of this crystal clear river. As we get within a few hundred yards from the crowd, I can see a line of people leading out into the water. I'm wondering what they are up to.

We settle down to the ground near a well-manicured park with a walkway leading in the direction of the crowd. I look around at Nipper and Allayer and realize their appearance has changed. Suddenly they are dressed in street clothes similar to what I am wearing, their wings are gone and they now look to be over six feet tall.

"What the heck guys?"

They both burst out laughing and continue for what seemed like a whole minute, and then I can't help myself. Their joy and happiness were so contagious I joined in, even after realizing the prank was on me. They weren't childlike Angels anymore; their age now looked to be around their early thirties.

Nipper, in between each burst of laughter, was letting me know that the look on my face was priceless.

"Okay guys, y'all have some explaining to do!"

"Well Chado, we could have come clean earlier in this special venture we're on. But Nipper wanted to have a little fun so I went along with it. We felt like you wouldn't mind if we gave you a small surprise."

"A small surprise? I wouldn't call that a small surprise, and where are your wings? You guys are almost as tall as my Guardian Angel. This is awesome."

Nipper asks: "Do you remember when you spoke the words 'God I guess you've got me?' Then you shut your eyes as you slowly sank to the bottom; you had completely let go of life and surrendered to God's mercy. Do you also remember briefly opening your eyes and you saw the millions of glowing phosphorus particles all around you and the peace that came over you?"

"Yes, I remember everything. I went from being so scared, gasping for air, helpless, until that very second when I opened my eyes and saw the glowing particles. That's when the peace came over me and I slowly closed my eyes for what I thought was my last few seconds of life. Then I felt what I thought were two rescue divers grabbing me, one on each arm, but when I opened my eyes I saw you guys. It was so pleasant seeing two childlike Angels with warm smiles, and then as you were helping me stand up, I felt safe and at peace. I was so confused at this point, thinking I was in a deep dream."

"Well Chado, God wants the transition from death to the afterlife, or should I say from mortal to immortality, to be as pleasant as possible.

As Angels with the duty of comforting and transporting souls at the time of their passing, we are commanded to first appear as a gentle child. When this takes place, no one realizes what's happening. When they see us they immediately have trust and the peace continues to grow with each passing moment. If we had presented ourselves like we are now, you may have gotten the wrong idea, been more confused, or possibly even feared us. Trust me; God knows what He's doing. He's only been at it since the beginning. Oh, by the way, your question about our wings and our whole new appearance: Do you remember the term 'shape shifters' used by some of the earlier Indian tribes?"

"Yeah, I have seen several movies that had the voodoo thing going. I never believed any of it."

"Well, you were wise not to believe such foolishness. Mortals don't have the power to pull that one off. But in the Spiritual Realm, angels and demons can, you need to remember this. Lucifer can disguise himself as anything that has blood running through it. You do recall, the Garden of Eden, right?"

"Yes, he appeared to Eve as a snake."

"Just keep that in mind; the Spiritual Realm can sometimes be a bit tricky. As Angels we don't usually take the form of anything other than what God gave us. And of course what you've known us as until now; it was just us as youngsters. Pretty cool don't you think?"

"Yes, absolutely cool."

"Oh, by the way, we hope the friendly little prank we pulled on you didn't hurt your feelings too bad."

"No, of course not. I've picked on y'all for some time now, so I guess I can take it as well as I can dish it out."

Nipper smiles, "You'll find out that God allows His Angels to have a bit of fun... as long as we don't really hurt someone's feelings too bad, and follow His commandments and do His will."

I follow Allayer and Nipper as we head off in the direction of the crowd that's gathered by the river's edge. Allayer whispers, "We can't tell anyone what we are doing, where we've been, or where we are headed. Remember, we need to blend in."

14

Second Chances

When we get within hearing distance, I'm able to make out someone preaching, and they were really going at it. *Whoever this preacher is, man does he know scripture, wow!*

Nipper starts heading for some benches and tables set up underneath what looked like one of my Granny's old peach trees back home.

I ask Nipper "Hey bud, has my granny been through here showing off her green thumb, planting peach trees?"

"No, your granny didn't have to come here, she went straight to Heaven."

"How do you know? Did you guys take her?"

"Well he asked you, go ahead Allayer, tell him."

"Sure, that's a big yes. We were the ones that brought all of your bloodline to Heaven, well most."

"Really? What do you mean, 'most'?"

"Well, there are a few that rejected Jesus Christ and didn't make it to Heaven. Remember the scripture Mathew 10:32-33? *'Therefore whoever confesses Me before men, him I will also confess before My Father Who is in Heaven. But whoever denies Me before men, him I will also deny before My Father who is in Heaven'.*"

"Yes, I remember those verses. A bit of fear would come over me whenever I heard or read that whole chapter. I would ask myself, which one of these do I fall under, deny or confess? I'm sure through my stupidity during my youth I have denied Christ somewhere along the line. As I grew older I felt the need to profess Jesus as Lord to as many people as would listen."

90

"Well, we hate to tell you this, but there were some in your family that continued to reject God all the years of their lives. They were so full of pride and embarrassed about what the world would think of them if someone saw them following Christ. This is so sad, when a person would throw away an eternity with God. The God who loved them so much that He sent his only Son to die for their sins."

"My goodness, if they could only see into the Spiritual Realm, surely all mankind would fall on their faces and be humbled before an almighty God."

Nipper jumps in "Here's the kicker. All the people that think they know what they're doing and just plain refuse to believe and trust in God are going to have a big wakeup call. In the final days at the Great White Throne Judgment, God says that every knee will bow."

"Wow that will be a scary time for a lot of folks. Hey, can you guys tell me if my dad made it?"

"Yes he made it, but it was by the hair of his chinny chin chin."

"Oh wow, I have often wondered if he really made it. He never wanted to talk about God with me. I tried bringing up the Lord with him only a few times and he would always get mad and want to change the subject. You know, come to think of it, it seemed harder to talk to my family members about God than anyone else. I know he confessed Jesus as Lord in his last few days on Earth, but I never knew if he really meant it. Wow, what a relief, thanks guys for sharing that. I'll get to see him, right?"

"Sure you will."

Allayer tells me, "Chado Cole, if it hadn't been for your mom praying so hard all through the years for your dad, he wouldn't have been spared. In the Holy Scripture, it tells you of

God promising to save your whole household. In your dad's case, God used Lucifer to strike him down with cancer and this allowed your dad time to realize his days on Earth were about over, in turn humbling him into submission. This is a good example of God's mercy. He heard your mom's prayers and God spared your dad from eternity under the rule of Lucifer and Hell. Just think if your dad had died suddenly before his sickness, when he was denying God and letting pride rule, he would not have had the chance to ask Jesus into his heart; he would have never seen Heaven's Gate."

"Thank you God, and thank you Mom for praying; gonna see Pop again, glory!"

* * *

"Chado, you want a peach?"

"Do I want a peach? Heck yeah! Hey, that's right we can eat in Heaven. Well, this is not exactly Heaven, but I guess Tabula Rasa is close, right?"

Nipper laughs, "You're in the spiritual realm and you can eat, get over it."

While we all kick back enjoying huge delicious peaches, listening to this preacher standing waist deep in water with God's Word flowing out of his mouth, I ask, "Well, who is this preacher anyhow?"

"That my friend is none other than John the Baptist."

"What? Do you mean THE John the Baptist from the Bible?"

"Yes, in the flesh, or should we say in the spirit."

"What's he doing here on Tabula Rasa?"

"Well Chado, you're looking at it and hearing it. He's been working here for a little over two thousand years preaching God's Word."

"What? Two thousand years? Wow! Okay, I'm confused again. I had no idea there were such a thing as a second chance after you die. You are either saved or you're not, right?"

Allayer explains "Well it's not a place you could actually call a second chance. This is the first time the souls of these immortals have been taught about the truth of God. You see, you were brought up in a nation where the beliefs were set on God's Word and Law. Just about everywhere you turned there was opportunity to understand about our Maker, whether it was a Bible in a motel dresser or a church you pass on the road or maybe even a Christian boldly sharing the Gospel. Let me put it to you like this, if you have knowledge of God and then turn away; you are in a world of hurt. But these souls that you are looking at were less fortunate and never had the opportunity or knowledge that God even existed."

"Okay?"

"Do you see the little teenager third in line from being baptized?"

"Yes, the dark skinned kid."

"Well, he was born into a family of desert people, belonging to a tribe that has worshipped idols for centuries, doing blood sacrifices unto their pagan gods. The kid has never known anything else other than what he was taught by his tribal leaders."

Nipper asks "Are you starting to get the picture?"

"Yes, so if a person on Earth doesn't have any knowledge of the one true God, they get to come here where they are taught the truth."

"That's right."

"Okay, so why didn't God send missionaries to teach the truth about Jesus to that tribe?"

Nipper boldly stated "He did, and the fools cut the missionaries heads off."

Allayer jumps in, "Nipper, calm down. Don't be so graphic."

Nipper mumbles, "Well they did, and I remember being there to transport both missionaries to Heaven. It was an awful sight, everyone in the tribe running around all painted up with their eyes rolled back in their heads chanting some crazy demonic language. And the heads of the missionaries stuck up on a couple poles in the center of the village. I wanted to kill them all and let God sort them out."

"Nipper, you need to cool it. You know God won't allow you to have that attitude but for a few seconds."

"I know. You're right Allayer. I get a little wound up when God's people are hurt. I know that little boy we're talking about would have never made it if God hadn't laid everything out so perfect. So Chado, do you understand now?"

"Okay, let me see. So if you have absolutely no knowledge of God, a soul gets to come to Tabula Rasa and then taught like a child the truth about God. Then what? Does everyone that comes here eventually go on to see Heaven?"

Allayer explains, "Well no, not everyone. Even here, God still gives a soul free will to choose. You see, everyone that comes here falls under a spirit of illusion and they think they are still alive and are on Earth. That's one of the reason we told you we can't let anyone know who we are or what we're doing."

"So the souls here at this stage can end up in Hell?"

"Yes, and you would be surprised at how many even after being taught still choose to rebel against God."

Nipper says, "Most of the older ones choose wrongly. The younger are easily taught. Sort of like back on Earth."

All of a sudden, I notice John the Baptist stops preaching and starts heading up the hill out of the river bottom in our direction. I whisper, "Hey guys check it out. John the Baptist is heading right for us. Do you think he wants to talk to us? "

Nipper says, "Be still and listen."

John walks straight up to where I was sitting and mumbles, "Hey bud, excuse me" then places one foot on my bench and with ease completely jumps over my head, landing directly on top of the stone table, barely missing my forehead with one of his sandals. I'm thinking, *what the heck.* I look over at Allayer and Nipper and they are laughing pretty hard at this point.

When I look back at preacher John, I wonder, *What's this guy going to do now?* All of a sudden he throws me a huge peach, then turns around picks three more; one for himself and the other two for Allayer and Nipper.

John tells Nipper, "My throat is dry and these peaches really hit the spot after a morning sermon."

Then he asks Allayer, "Who's the new guy?"

Allayer says, "John meet Chado Cole, he is our special assignment, God is up to something and we don't have a clue."

"So, Mr. John, Sir..."

John quickly states "Hey, new guy, I am a nobody, doing the work of the Lord. Don't call me Mr. or Sir, please just call me John. So what's your question?"

"So you guys all know each other?"

Nipper joins in "Yup, yup, yep. We had a hand in bringing John to Heaven."

"John, do you mind me asking, why you chose to live here instead of Heaven?"

John takes a deep breath, looks around at Nipper then back at me with a smile and says: "God designed this place for a special purpose; I am just a tool designed by God to teach the Gospel, so that the unknown will be known and the unsaved will be saved. He desires that no man would perish, but all who love Him would have everlasting life. The mortal would put on immortality, and all who have breath, look on the One that is greater than all, the Lamb, the Most High, the King of Kings and Lord of Lords, Jesus Christ. God has overflowed my soul with the gift of preaching, and every morning He gives me a renewing power for the Word of God to flow freely from my lips. If there were no souls to preach to and I was the last one here, I would preach to the rocks, the trees, the birds of the air. I say the Word of God will pour from my soul for eternity."

"Amen, John. I am speechless. I thank God I had the opportunity to meet you. I hated the way the Pharisees and Herod treated you back in those days."

"Chado Cole, it was a pleasure to meet you. Don't sweat King Herod; I know now he wishes he had listened back in those days. He stands where the worm never dies and the thirst is never quenched. Nipper, Allayer, if God reveals this mystery, let me know, I might be able to use it in a sermon."

John the Baptist walks away heading in the same direction as a few stragglers from the crowd were heading. He slowly turns around, looking back in our direction and with a big smile, winds up like a baseball pitcher and throws his peach seed at me, almost hitting me square in the chest.

"What the heck was that about?"

Allayer and Nipper were having themselves a big hootenanny laugh. I look back at John and he gives me a big smile then held up his hand with a warm wave.

I turned back to Allayer and Nipper and ask, "Is he usually like that? When I first met him he almost kicked me; and on his departure he almost got me with a peach seed."

Nipper laughs, "John the Bee was just checking out your reflexes and to see if you could catch."

"What do you mean John the Bee, and why would he want to know about my reflexes"?

Allayer looks over at me with a big smile, "The Bee is his nickname and he loves to play baseball; who knows, he might ask you to play."

"You got to be kidding! I might get to play baseball with John the Baptist? That is awesome!"

Nipper, with excitement in his voice, "Wait till you see who else might be playing! God has a pretty good list of people you might have read about in the Bible that are here serving Him on this planet. Well not all of them play baseball, but some do."

"So John's not the only one here on Tabula Rasa from the ancient times, I mean the people from the Bible? That is so exciting! Who are they?"

"We aren't going to name everyone God has assigned to Tabula, it would take all day. You have to realize this is a huge planet with millions of souls that are in transition. God has His chosen scattered all over the planet teaching and preaching."

"Okay, I get the picture. So is John a good ball player?"

"Oh yeah, he didn't get his nickname the Bee for nothing. You could even say he's as good as or better than the pros on Earth. You don't want him pitching on the opposite side. His strike out percentage is unbelievable!"

"I'll keep that in mind if I get a chance to play."

* * *

"Hey guys, can I ask a question?"

Nipper said, "Chado Cole have we ever not let you ask a question?"

"Well, I was just wondering, if God's chosen have been here for thousands of years, how long will they have to stay before they move on to Heaven? "

Allayer tells me, "It's like this. God gives everyone assignments. You do know we don't just drop people off in Heaven and they lay around with someone serving them tea. God has carefully chosen duties that fit each ones character. He knows what they have a love or passion for."

"Okay, but when can John the Baptist and the other teachers leave the planet?"

Allayer continues to explain, "After God destroys every living thing on Earth and all souls of men are spiritually evacuated, each to his own destination. God's redeemed will go straight to Heaven; the unrighteous will be condemned under the rule of Lucifer to a devil's Hell. The few people of Earth without any knowledge of God will come to Tabula Rasa. After these last few are taught and have made decisions, they will then be transported to either Heaven or Hell depending on their choice. When the last person on Tabula Rasa has made his or her decision and the planet is without souls of men, that's when God will call all who have labored for so many years back to Heaven."

"So do y'all have an idea how long Earth has left?"

"No, but all the Angels believe it's very close! Nipper and I both believe the special instructions of having to show you everything has something to do with the final days."

"Are you guys sure you've never had to do this with anyone else?"

"Nope, you are our first. Everyone else, go straight to Heaven."

"Yeah, I'll be happy to find out what God's up to."

...

After enjoying several peaches while sitting on the shaded park bench, Allayer decided it was time to move on. We start walking toward a small town that is only a few hundred yards from where the baptism had taken place. I noticed the people there were using horse and carriages for transportation. "Hey Nipper, If this was like Earth, where were all the cars and trucks?"

"We don't think God really cares for motorized vehicles. If you have to have fuel for everything, that leads to industrial disease. Take a look at Earth after a couple hundred years of what they call intelligent progression. Mankind has destroyed mother Earth from the inside out. I don't know if you've noticed but the whole Earth groans and suffers as a woman with pain in childbirth, right along with the sickness of men's hearts. They sacrifice the air and water for profit, even some of the ones that claim to protect the Earth are hypocrites. They embrace lies and spit at the truth. They sneer at God's Holy Word and believe the lies of hell. These souls are brought here for a very short time, so there is no need for them to have jobs like they had back on Earth. It's all designed for having knowledge of the truth about the Holy Trinity, not cruising in a Camaro."

"I understand, I always have wanted to live back in the old days, you know the horse and buggy days. Well I have been spoiled to electricity and running water. I would miss that and cable TV."

Nipper laughs, "Don't worry God provides everything, we guarantee you will be well taken care of, and you won't miss cable TV. Chado, if you had the power, wouldn't you do the same for one of your children?"

"I reckon so Nipper, I reckon so."

As we walk through a large stone gate entering the city, a group of small children came running up to us. They were all speaking in a different language, and at first, I couldn't understand a single word they were saying. Then I noticed I was able to make out a few words in between their non-stop chatter. This language that I had never heard before was now making sense.

"Wow, I can tell what they are saying. They are telling me, 'Welcome to our village stranger, welcome. May God bless you and keep you'."

I look at Allayer and he's shaking his head yes and reminds me, "Do you remember what we told you about your thought capacity after you leave Earth?"

At that point I turn back around to the kids and to my own surprise, I tell them in their language, "Thank you guys and May God bless and keep you also."

While we were slowly making our way down the street, I see a small child heading in my direction that looked like a Mayan Indian. This little girl is holding a cup full of what looked like grape juice. She's smiling while trying to hand me her cup, and at the same time asking me if I was her father. I look around at Allayer and Nipper expecting them to be rolling on the ground, but it was just the opposite. They were both looking down with sadness on their faces. I slowly turn, having to face this precious little child, "No Sweetie, I'm not your father, but if I see him I'll tell him you're looking for him."

As I look back at my two faithful Angel buddies, they are both shaking their heads no. "No, what did I do?" After we move up the street away from the little girl, Nipper whispers to me, "Chado, a lot of the kids that come here have lost their parents. The parents had knowledge of God but continued to reject the truth of salvation and they didn't make it. So the kids after passing are brought here. That little girl's whole village was wiped out from smallpox and she still has some memory of her family. That part of it is very sad."

"I thought everyone is under a spirit of illusion and doesn't really know what's going on?"

"Well, they don't. But God, for whatever reason allows everyone to have some memory of family. We think it might be some way to allow their hearts to become tender to the true love of Jesus."

Nipper tells me, "Remember when you lost your daughter Summer and you became closer to the Lord than any other time in your life?"

"Oh yeah, how could I forget?"

"Well, we believe that could be one of the reasons God allows those who come here to have a memory of their family."

101

As we move up the street, I ask Allayer and Nipper "Hey guys, are y'all wondering why I haven't asked if my daughter Summer made it to Heaven?"

Allayer lets me know, "We understand, you don't want to know until you get to Heaven, right?"

"Right, I guess my fear ever since she got killed comes from how she was living on the edge, and a little on the wild side. I'm just thankful to a Christian lady I was dating a few years ago that told me she had prayed the prayer of salvation with her; actually, several times. I pray Summer meant it in her heart." As I was looking down at the cobblestone street, making our way through this small village, a heavy feeling of despair came over me. Without realizing it, I felt the tendency to shrug my shoulders with a feeling of defeat.

I looked back up at the guys and said, "I just hope she made it, I can't stand the thought of living in Heaven for eternity without my little Sweetie."

I notice Nipper and Allayer are not successful trying to hide their childish grins. As we move along the narrow street, I'm thinking, *that was a good sign, the grins I mean; maybe she did make it!*

15

Bad Day for Pagans

As we pass by a two story building just to our left, I hear loud voices coming from inside. The building has two large doors that are wide open and you can easily see inside. To my surprise, I have a clear view of some sort of a statue in the center of the room. There are prayer rugs placed all around the statue, and several people are kneeling, praying and worshiping the statue. In the back of this weird house of worship, there is one old man surrounded by a group of younger men having a heated discussion.

Allayer taps me on the shoulder and points to a table and chairs sitting around what looked like an old timey water well. The well reminded me of what you would see in a movie about the Bible in ancient times. This well had an old pulley system with a rope and bucket. The well and the sitting area had an awning covering it. I'm thinking *this is actually very nice.* As we sit down a gorgeous young lady walks up to us coming from a basket weaving shop just across the street. She has three silver chalice drinking cups with her and as she sets the cups on the table, with a foreign language she tells us, "*Trust in the Lord with all your heart, and lean not on your own understanding; in all your ways acknowledge Him, and He shall direct your paths.*"

She then turns and drops the bucket over the edge and with the weight of the bucket, the rope quickly uncoils and we hear the bucket as it hits the water. I stand to help her draw the water back up when Nipper grabs my hand, shaking his head no, he whispers, "It's their custom to serve you, we shouldn't interfere."

I sit back down thinking, *"If that had been my dad and I didn't try to help a female, he would have popped me behind the head and said, 'Boy, you better get off your butt and help that lady'."*

Nipper giggles as he hears my thoughts, *"Well Chado, we aren't in Kansas anymore."*

We all three laugh a bit and suddenly hush as the young lady approaches. She walks over with a ladle made out of what looks like an old timey gourd; she then fills each of our glasses to the point of almost running over. When she finishes, she places the gourd back in the bucket, sets it on the edge of the well and turns back to us, giving us an elegant bow saying, "May God bless you and keep you, and that you will always thirst for the Word of God."

We all give her a nod and thank her for her kindness. She smiles, turns away and heads back to her basket weaving shop. I can't help myself, in a daze watching her walk back across the street, I'm thinking *what an awesome lady, Earth could use more people like her.* Suddenly Allayer lightly kicks me on the leg.

I look over at him and ask, "What the heck Allayer?" He's motioning with his eyes to look over at what's going on in the pagan worship center.

With a clear view of the heated disagreement still going on with the old man right in the middle, Allayer tells me, "Watch and remember", and then holds his finger in front of his lips letting me know to be quiet and listen.

I whisper, "Who is that old man?"

Nipper leans over, takes a drink of water and tells me, "That's Elijah."

"What? You're telling me that old man, is the Elijah from the Bible? The Elijah that God took up in a whirlwind and he never saw death, that Elijah?"

"Chado, why are you so surprised every time we see someone you've read or heard about?"

"I know, I know. It's just so cool getting to see these people. I've been taught about these Bible characters all of my life. I remember sitting in our little Sunday school classes as a kid. Not to mention on through my adult life and now boom! I'm seeing it all first hand. You guys need to give me a little room for excitement."

Allayer whispers, "It's a joy for us to witness and be a part of this assignment, but you need to pay attention to what's going on across the street."

I turn to where I can see what is unfolding inside the mosque. The younger men are slinging their hands in the air and some are pointing their fingers in the face of Elijah. I can make out some of what they are saying and they are defending their statue and claiming it to be a god. One dressed like some noble priest starts blaspheming the Holy Spirit while lighting incense around the statue. Another one of their priests comes from the back and the rest hush, like he was something special. He stands in front of a podium a few feet behind the statue and tells Elijah to leave and never return. He says they will see to it that all who live in or enter this village will either bow to Hurrian, the god of wisdom, or die by the sword.

I'm thinking *this is unbelievable, if they only knew what was really going on here. Good lord, what are they doing?*

Allayer bumps my leg again and points down the street. As I look I can see three people walking toward our location leading several horses. The one guy in the middle looks like a young kid no more than twelve to fifteen years old. The other two guys look like linemen for a pro football team. They all three are dressed in sackcloth and sandals. The two big guys are wearing leather belts strapped across their breast with each having huge swords attached to the belts. I'm thinking, *it's about to be a showdown.*

I look back and I hear Elijah, "Hear me worshipers of Hurrian, you have turned your face from the prophets and the Word of God. As the Lord of Host has cried out in the wilderness, you closed your ears. He shouted from the mountains, you turned away. He opened the Heavens and your hearts became like stone. Thus says the Lord, He knows your heart. I tell you this now, you will see the truth, and you will meet the darkness where the worm never dies."

Elijah turns and slowly walks toward the door with several men running up to him, spitting and cursing. Elijah, with a stern look on his face manages to walk past and through the angry mob. He then turns and walks toward the three men coming up the street without speaking or even looking at them as they pass. He continues on while lifting his hands to the Lord, praying and singing as he walks.

I was hoping he would have come over and hung out for a while. Allayer tells me, "This isn't a good time for a visit if you get my drift."

"I totally understand. So who are the three guys with the horses coming up the street?"

"You want to tell him Nipper?"

"Sure. They are all Angels; the two big guys are Warrior Angels and the little guy, well, he's kind of special."

"What do you mean special?"

106

"He has a power of persuasion. He can pretty much have a person stand on their head if he wanted them to."

"So, why does he have the two Warriors with him?"

"Sometimes Lucifer allows some of his followers to be numb to his ability, so God sends backup, just to keep all this on the quiet side."

"So Lucifer has power here?"

"Not really, he's very limited here. His power hangs onto the free will of some of these souls."

"Okay, I'm confused now."

"Just watch and learn."

The three Angels stop right in front of us; they dropped the reins to the horses without having to tie them up. Apparently these horses are trained and have done this before. Allayer, Nipper, and I have to stand because our view is blocked by the horses. We take a couple steps closer as the three Angels enter.

Immediately, the spiritual leader of the group starts raising his voice. "You aren't welcome here infidels, you are filthy and have no right to set foot in our holy temple. The very sight of the dirty rags you wear is an abomination. You must kneel in the street before our god of wisdom, Hurrian. Then you must bathe and wear pure white cotton robes and bring a sacrifice of blood before our god. Leave now, or we will have your heads."

The others join in, shaking their fists and start moving toward the three Angels now standing just inside the doorway. The small Angel pulls out a handful of dirt from a leather pouch tied to his side. He walks through the angry mob and tosses the dirt up into the air over the statue. The mob becomes furious, with the leader shouting, "How dare you defile Hurrian. Kill them, Kill them all!"

Suddenly I hear a loud booming voice from the little Angel, "SILENCE!"

I look over at Allayer and Nipper, "Wow, did you hear that?"

Allayer bumps me in the ribs with his elbow, "Be quiet."

You could have heard a pin drop, they were all speechless. A few seconds passed, then suddenly I notice the dirt that the Angel threw on the statue seem to be eating away at their golden idol. Within just a couple minutes it is completely gone. After the idol is destroyed the small Angel tells them, "You will all go out and mount the horses, you are going on a journey."

Each one comes through the door, without any expression on their faces, gets on the horses and waits. The two Warrior Angels grab onto the reins of the front four horses and start back down the street from where they came. The leader of this pagan religious group has to ride on the last horse, this being another touch of humiliation.

The small Angel walks by us and smiles as he nods his head in a friendly gesture. We all nod back and smile as he turns and follows after the group.

I look over at Allayer and Nipper with my eyes blared wide open in amazement to what just took place. "Guys that was unbelievable, can I ask where are they taking them?"

Nipper points to a mountain range that looks to be several miles away from the village. He looks over at me as we walk back to our table and tells me "You'll see. Finish your water, we're going to follow."

As we make our way down the cobblestone street leading us out of the village, the three Angels and the group of condemned men are only a few yards ahead. We pass several people from the village on our way out of town and they all seem to be smiling or making friendly gestures as we walk by. I ask Allayer if they have any idea on what's taking place.

"Chado, do you remember what we told you about the spirit of persuasion?"

"Yes, so I take it they don't know?"

"That's right, and they won't even miss these characters."

"What would have happened if Elijah hadn't confronted them?"

"Well if God would have allowed this to go on, they would continue to force their false religion on everyone in the village. They would have grown stronger over a short period of time, eventually spreading completely over Tabula Rasa. Sort of like a plague that would destroy millions. This would start religious wars and eventually turn Tabula into another Earth."

"Wow, just like on Earth."

"Now you've got it. With all the man-made religions on Earth, it only took a few thousand years for the complete fall of man."

"What do you mean the complete fall of man? Is it over for Earth?"

"Nipper and I both feel, well I guess you could say all of the Angels can tell, it's just a matter of time before God takes everyone that loves Him in the great rapture."

Nipper explains more, "Lucifer didn't just start his job today, he has been at it for thousands of years and he is good at stealing the minds and hearts of men. He has used religion as one of his best traps. Oh yeah, he's a sly dog. He has fooled man with a spirit of deception. Can you imagine how stupid it would be to worship a statue or some gold idol? That's hilarious, and people have fallen for that deceiving spirit for centuries. If you fast forward to your time on Earth the idols changed from being a statue to money, fancy cars, bigger homes, sports, movie stars, oh yeah rock stars; anything that people loved more than God.

So to answer your question, God has sent some of His key people here to Tabula Rasa. They teach and give the ones without knowledge a chance to know Him, and when they refuse to acknowledge Him as God and turn to idols, His wrath is certain. Chado, do you get the picture?"

"Yeah, thanks Nipper."

As we continue following the three Angels and their captives, I see the priest on the last horse turn and look back at us. He has an empty, lost look on his face; his eyes seem to have sort of a glaze covering over them. He reminded me of an old black man I had the opportunity to meet years ago. The old man's speech slurred to the point where I couldn't understand him. A great grandson of the old man kindly told me his grandfather was one hundred and five years old. His eyes were sky blue and had the same haze covering both eyes. This was the oldest man I had ever come in contact with back on Earth.

The priest calmly turned back around and slumped in the saddle as we near the base of the mountains. We turn off the cobblestone road onto a narrow trail that twisted around and up, paralleling a river that was flowing between two huge mountains.

I could now smell the evergreen trees growing along the trail and feel the cool mist coming off the river as it rushes across the boulders and the small waterfalls that were numerous up the river. I look over at Nipper and tell him, "Doesn't this kind of remind you of Montana; what do think?"

He reaches over and breaks off a small twig from one of the aspen trees and says, "You know partner, heck, I believe you're right, it does feel a little like Montana."

I laugh at his new western accent, "So Nipper you've been to Montana?"

Allayer laughs, "We've been around since 1116 BC, don't you think we've had enough time to make that trip?"

"You guys are too funny, and to be so old and still have a sense of humor." We all three continue to laugh as we come to a sudden stop.

I walk over and stand as close to the river as I could, in an attempt to see around the bend to find out why we've stopped. I start to walk ahead and Allayer tells me to hold up. Within a few more seconds we start moving again.

"Hey guys I wonder what's going on up ahead?"

Nipper says, "We are probably at the hidden cave."

"The hidden cave?"

"Chado, why do you feel the need to repeat everything that has any kind of excitement attached to it?"

"Well, I don't know... because it's exciting?" I start giggling and look over at Nipper and he's smiling from ear to ear shaking his head.

"Hey guys, I see what's going on. The two big Angels are removing heavy brush away from a narrow passage. Is this some kind of secret passage or do the town folk know about it?"

Nipper animatedly replies, "Absolutely not, this is definitely off limits to everyone."

"Well, just a little brush covering the entrance wouldn't keep me out, especially when I was a kid. Adventure was my name and meddling was my game."

The little Angel ahead of us starts laughing and turns around, holds his finger over his lips with the universal sign to be quiet. Nipper tells me, "Now you've done it."

"What? Am I in trouble for joking around?"

Allayer whispers, "No you're not in trouble; it's just the little Angel has to keep his concentration to be able to control the minds of those wicked men. Remember, he has the power of persuasion and he's locked in on the bad guys. We just need to tone it down a bit. As for your question about someone finding this opening, if they do, they won't make it past the next obstacle."

"What next obstacle?" Nipper chuckles; "How did we know you were going to ask?"

"Okay guys, I'll wait and see for myself."

All the horses, without any effort from their riders, lined up single file and squeezed through the narrow opening. It reminded me of earlier when they all stood in the street back at the village without being tied. I was now certain that this was not the first time these horses have been through this passage with the condemned saddled on their backs.

We stop again; I mumble, "It looks like a dead end. What now guys?" Allayer and Nipper wave their hands, and tell me, "Wait for it, and be quiet." I'm thinking, *Surely we didn't make a wrong turn somewhere behind us.*

I see the two big Angels pull out their swords. They stick both blades in the soft ground, and then they kneel down as to rest their foreheads on the handles of their swords and seem to be praying.

After only a couple minutes pass, the Angels stand, walk up to the face of the cliff wall, one on the right and one on the left. Both reach up well above their heads and at the same time thrust each sword into what looked like, keyways.

As they pull the swords from the cliff wall, I feel movement under my feet and start to hear the sounds of stone rubbing against stone. The floor of the narrow path was vibrating, and several small rocks from overhead sprinkled down near where we were standing. Finally, silence.

As I'm still looking up to avoid getting hit with falling rock, Allayer bumps me with his elbow and nods toward the dead end. To my surprise, 'Shazam', a cave opening has appeared. I turn and whisper to Allayer and Nipper, "I guess you guys were right, no one in a million years could ever find this place."

We slowly enter the cave and I see one of the three Angels walk over to a small pool of burning liquid, he grabs a torch and dips it in the pool. As he picks it back up his torch ignites with the same bright bluish white fire as the pool. He walks a few feet ahead of the group, reaches up with his torch and touches a long trough. The sound of the liquid igniting from the trough echoes for several seconds. This bright white fire races down the trough, illuminating the entire cavern.

I am speechless; the size of this cavern would dwarf Carlsbad, my goodness, and the colors are unbelievable. I could see streaks of gold several feet wide layer after layer across each wall. There were clear bluish pools of water as far as the eye could see.

As I walk over and stick my hand in one of the pools, I had a thought, *what a nice place to bathe, especially with the thermo heat causing all the bubbles.*

I hear Nipper "Come on, quit fooling around. We need to catch up."

I jump up and get into a little trot. I didn't realize that the few minutes I spent exploring the cavern had allowed almost everyone to make it across. I can tell they are headed for an opening that's giving off light from the outside. That's got to be the way out.

We catch back up with the condemned, just as they walk out into the sunlight. We are now on top of the mountain; wow, what a view. This reminds me of God's mountain back on Earth. "Hey that's right. Allayer, Nipper, has this mountain got portals like the one we came through?"

Both Nipper and Allayer shake their heads yes, as they both turn and continue following the group along this huge plateau.

16

Iron Collars & Chains

We only walk a couple hundred yards through the scattered trees when we come out in an opening. "Oh, my goodness, hey guys, this is exactly like the other one! I mean God's mountain, with the portals."

This place had the same rock formations and bench that was on God's mountain, including the portals. I bump Allayer with my elbow and whisper, "I still say it looks a lot like Stonehenge." I ask Nipper, "Hey bud, which one of these portals leads to you know where?" Nipper shakes his head and tells me to follow Allayer.

The horses walk through a small opening that leads to the inside of the rock circle, each one stopping near the middle allowing the rider to dismount. After dismounting, the men were directed to sit on the stone bench and wait. The horses all walked out of the arena and started grazing just on the outside of the stone circle behind us.

While sitting on the far side of the rock circle, we could see the faces of the condemned men and also have a clear view of all three portals. The men still have a blank look on their faces and their eyes are covered with a dull bluish sheen.

I whisper to Allayer and Nipper, "That little Angel with the power of persuasion, how long can he control them like that?"

Nipper shrugged his shoulders, "I guess as long as he needs to."

We sit for a few minutes and my anticipation gets the best of me and I ask Allayer, "What are they waiting on? I figured they would have just herded them through and we would be on our way by now."

Allayer holds his hand out with a gesture, like you would if you were going to pat a kid on the head. "Have patience and watch."

I hear what sounds like a wagon and horses coming up from behind us. We all turn, sliding our butts on the rock bench, positioning ourselves to see what is slowly making its way through the scattered timber, when finally it appears. It is a two wheeled cart, being pulled by mules. This thing looks like it's a thousand years old, and the guy driving this ancient cart looks like a great big bodybuilder with long black hair reaching below his belt.

He stops the wagon just on the outside of the rock circle, gets off, walks around to the back of the cart, reaches in and grabs a hand full of chains and what looks like iron collars. He walks inside the circle directly in front of the men and drops his heavy load of medieval chains and collars on the ground.

He then turns and looks over in our direction as he reaches for a lamb skin wine pouch hanging at his side. He holds it up over his head with both hands squeezing it with his mouth wide open. The stream of wine makes a hollow sound as he fills his mouth. He then holds it up at us, as if to ask if we want any. We all three gave him a friendly wave letting him know, thanks but no thanks.

I ask Allayer and Nipper, "Who is this guy?"

Nipper answers, "You want to guess? Here's a small clue; he kicked a lot of butt in his day and had his power stripped away when a cunning woman cut off his hair."

I laugh, "Well that was easy, it's got to be Samson!"

"Yep, you got it, Samson."

After Samson gets his refreshment, he turns back to the job at hand. He reaches down and picks up the iron collars and locks each one on to the necks of all the condemned men. Each collar has a four to five foot chain already attached. Samson goes back to his cart and retrieves eleven sections of rope, comes back and starts attaching a single rope to the end of each chain. The ropes look to be at least ten to fifteen feet long.

I ask my Angels, "What are the chain and ropes for?" Allayer and Nipper at the same time, "You'll see."

After tying each rope securely to the end of each chain, Samson walks back down the line of men, carefully coiling and placing each rope directly in front of them.

To my surprise, after he finishes he walks over and sits down right beside us, smiles, holds his hand out and shakes our hands. I'm thinking, *Now how cool is this? I just shook hands with one of the heroes of the Bible.* He doesn't say a word as he lies back on the rock bench, takes some of his long hair and drapes it across his eyes to block the sunlight and immediately goes to sleep.

Allayer looks over at me with a grin, "Samson must have been putting in a lot of overtime."

Nipper and I both giggle.

The sun starts to set behind the mountain range and I mumble, "Well what do you think?"

Allayer tells Nipper, "Looks like it won't happen until morning, too risky for this late in the day."

Nipper replies, "Yes, I believe God will delay the passing until morning."

"Hey guys, what's going on? Why's God delaying, what did you call it, the passing over?"

117

Nipper shakes his head yes, "God probably has someone coming for this one. Who knows what Lucifer might have up his sleeve? God might be sending backup."

With my eyes blared, "Backup, we might need backup?"

Allayer explains, "Chado Cole, here on Tabula Rasa, the fallen angels aren't allowed to come and retrieve the souls of men without permission; on Earth when the lost die, they have a right through the authority of Lucifer. Remember he is the prince of the air on Earth. On Earth as the lost die, at that very second the demons of Hell grab them by the hand just like we did you, and they are immediately taken straight to the pit.

Here on Tabula we have to wait until an appointed time, and that appointed time is exactly when God allows it. You see those two big Angels over there? When all this goes down, you'll get to see them do their job; and sometimes they allow Samson to complete the task while they stand guard."

"I have to ask, what's their job?"

Nipper mumbles, "Well they sort of feed the demons those ropes as they poke their nasty heads out. Trust us, it won't be pretty."

Allayer asks "Can you see that gold threshold in front of the portal to Hell?"

I stand to get a better look, while Allayer continues to explain. "It's about twenty-four inches wide and embedded in the rock about six feet in front, circling all the way around the portal. Can you see it from here?"

I take a few steps toward the portal, "Yeah, I see it. What's it for?"

Nipper stands and walks up beside me, "Chado, the fallen angels are scared to cross that threshold, because if they happen to get brave enough and try it, they lose almost all of their power. When this happens, the fury of those two big Angels will be unleashed!"

Allayer tells us, "Let's find a place to rest for the night." We all head for a dark green grassy spot underneath an evergreen tree leaving Samson lying on the rock bench.

After only a few minutes I fall into a deep sleep and I dream of meeting God. When I first saw Him from a distance, His face shone so bright I couldn't quite make out what He looked like, but I could hear His deep soft voice. "*You will be given two scrolls, each having one page. They will be made of papyrus sheets; the length of each is eighteen inches and the width of each fourteen inches. Each scroll on its own attached with two pieces of cedar wood. The print of your bloodline will reveal to each, a mystery.*"

I feel someone bumping my shoulder, rousing me out of a deep sleep. I slowly open my eyes and see Samson standing over me with his huge body blocking the morning sun. He doesn't say anything, he reaches down and gives me a handful of figs and drops his lambskin wine pouch beside me. I turn to say thanks as he heads back toward the portals. As I'm thinking, *How in the world, is that fig tree making it up here at this altitude?*

Allayer asks me, "Chado, did you sleep well? This was your first time to sleep since they woke you up for your last dive on the barge."

Before I can answer Nipper interrupts, "Hey Chado, did you dream about a scroll last night? Allayer and I both dreamed about a couple scrolls."

With excitement I reply, "Yes I did, God told me the sizes, what they're made of, how they're held together with cedar wood and something about my bloodline would reveal mysteries, and that's about it. Samson woke me up."

Nipper tells me, "Yeah, that's about all He allowed us to see also. God loves to give us little hints in our dreams about things to come."

Allayer takes one of my figs that Samson gave me and pops it in his mouth, "Come on, we need to get back to the portals, I believe it's going to be a wild morning."

* * *

As we walk back over to what looks like Stonehenge, I see the condemned men were still sitting in almost the exact same position. From the weight of the iron collars and the heavy chains they are all slumped, leaning forward. Each one having to look down and being forced to bow before God.

The two big Angels dressed in sackcloth are standing, one on each side of the gold threshold in front of the portal to Hell. Each one with the tips of their swords lightly stuck in the ground, they rest their hands draped on the handles of their weapons. They both stand at attention staring across the threshold at each other.

I can feel the warm rays of the sun now peeking over a nearby mountain, thinking what a beautiful morning to be witnessing such a dreary scene.

Allayer hears my thoughts, reaches over, places his hand on my shoulder, "Chado, they had their chance. From the time they died on Earth until yesterday, they were presented with the Gospel of Jesus Christ and their free will got the best of them. Remember, God designed this place to give all without knowledge a chance."

Nipper joins in, "Yeah, remember what Tabula Rasa means; chance without prejudice."

"I reckon so."

Suddenly, I feel a warm strong wind hitting my back. Allayer wheels around and points behind us, I turn and see heavy dark clouds moving in our direction. I ask Allayer and Nipper, with a whisper, "Hey guys, is it about to go down?" Nipper shakes his head yes.

Samson gets up and slowly walks across the opening, with his size and weight the small stones crunch under his sandals. He walks up to the first man reaches down and takes hold of the chain in one hand and the coiled rope in the other. He slowly turns, looking at the portal.

I see the little Angel of persuasion positioned just to the right of the eleven lost souls. He kneels and raises his hands to Heaven.

I look up at the heavy dark clouds now starting to cover the morning sunlight. Allayer reaches over with his foot and bumps me on the leg, "Can you hear it?"

"Hear what; the wind?"

"No, it's coming from the portal. The dark angels are on their way; you can't hear that?"

With the wind from the storm, I can't make out what Allayer and Nipper are hearing. I then turn my head and lean forward, as a few seconds pass.

"I can, I can hear it. That sounds just like when my Warrior Angel spooked me on our way here. Without any warning he flew over and then suddenly slowed down right in front of us. The air rushing over his wings made that same noise. Yes, I hear it."

The two Angels standing on each side of the portal pick up their swords and hold them in a position ready to strike whatever comes across the golden threshold. The portal opening, which had been transparent allowing a clear view of the forest behind it, is now becoming darkened, covered with a burning, reflective liquid. The sounds of the dark angels' wings have stopped, a silence comes over the whole place, even the wind from the storm has ceased.

I look at Nipper and whisper, "Hey bud, this is freaky." They both at the same time reach up and place a hand on my shoulder, then turn, continuing to watch this scene unfold.

As I look back at the portal, "Hey, I see something coming out."

Allayer tells me, "Be quiet."

To my surprise, a nasty little three foot demon walks through the portal. This spawn of Satan has black tar dripping from its hands and feet. His face looks half rotted with parts of his chin bone exposed, and suddenly, his smell makes it to where we are sitting. This gross, pungent odor of sulfur mixed with rotting meat would gag a billy goat. It slowly gazes around like he is on a mission to see the strength of his opposition. After taking his time at looking everyone over, he turns and retreats back toward the portal opening. Just before he steps through, he turns and snarls loudly at one of the Angels standing at the threshold.

I don't need Allayer or Nipper to explain what just happened, that thing had a mission. I'm wondering if this is normal and I see Nipper shaking his head no.

Allayer tells me, "Hey Chado, let's move back a few feet. We both think they are up to something."

"Aren't we covered with the two big Angels and Samson?"

"We are usually covered, even with one Warrior Angel. The thing is, Lucifer knows that time is running out and will try every trick in his play book to harvest the souls of this planet. And here's the tricky part: If they get their hands on either one of those two Warrior Angels' swords, the threshold won't have any effect on their power."

"Well, if they can't cross the threshold due to losing their power and being destroyed by the Warrior Angels, how can they do it?"

Allayer asks me, "Do you remember in the Bible about the Nephilim Giants?"

"Yes, they were enemies of God. In the Bible, Lucifer devised a plan and used a select group of angels to go down and lay with women for offspring that would contaminate the gene pool of mankind. The theory of some folks said Satan's reason was to prevent the birth of Jesus Christ. So God destroyed them all... right?"

"Wow Chado, your gift of knowledge is coming along. You hit the spike right on the head. But here's the kicker, Lucifer took the fallen angels offspring, and gave them power to actually do battle with our Warrior Angels. At this same location a little over three hundred years ago, they made a stab at stealing one of our swords."

"What happened?"

"Well I'll put it like this. It didn't end well for the Giants."

Nipper chimes in. "We think this might be why God delayed this from happening yesterday. He knows that Lucifer is up to something."

* * *

A bit of black smoke belches through the portal and one by one dark angels walk through. They are all just a bit smaller than our two Warriors, each having a look of hatred in their faces. I notice several of the little short demons walking in and around the fallen angels legs, like cats around their master.

Samson wastes no time as he takes the rope of the first condemned man and tosses it over the threshold. One of the demons reaches out and catches hold of the rope, turns and walks through the portal.

At the very same time the demon catches the rope, the little Angel of persuasion releases the mind of the condemned soul. I could see his face, the glaze over his eyes vanished and the expression on his face told me he was now aware of his surroundings.

The rope was now uncoiling as the demon continued to pull, and we could hear the sound of the chain being dragged across the rocks. He starts struggling, leaning back against the chain with his heels dug in. With the resistance, two more of the small demons join in and grab the rope; skidding the man across the ground.

The man is now lying flat, trying with both hands to get the iron collar off while he is slowly dragged across the threshold. Finally we see the bottom of his feet disappearing through the portal. One by one, the demons drag the condemned men through the portal until there is no one left except the priest.

I hear the swooshing sound of wings; we all look to our right and out of the portal of Heaven, to my surprise, my

124

Guardian Angel appears. He looks over at me and smiles, then immediately turns and regains his stern Marine Corps stare and heads in the direction of the portal to Hell.

Not far behind him, six more Warriors walk through Heaven's portal. Nipper and Allayer stand, one on each side, and place their hands on my shoulders. Nipper chuckles, "How's that for backup? Let Lucifer try something now."

Allayer points at the rock bench, "Hey guys, I think we can all sit back down."

I look back about the same time Samson tosses the end of the last rope over the threshold. The arrogant priest, released from the little Angel's spirit of persuasion, comes alive and starts yelling.

Still thinking he's back at his mosque, "We will have your heads, bow to Hurrian or die!"

He reaches up and feels the iron collar attached around his neck, "What's going on here? Release me immediately!"

He looks over at the seven Warrior Angels then back at the gate to Hell. He sees the demons pulling the rope attached to his chain. "Oh no, have mercy, don't take me, I am a priest of Hurrian, have mercy!"

The demons standing at the threshold are laughing and jumping up and down as they look up at the fallen angels for gratification.

Another demon much larger than the rest walks out of the portal and starts popping his fanged teeth together. The sound of this pop, pop, pop, was echoing across the opening, sounding like someone banging two hollow wooden boxes together.

The priest now begging to his false god, "Help me Hurrian, rescue me from these infidels." Now on his stomach clawing at the ground with one hand and pulling at the chain with the other, the demons pull him over the threshold.

One of the fallen angels reaches down with one hand and grabs the priest by the hair of his head. He lifts him completely off the ground, holds him face to face and tells the priest, "Hurrian is not real, you hunk of flesh."

The fallen angel lowers him down a couple feet and the demon that's still popping his teeth reaches up and bites the priest in the forehead leaving fang marks on his flesh.

The dark angel lifts him back up, "I've marked you, now you're mine forever!"

At this point the priest is screaming, "Have mercy, please have mercy!"

The fallen angel turns and throws his limp body through the portal snarling, "There will be no mercy this day."

The very same fallen angel looks over at the Warriors and starts laughing, and suddenly I hear the sounds of swords being unsheathed. Several more dark angels appear out of the portal; followed by two Nephilim Giants, both having to bend down, just to make it through.

They looked to be twenty feet in height, their shoulders as wide as a truck hood. They were carrying battle axes and their shields looked like the skin of a dragon.

I hear the little Angel with a loud voice, "If you giants cross the threshold, your existence will end!"

One of the giants pushes his way through the fallen angels, with the other one close behind. As the first giant's foot crosses the threshold, he swings his axe at the Angel standing on the left side of the portal. The Angel leans back like tall grass swaying in the wind, with the giant's axe missing him only by inches.

The two Angels wearing sackcloth positioned on each side of the portal swing their swords at the exact same time. With the sweeping sound of their blades moving so fast, the naked eye could only catch a glimpse as they cut both the right and left legs completely off of the first Nephilim Giant. We feel the vibration of this huge monster when his heavy body hits the ground.

The seven Warrior Angels are already advancing and strike the second giant, causing him to land on top of the first one. A couple demons run out past the blades of the Angels as they turn to try to get behind the two Angels wearing sackcloth.

Out of nowhere, Samson grabs the two demons by their feet. Twisting like he is playing shot-put, he throws both demons against the stone entrance, leaving them injured and staggering as they crawl back across the portal to their safety of Hell. As I look back at the battle between the Angels, I catch a glimpse of my Guardian Angel taking off the head of both giants.

Several of the angels from Hell that had been attempting to cross the threshold, now retreat by jumping back through the portal.

The fallen angel that was laughing when all this started barely escaped and had to dive through the portal with one of the Warrior Angels' blades just missing him.

After the dust settles, Samson takes one of the giants' axes and goes out and cuts down a couple trees. While he is doing that the other Angels roll the two giants' bodies over to the edge of Hell's portal. Samson brings the two trees over and everyone together uses the trees to shove the dead giants through the portal.

With his feet, Samson rolls the heads of both giants just inside the threshold. Then he backs off a couple of feet, turns like he's playing football, and kicks each head through the fiery portal. The two big Angels dressed in sackcloth both throw their hands in the air, with their swords dripping with blood and shout, "Touchdown!"

Samson had not said a word the whole time he'd been here, but then looked over at us and smiled. "You know, they weren't the Philistines, but it was still a good fight."

He walks back over to his cart, and as he's climbing aboard, the seven Warrior Angels, who are still standing in front of the portal to Hell, give Samson a wave of appreciation. Samson smiles and bows his head while popping the reigns against the mules' backsides. As he turns this ancient wagon, we have to take a couple steps back to give him room. I suddenly remember his wine pouch still lying on the ground where I had slept.

"Hey Nipper, I'll be right back." I trot over, grab the wine pouch, then hustle back to catch his slow moving cart.

"Hey Samson, you forgot your wine pouch." He reaches down grabbing the lamb skin container, holds it up over his mouth while squeezing out a mouth full of wine. With his huge hand, he wipes off a bit of dribble from his thick black beard while handing the pouch back to me. He smiles and with a deep gentle voice, "Keep it, there's plenty of wine where I'm going."

"Thanks Samson. Hey just so you know, you were one of my favorite heroes of the Bible."

He humbly grins, pops the reigns and starts heading back down the mountain. I stand and watch as he goes out of sight, twisting and turning through the evergreen trees, thinking: *How cool is this? I just had a conversation with the mighty Samson, and he gave me his lamb skin wine pouch!*

17

The Bad Guy

I hurry back to Nipper and Allayer as they are still standing, watching the Warrior Angels that seem to be guarding the portal.

"Hey guys, what's going on? Isn't all the excitement over?"

"Not quite, they have to guard the portal until God closes it."

"Oh. Why didn't He close it as soon as the battle was over?"

"We don't know; this is a bit peculiar. He usually closes it as soon as the last condemned soul passes through. Let's sit and watch for a while."

As I look up at the blanket of heavy dark clouds continuing to cover the sun, a chill passes over me and as I shrug my shoulders to shake it off, Allayer looks over at me. "Chado Cole, we feel it too."

"What's going on? Is something bad about to happen?"

Nipper mumbles, "The last time I felt that, I got to see Lucifer".

"Lucifer, what the heck? Are you kidding me? Is he about to come through that portal?"

Nipper asked Allayer, "Do you think he's coming?"

Allayer starts shaking his head, "Yes, I believe so."

Fear grips me, "Guys should we get out of here?"

"No, don't worry. He has power on Earth to go and come as he pleases, but here he has limitations and only is allowed access by the Almighty."

Nipper reminds us of scripture. "Remember the book of Job, it's the oldest book of the Bible written back in two thousand BC, and it says:

'Now there was a day when the sons of God came to present themselves before the Lord, and Satan also came among them. And the Lord said to Satan, 'From where do you come?' So Satan answered the Lord and said, 'From going to and fro on the Earth, and from walking back and forth on it.' Then the Lord said to Satan, 'Have you considered My servant Job, that there is none like him on the Earth, a blameless and upright man, one who fears God and shuns evil?'"

"Okay Nipper, what's this got to do with Satan coming here?"

"Well the story of Job is a good example of Satan having free rein on Earth and God having trust in his servant Job to do the right thing. I guess you could say we are giving you a heads up. We both believe Satan has heard about you and realizes God is up to something. Just beware, Satan will try to sift you for every bit of information he can. Not to mention temptation of no telling what. Remember, he still thinks he'll win the final battle."

"What the heck guys, I don't want to talk with the devil, nope, not going to talk to him."

"Chado Cole, don't worry, you are well protected, and remember what we told you; Lucifer's power is limited here on Tabula Rasa."

"Okay, okay, what do I say?"

"Chado, remember your scripture."

"What scripture would that be?"

"Try Mathew 10:19."

"Yes, I remember that one, '*But when they deliver you up, do not worry about how or what you should speak. For it will be given to you in that hour what you should speak; for it is not you who speak, but the Spirit of your Father who speaks in you'.*"

"So, let the Spirit of the Lord guide you, we promise you'll do just fine."

I find myself staring at the portal and trying to imagine what I'm about to witness coming out of this pit of Hell, when I feel Nipper punch me on the shoulder, chuckling, "It's going to be okay."

I see my Guardian Angel wave his hand in a gesture for me to come over to where the seven Warriors are standing. When I get up from the rock bench, I feel weakness in my knees and fear coming over me. On my short walk across the opening, I want to be anywhere but here. The dark clouds hovering over this mountain range and the grey background of the rocks and forest make me feel dread and defeat.

Suddenly I feel a warm breeze with the smell of cedars and as I look up a small ray of sunlight had broken through the heavy canopy of dark clouds. The small ray of light is hitting the ground right beside my Guardian Angel. I can tell my fear was leaving and is being replaced by a spirit of bravery, I can tell the Holy Spirit of God is with me. The weakness in my legs has been replaced with strength, my slow lazy walk turned into a sprint.

We are standing about thirty feet away from the portal. No one is speaking, and all eyes are fixed on the portal.

We hear the sound of wings roaring coming from the other side of the portal and finally dead silence.

Just like before, two small demon scouts poke their heads out and then vanish back to the other side. We hear the sound of more wings and then quiet.

We hear the sounds of thunder with lightning striking the ground just outside the portal. This opening to Hell belches out black smoke with six fallen angels appearing. They all line up three on each side like an honor guard or military unit. These fallen all stand at attention with their hands on their swords, ready for battle.

As we are waiting for the dark lord of Hell to walk through, I am having thoughts of him appearing as a huge, scaly dragon spitting out fire. To my surprise, I see a tall, thin figured man step through the portal. He is wearing a black suit with a matching flat brim hat, a white shirt with a small black bowtie. The way he is dressed reminds me of what you would see a preacher wear back in the late 1800's.

I feel there was something familiar about him, and I can't seem to put my finger on it.

He looks over at my Guardian Angel, "So, you're the ones that killed my Nephilim Giants and threw their bodies back over."

Not replying to Lucifer's comment, my Angel moves his fingers as to slightly reposition his grip around the handle of his sword.

The author of darkness takes a few steps over the golden threshold and now we are eye to eye with the most evil entity in God's creation.

I suddenly can hear Allayer and Nipper in my thoughts, "*Chado Cole, protect your mind. When he's that close, he can tell what you're thinking. Don't think about your mission. Concentrate on scripture.*"

Satan looks over at me with an odd looking stare. It's like he's wondering... How can I get in this guy's mind?

I can't stand him looking at me. I turn away to look over at the Guardians and he takes another step closer.

He reaches out to touch my face when I hear the Guardian's start to unsheathe their swords.

Satan pulls his hand back, looks over at the Guardians and with a commanding voice, "Put your weapons away! I mean the boy no harm. I believe I know this young man."

I couldn't hold my tongue, "You don't know me, Lucifer!"

"Oh yes, I remember you. Do you recollect a dream or should I say a vision of the Christ when you were eight years old?"

"Yes I remember one night being awakened and drawn to the window of my bedroom. As I looked up over the top of the tree line into the night sky, I saw the heavens open up. Jesus was standing in the center, and was surrounded by a great cloud of witnesses along with the Host of Heaven. I felt a sense of peace and comfort, and I know it was real because I can remember it like it happened yesterday."

"Oh yes, Little Soul, it was real."

"Lucifer, how do you know it was real, were you there?"

"I don't like to tell the truth, but no, I wasn't there. Let's just say I had a representative honoring my absence."

"What do you mean? You had someone at my house?!"

"Let me explain to you, Little Soul. Your father's family had a curse against them for several generations, and each generation continued to regenerate the curse from their continued sin. I guess you could say it's a curse that would never end unless someone like you broke the curse by worshiping

133

God and having a relationship with the Christ. I've had several demons oppressing your father and his two sons for years. My demons were there the night of your vision."

"So that's why my dad would get so angry when mom brought us to church! You had demons hovering around our home, causing him to act like that!"

"Yes, I got your grandfather and if it hadn't been for your mother's prayers, I would have got your dad, your brother, you, and all your kids and their children's children."

"So why were you so interested in my vision of Jesus?"

"Well, we thought you were going to turn out to be some great man of God, rescuing thousands of souls, but you were a disappointment to Heaven for the way you fell into a life of sin and rebellion. I played you like a new fiddle; you were so easy to steer away from God's original plans."

"Lucifer, I know I didn't always live according to God's will and I regret my mistakes. During my last years on Earth, I tried my best to be pleasing to God. I know my best days were as filthy rags, but you can't hold that against me because my Savior paid the price on the cross."

"Little Soul, spare me the scripture, I know it all. Let me allow you to revisit a time when you had a dream, a vision, or was I truly standing before you? One warm summer night exactly one year after your vision into the Realm of Heaven, I stood at the foot of your bed. Can you remember?"

"Yes, I remember. It was at the old house in Fairfield."

"Yes that's right, the very same house my demons spent years promising to me the souls of your entire bloodline. So tell me Little Soul, what do you remember about my calling?"

"I remember my brother not being there. It was just Mom, Dad and I. We had no air conditioning in the house and

Dad had installed an old attic fan we would use to pull cool air from the outside. I remember Dad turning the fan on and the summer air being pulled through the open windows, causing the curtains to move around like they were dancing. The rumbling sound of the attic fan was so comforting it would put you to sleep within minutes.

On the night you came to my room, I was in my bed but just a few minutes when I attempted to readjust my pillow, I happened to look up and saw you standing at the foot of my bed looking down at me. You were dressed exactly the same as you are now. Your dark presence startled me. I immediately started kicking at you, asking, who are you? I started hollering at you over and over. 'Get out, get out of my room.'

My dad yelled out, 'Who are you talking to?' You then walked right beside my bed. I scooted as far over as I could to the opposite edge, hollering back at my dad, 'There is someone in our house!' I leaned over after you walked out of my room and watched as you slowly walked down the hall.

My dad got up and checked for an intruder, made sure all the doors were locked, then walked by my room and with a harsh tone, said 'Go to sleep!' Apparently my dad didn't believe anyone had been in the house."

"Yes, you do remember, that's right, I was there looking down at what I thought would someday be a great man of God. I ordered some of my best demons to try to steal whatever plans the Creator had for you. Apparently it worked, you spent most of your life driving fast cars, chasing women and having a great ole time.

So tell me, Little Soul, why has the Creator not allowed you to enter Heaven? Why has He brought you here to Tabula Rasa? What have the Angels of comfort told you? You weren't much good for Him on Earth as His servant. What makes you think you can be of service to Him now?"

"There you go again bringing up my failures. I served God while I was on Earth. I had several good years of service. God allowed me to write music, sing His praises and I bet it impacted someone's life. It might not have been thousands as you had feared, but by confessing Christ to as many people as I did, maybe, just maybe, there might be at least one who would lead thousands to know Him.

One other thing, I confess, I didn't live for God during my youth. I was a foolish young man. Not living for Jesus Christ, I was a terrible father to my children and they have suffered because of it.

But here's the ticket, I have asked for forgiveness and God is faithful to forgive. So trying to condemn me by reminding me of my sinful past, is I guess pretty good conversation, but has no meaning to me or God. *He has cast my sin as far as the east is from the west."*

"Little Soul, I have walked among the sons of God and I have heard your name. I walked among the demons of Hell and a second time I have heard your name. I know the Creator is going to use you in some way. Come with me and let me show you the kingdoms of Earth where I will give you reign over millions of my servants. Let me fill your heart with the pleasures of the most beautiful women. There is nothing you could imagine that I can't provide for you, just take my hand. Remember you've failed God on Earth before, what if you fail him here? Don't you think He may cast you out, as he has cast me down to the Earth?"

"Lucifer, I have what I want, and that is to serve the God of Abraham, Isaac and Jacob, the Creator of all things above and below. I answer to only Him."

Lucifer shakes his head, "Whatever the Creator is up to with you couldn't have much effect on the final days. Just look around on Earth, it's in the season of the great falling away. I have the souls of men right where I want them. The rivers of pride run deep."

He turns and walks back through the portal with his six angels following close behind.

I take a deep breath with a long sigh of relief, and I hear the sound of a strong wind and turn just in time to see the portal close. You could now see right through the rock doorway as the fiery blue portal window vanished. The fresh smell of the mountain air has returned as the stench of sulfur dissipates. The dark shadows from the heavy canopy of clouds disappear. I look up and feel the warm sunlight hitting my face as if to have assurance God is in control. I turn and see Nipper and Allayer smiling, heading in my direction.

* * *

I look back at my Guardian Angel and notice something about his face, arms, and legs that I hadn't noticed before; he has deep scars all over him. *What could have happened to him?* Even though I feel the urge to ask and want to talk to him, I realize this isn't the time or place. I'm not sure if I could find the right words anyway. He must have noticed me watching him, because he gives me a short smile and places his right hand on my shoulder as he passes. They are all now heading for the portal to Heaven.

I ask Nipper and Allayer, "Are we going with the Warriors? Can we go to Heaven now?"

"Not yet, we have a few more things to show you here on Tabula Rasa."

"Well dang, I was ready to hit the road Jack. After the long conversation with the most evil being in God's creation, I am definitely ready to get off the top of this mountain!"

I look over at the portal as the first six Angels go through with my Guardian giving us a small wave as he turns and disappears through the portal.

"Allayer, when will I see him again?"

"You'll get to spend a few days in Heaven with him before he's reassigned."

"Sounds great, are we ready to go?"

Nipper grabs my wine pouch, takes a little sip, and then passes it around to Allayer. After we had a small refreshing taste of Tabula Rasa wine we start our journey off the mountain. As we make our way through the scattered saplings, I can now see the two Angels wearing sackcloth and the Angel of persuasion just a few yards away from the entry back into the cavern.

Nipper tells me, "We need to catch up before they go through the hidden gate."

As we make our way through the cavern and down the mountain trail, I can't help but think: *How strange is the event that had just taken place on top of that beautiful mountain.* As I tried to make sense of it all, I hear Allayer and Nipper talking. I keep forgetting they can hear my thoughts.

"Hey, guys."

"Yeah, Chado, go ahead ask away."

"Well, I was wondering about a few things I'm not real clear on, like, why don't the Warrior Angels ever say anything?

138

As a matter of fact, the three Angels walking ahead of us haven't said anything either, except when they were talking to the condemned men; and you two don't mind having conversation at all."

"Chado, Nipper and I were once human. Remember us telling you how we got killed back around the time when the Ark of Covenant was stolen from God's children? At our time of death, God gifted us with knowledge, a spirit of comforting and transformed us into a type of Angel. There are millions just like Nipper and I. You've already seen how different we are from the others. We don't have the same power as the Angels of God. We are limited and different in a lot of ways."

"Different, can you tell me how?"

"Sure, it's actually pretty easy to explain. In the beginning, God created man in his own image. Nipper and I both still have a lot of human characteristics remaining, proving we aren't much different from you. We still love to joke around and have fun like we did as mortals. When you eventually reach Heaven, God will gift you with several angelic abilities, you'll see."

"Abilities, like what kind of abilities?"

Allayer and Nipper both laugh, "Patience, Little Soul, patience."

"Yeah, why did Lucifer keep calling me 'Little Soul'? I started to ask him why, but I didn't want to lengthen our conversation any longer than I had to."

"We don't know, maybe he calls everyone Little Soul, or it was his way of trying to get you angry so you might spill the beans about your assignment."

"Yeah, maybe so. I know I didn't like it. Hey you guys finish explaining about the Angels."

"Well, God designed the Heavens and the Earth and saw that it was good. He didn't stop there, He continued forming and designing every living creature including Angels. I guess you could say He needed help to run it all, and what better way than to have Angels of all sorts to help Him do just that. The Hosts of Heaven were designed by God as creatures of light. You and every believer on Earth, Heaven and Hell know them as Angels. God designed each one in a very special way. They all have commonalities, but each being has its own unique gifts. The Angels of Heaven or Hell have no idea what it's like to be human, so don't be alarmed when they don't show the same characteristics as mortals. We know without a doubt, you'll feel right at home with the Angels after you've been in Heaven for a while."

"Allayer, do you think when I get to Heaven; my Guardian Angel will talk with me?"

"Sure, he will. The Angels of Heaven open up a little better when you're one on one. My advice would be to go a little slow at first. Trust me; he'll open up to you."

Nipper chimes in, "Remember, they have never been mortal, so their conversation will be more rigid or should I say direct and to the point. Oh yeah, they don't really joke around as much as we do."

"Thanks for the heads up guys."

We finally get to the bottom of the mountain where the stone trail meets the cobblestone road. Allayer and Nipper continue following the three Angels ahead of us as we turn to the right heading away from the village.

"Why are we still following the Angels? Aren't we going back to the village?"

"No, we're not going back to the village. But we aren't really following them, we just happen to be going in the same direction as they are."

We continue walking down the long, winding cobblestone road for several miles. As we walk, I see a few scattered homes nestled in the foothills of the mountain range that we were leaving behind us.

"Hey guys, I have another question."

"Go ahead, shoot."

"I'm curious about the portals. How are all the people here coming from Earth and leaving for Heaven? I know they're using portals, but the whole thing on top of the mountain with the secret passages, surely everybody that comes and goes doesn't have to make their way through all that, right?"

Nipper chuckles, "No, of course not, what you saw on top of the mountain was designed for the condemned and the coming and going of God's Angels. No one else here will ever see that. The portal to Hell that's on top of the mountain is the only one on Tabula Rasa."

"So where are the other portals located?"

"God has them scattered all over the planet."

"Well, why don't the souls here just go find a portal and zoom off to Heaven?"

Allayer grins, "Chado that would defeat God's plan for the citizens of Tabula Rasa. It's like this, they arrive here as lost souls without any knowledge of God. After they are here for a while and fully aware of the truth and know Jesus as their Lord and Savior, at that moment, God allows their eyes to be opened and they see the path to Heaven."

"So the portals become visible only after they surrender their hearts over to Jesus?"

141

"Yes, not only can they see the portals, they are led to the portal locations by the Holy Spirit."

"Now that is really cool. Why isn't it like that on Earth?"

"Well, Satan kind of messed that up. Remember he has full reign over the Earth, at least what God allows him to reign over. When a Christian dies they are met at that second by Angels like us and we transport them straight to the Gates of Heaven. It's kind of like the flash of light you talked about. When someone passes that's rejected the Lord, in that very second they are met by some of Lucifer's demons, or on special occasions, his fallen angels do the transporting to Hell's gates. Chado, can you imagine dying and in the next second you're facing something like what you saw on the mountain that came out of the portal of Hell?"

"No, I couldn't imagine. That is a scary thought. You know some of the rich and famous that make their living joking about Christians claiming to be atheist are going to have a rude awakening. So what happens when there's some kind of huge natural disaster or terrorist attack where hundreds or maybe even thousands are killed? Do we have enough Angels to take care of that many at one time?"

Nipper stops in his tracks looks over with a smile, "Remember God has designed legions of transporters like us and if needed, one Angel can transport ten thousand."

Allayer reaches for my wine pouch before we start walking again, "You know transporting that many souls at one time isn't the problem. The problem is sorting them out. The saved are transformed from mortal to immortal at the same time the lost are."

"Why is that a problem? Y'all can't tell them apart when the saved and the unsaved die?"

"Oh yeah, we can tell them apart because the saved have a glow or an aura around them, and the lost, well they have a type of darkness surrounding them."

"An aura, what do you mean?"

"Well it's like this, when you were back on Earth living the life of a Christian, God gave you a spirit of discernment. When you were walking through your church on a Sunday morning, mingling with fellow believers, did you ever notice a special glow in the faces of certain ones?"

"Yes, I have, I've even shared my thoughts about that with close friends. It was something different in their faces. You could see and tell they had the love of Christ."

"That's right, even some of the lost can see it, they know it's something different about Christians but just can't totally understand. With that curiosity and hearing that soft, still voice of God, some are drawn to it and eventually are saved. The sad thing is that millions hear it, feel it and then reject it."

"So tell me why it gets tricky when you have to sort the saved from the lost during a large disaster?"

"Chado, do you remember the Parable of the Wheat and the Tares?"

"Sure I do, Mathew 13:24-30."

"Quote it to us, we have time."

"Okay. *'The kingdom of Heaven is like a man who sowed good seed in his field; but while men slept, his enemy came and sowed tares among the wheat and went his way.*

But when the grain had sprouted and produced a crop, then the tares also appeared.

So the servants of the owner came and said to him, 'Sir, did you not sow good seed in your field? How then does it have tares?'

He said to them, 'An enemy has done this.' The servants said to him, 'Do you want us then to go and gather them up?'

But he said, 'No, lest while you gather up the tares you also uproot the wheat with them.

Let both grow together until the harvest, and at that time of harvest I will say to the reapers, first gather the tares and bind them in bundles to burn them, but gather the wheat into my barn.' "

Nipper says, "We believe the meaning behind that scripture relates to the final rapture, but it mirrors the same sorting out we have to do when a multitude of mortals die at the same time. To answer your question, you need to understand, even though the demons have no right to the saved, they still try to drag them away. We think they know, it's just they are mean and hateful and are trying to scare the saved and make trouble for us. Remember they hate the Christians and despise the Angels."

"That sounds like what happened when we had the little run in with that demon back on Earth."

"Yep, same thing, we always have a Warrior Angel nearby as we transport. And usually some of the Christians have their Guardians with them at the time of passing. So we don't usually worry about the demons."

"That reminds me, I'm glad my Guardian was with us when you guys picked me up from my ocean floor death bed. The nasty demon that grabbed my ankle gave me a pretty good scare. However, that demon tucked his tail and vanished when my Warrior Angel's sword lit up as he unsheathed it."

Nipper asked, "Yeah, but what about your other question?"

"Oh yeah, back on the mountain, when the Nephilim Giants attacked, why didn't the Warriors' swords light up like my Guardian's did before?"

"Well, Chado, back in the Gulf of Mexico your Guardian was sending a message to Lucifer that you were off limits. The battle on the mountain, the Warriors had no need to use that much force to defeat the giants or the fallen angels. Lucifer knows that his crew is no match for God's Angels."

Nipper takes one more swallow of wine and hands me the lamb skin pouch as we continue down the cobblestone road.

Allayer points up ahead, "That's where we're headed, Chado,"

* * *

As I look, I see a row of trees standing on the edge of a hill. These wooden giants all planted in a perfect line, as if they were meant to watch over the small village at the bottom of the hill. Their huge limbs swaying in the wind almost like a dance. I continue to follow Nipper and Allayer as we walk off the cobblestone path onto plush green grass and finally, we all plop down underneath a huge elm tree. "Chado, keep an eye on the crossroad at the bottom of the hill."

As I look I see several people gathered together underneath another big shade tree just a few feet from the road intersection, when suddenly I notice a flicker of light in the center of the crossroad and two people appear. I rub my eyes and wonder, what did I just see? I notice Allayer and Nipper are now grinning, as I look back, two of the people sitting under the shade tree immediately get up, walk over to introduce themselves, and then all four walk back to the shade tree and sit

145

down. I see it again. Another flicker of light, three small children appear right in the same place as the others.

Before I could ask, Allayer starts to explain, "This is one of many portals of salutation that are scattered all over the planet. These portals are used to transport the people of Earth that have died without any knowledge of God here to Tabula Rasa."

"Wow, so that was the flashes of light coming and going we saw just before we arrived?"

"Yes, that's right."

"Who are the people greeting them?"

"Well it could be anybody that God gave the task to. He usually chooses souls that He knows will be really good at it. It might be someone from three thousand years ago or He might even have people from your time."

"So when they arrive you say they have no understanding of what's happening?"

"We know... it's a bit strange. When they get here their minds are a lot like those of very young children. God does this so that everyone is easier to teach. But some of the older people are so deeply rooted in hatred and sin that it sometimes shows up later as God allows the free will factor."

Nipper chimes in, "God gives them a sense of peace and a hunger to learn. After they arrive, they are brought to these villages, where they are made to feel at home and are comforted by some of God's teachers. The teachers encourage some of the younger new arrivals to be mother or father figures to the children here."

"Guys, you know this is an almost foolproof setup. A person can get here, be taught, and accept Jesus as Lord and then move on to Heaven. It makes you wonder, how in the world does anyone fail to understand the truth - or just reject Christ - like the condemned we brought to Hell's portal?"

Nipper mumbles, "Like we just said, free will is a killer."

Allayer shrugs his shoulders and sighs, "That question has been asked for a couple thousand years. When you think of it, it's a lot like Earth. Most people are exposed to God all their life and just don't get it. Men are born with a sin nature, and even with an opportunity, or should I say a second chance like this one, they still turn away from the love of God. We believe some are just born for destruction."

"I know; that's a sad thought. If they only knew what they were missing out on."

We grab a couple apples and oranges on our way past a small grove of fruit trees near the bottom of the hill. I ask, "So where are the portals they use to get on God's freeway to Heaven?"

Nipper and Allayer point to a building located on the opposite end of the village from the crossroad. At that point, I hate to ask if the portal is in the building, thinking the question would be really dumb. Nipper laughs, "No it's not in the building, you'll see."

We get within a few yards of this bamboo shack and I see several people walk out and start heading out of town. Nipper, leading the way, starts to follow this small group. Just over a couple small foot hills we come to another river, and low and behold, John the Baptist. He was at it again, waist deep in water with a long line of people, all waiting to be baptized. You could hear him from a long distance boldly preaching, "No man can come to the Father but through His Son Jesus Christ!"

Splash, another submerged, and then another, with John never missing a breath continuing his preaching. It was truly a spectacular sight.

We watch as the ones who had already been baptized and accepted Jesus as Lord start heading away from the crowd further down the river bank. With Nipper still in the lead, we all follow the new believers. As we make our way through a few weeping willow trees growing along the river bank, I am reminded of home. The branches hanging low over this crystal clear river makes me think of the swimming holes of my youth.

I hear Nipper, "There it is!" I look up and see a stone doorway just a couple hundred feet away with trees lining the path on each side, their branches all hanging over the road creating a tunnel. It is simply beautiful. The stones in the doorway look like they are from an ancient castle, each stacked unevenly but giving the appearance of being perfect.

There are dogwood trees blooming on each side of the door with roses of many different colors twined around the base of each tree. Just to the right of the portal, I see an old man seated on a huge wooden chair. He has a large scroll set on a rock stand in front of him. As each person steps over the threshold to the portal, he writes on his scroll.

Before I can even ask, Allayer hears my thought, "No that's not the Lamb's Book of Life. He's just documenting each person leaving Tabula Rasa."

"Who is the old man?"

"We don't know for sure, some of the Angels say it's Methuselah. He doesn't talk to anybody and he's usually too busy doing what you see. So we never bother him; as a matter of fact we've only seen this place one other time."

"So how many portals to Heaven are there on Tabula?"

"We think there are several hundred scattered all over the planet. We know every village and town has at least one around their location."

"So is there someone like Methuselah at each portal documenting everyone that goes through?"

"Yep, all are volunteers, and they won't complete their mission until the last soul passes over. That won't happen until there are no more coming from Earth."

"Right, if they run out of souls here that means Earth is toast."

"Yep, pretty much. That's when we'll see God fulfill scripture with the two thousand year reign of peace, a new Heaven and a new Earth. It's going to be awesome."

"So, what now guys?"

Nipper and Allayer look at each other then back at me, "Let's get in line, it's time to get you to Heaven."

"For real, y'all aren't pulling my leg again, are you?"

"Nope, let's get in line."

All three of us edge closer to the back of a very long line. The glow we talked about earlier was evident in the face of each person there. I'm sure my face was now shining as bright as anyone's. The thrill and happiness is starting to overcome me as I try to keep my composure. I hear the chattering of several different languages as I stand in line with people from all over the world.

My thoughts of Heaven are overwhelming! *Will I get to meet my great-great-grandfather? I wonder if some of my kin, maybe my daughter, will meet me at the gate of Heaven. Probably not, I'm sure Jesus will be at the gate. What if no one meets me there and I have to wander around Heaven to find everyone? Well I guess that wouldn't be a bad problem to have.*

Wait a second... God is in control and I know He has this. I'm letting my mind get way too far out there.

We slowly move closer to the portal, ole Methuselah is continuing to jot everyone's name down as the line shortens. It looks like we are only a couple hundred people back from the entrance.

As I'm looking around at all these people, I start wondering about my dad again. *I'm still not sure if he made it. Oh yeah, I remember in the conversation with Lucifer, he said he got my grandfather and almost got my dad and he would have if hadn't been for my mom praying and fasting for my dad. So he's definitely up there. Okay, that's a relief. But Summer? My sweet daughter, did she make it? Well duh, I remember Allayer and Nipper grinning when we were talking about my daughter. So I think that means she made it also.*

Pondering over these thoughts, faces of old friends I lost years ago pass through my memories. *I wonder if...* Suddenly, my deep thoughts are interrupted as Allayer turns and looks at me and with a stern voice.

"Chado Cole, you stop that right now! You're going to have a heart attack and die again if you keep worrying about who did or didn't make it to Heaven." We look at each other and burst out laughing.

"Heart attack, Allayer you are crazy."

After our comic relief, our laughter dies away and we find ourselves standing right in front of old man Methuselah. When he died on Earth he was only 969 years old, the oldest man in history.

As the two people in front of us stepped through the portal, Methuselah never changing expression, looked up at me and with a deep, crusty sounding voice he says, "They told me you were coming."

I was speechless. While I was trying to think of something wise to say back, he looks down writes our names on the tablet, and then motions with his left hand to move through. All I could manage to squeak out was, "Thank you, sir."

18

Next Stop, Heaven!

I look at Allayer then back at Nipper; both I think are as excited as I am. We all three step through together with our arms locked at the elbows. I get the same sensation as before with my whole body being submerged in warm wax.

As we move forward past the portal, I feel a pull that I imagine to be like that of a giant vacuum. I see ahead of us what looks like a glittering dust trail. It must be from the two people that had just gone through ahead of us. The surrounding stars and their shapes seem to be changing as our speed increases. Instead of appearing round and clear, they are becoming elongated and distorted. I'm wondering: *Could this be light speed or something even beyond?* All I know, we were now traveling so fast the stars look like long strands of light all intersecting into a mass of distorted rays. I feel a small vibration coming from Allayer and Nippers arms as I look back at Tabula Rasa. Everything behind us has the appearance of a distant galaxy, just as you would see standing on Earth staring into space. I notice we have a glittering dust trail behind us also.

I look over at Allayer as he points in the direction we're headed. I can tell we are now starting to slow down, but can't quite make out what he's pointing at.

Nipper and Allayer are smiling and excited. They remind me of a couple kids who are approaching Disney World for the first time. They both laugh at me with Nipper saying, "You think we look excited, you should see your face, I wish I had a mirror."

As a few more seconds pass, the stars are now slowly coming back into focus.

I ask Allayer what he's pointing at, and before he can answer; I see a large cluster of stars with one in the center that looked a hundred times larger than our sun back on Earth. The planets surrounding this star look a lot like our solar system. The only difference between our solar system and this one is we had nine planets orbiting the sun and I count thirteen here.

I'm wondering if there's significance to the number of planets surrounding this star. Nipper hearing my thoughts, "Yes, the number twelve is important; there were twelve tribes of Israel and twelve disciples. Now, what do you think?"

"Well, are the planets named after the tribes or the disciples?"

"Neither, the twelve tribes of Israel were named after the planets. God designed these planets way before there was an Israel."

"Okay, I understand, so if there are thirteen planets, does this mean one of them could be Heaven?"

"Yes sir, number thirteen is your lucky number." We all burst out laughing again, knowing there is no such thing as luck. We continue to decrease our speed as we enter into this beautiful solar system of Heaven.

The huge star in the center is casting an almost blinding light, and then darkening as we pass through the shadows of the outer planets. This scene reminds me of the solar eclipses we experienced on Earth.

I try to make out which planet could be Heaven, but they all are beautiful, each having their own unique colors. As we get closer, I notice each one has a close resemblance to

Earth, with the unmistakable light blue color of water covering a large percentage of their surfaces. I'm so excited I could burst!

Nipper points at a small speck that seemed to be floating across space. It was quite easy to see due to having the background of the blue planet ahead of us. I notice the speck was moving in the same direction as we were. Before I could ask, "That's the people that went through the portal before us."

"Guys, you know I always wanted to be a jet fighter pilot when I was a kid, heck, I even dreamed of going supersonic speeds as a grownup. This is so far beyond an F-18! We just traveled across the galaxies at or beyond light speed, and now we're cruising through these planets probably faster than any jet on Earth. This is the best time I've ever had."

Allayer and Nipper unlock our elbows and completely let go. I quickly reach back to grab onto Allayer and Nipper's arms, but they pulled away just out of my reach. Fear came over me as I realized I couldn't reach either of the two. I look back in the direction we're headed and; oh my goodness, I'm flying through space. Hey, I'm flying guys! I'm really flying!

Nipper darts around me like he's Peter Pan's cousin, laughing the whole time. "Chado you can do it, just relax and feel it."

For the next several hundred miles, I flop through space like a wounded goose trying to get the hang of this new talent God has blessed me with. My biggest problem is I can't seem to distinguish between what's up or down. "Hey Chado, there is no up or down, you're in space for God's sake."

"Duh, thanks for the info Nipper."

After a little help from Allayer and Nipper, I'm now gliding along like they were, grinning from ear to ear like a kid at Christmas.

We've passed several planets, all looking like they would sustain life.

"Tell me guys, are there people living on any of these planets?"

"No, but you can visit them if you ever want to do a little exploring. God has all sorts of animals living on these planets. There are species you've never heard of, all scattered throughout the planets in this system."

"That is so amazing. Are they friendly? I mean is it safe to go walk around?"

"Sure it safe, all of God's creatures are friendly. You do remember the saying; the lion will lay down with the lamb?"

"Okay, okay, I remember, just asking."

The people that were ahead of us seem to be changing direction and circling around the back side of what looked like the largest planet in the system. We continue following their lead and I notice we're starting to close the gap between us and them. They are no doubt slowing down.

Could this huge planet be Heaven? I see Allayer shaking his head no. "Well dang, I thought it would surely be Heaven."

* * *

I can now see a light coming from something located on the backside of this behemoth of a planet. I look back at the guys and they are both smiling. This must be it; it's got to be Heaven. We travel a few hundred miles and I start to see more and more. With only a small piece of this planet exposed, the rotation of this system circling the sun allows my view of Heaven to be slowly unveiled.

At the same time we all come to a complete stop, as if we have arrived at an imaginary overlook. Now suspended somewhere out in the darkness of space, the grandeur of Heaven has almost come into full view. With the deafening silence and the overwhelming beauty I start to cry tears of joy. I search for words; there aren't any to be found. Suddenly a poem came in my heart. With Allayer and Nipper smiling, as they hear my thoughts, "Okay Chado, we want to hear it."

"Oh Lord my God,
We witness your awesome wonder,
We see the universe, Thy hands have made.
The stars and planets you have set in place,
I stand unworthy of your grace.
My God My God you've shown your love,
Let us always seek your face."

After I finish the humble little poem to the Lord, the unveiling of Heaven is now complete. This beautiful planet that I can now call home is in full view. To explain what I'm seeing is almost impossible to put into words. Without saying anything, Allayer and Nipper place their hands on my shoulders telling me, "Hey bud, we have been here thousands of times and upon each arrival, it still seems like the very first."

We slowly start making our way across the atmosphere of Heaven. As we get closer, I see something very strange about the planet. It looks like this peculiar world is sitting on a sheet of glass that is several hundred miles thick and extends outward past the equator. There's a white ring that seems to be several miles wide circling the whole planet around the edge of the glass.

"Can y'all fill me in on what's with the sheet of glass and the white ring underneath the planet?"

Allayer chuckles, "That's not glass, that's water, and the white ring is white sand."

"So God has a super cool beach underneath Heaven?"

"Yep, He sure does. Get this, you can wind surf on the sea side or walk to the edge of space on the other. He has tunnels that go underneath and through the sea bed. You can see face to face all kinds of sea creatures that live in the deep. There is no vacation place in all of God's creation that will compare to what you're going to see in Heaven."

As I continue to admire this beautiful planet of Heaven, I try to compare from memory the difference between Heaven and Earth. The best I could come up with is Heaven has to be at least three times the size of Earth. I remember wondering if Heaven will be large enough to house all the people that have died over the last few thousand years and the ones yet to come. After seeing the size of Heaven, there is no doubt there is plenty of room.

We are now just a mile or two behind the people from Tabula Rasa. I feel the dampness from the grey and white clouds as we pass through the upper troposphere. We were now only seven or eight miles to the surface of Heaven.

The people we were following suddenly vanished as they went through what had to be another portal and we changed directions heading away from their entry point.

"Hey guys, we're not following them through the portal?"

"Nope, we have to bring you in through another entry point. God wants you to see everyone coming in from a distance, or I should say where you can get the big picture; because only the Angels are allowed to use this route."

As we get closer to the ground I can make out a narrow road leading through rolling hills. Clover everywhere, the hills are covered in crimson clover. The narrow road looks like it's made from the same cobblestones as back on Tabula Rasa.

Before I could ask, "No it's not made of gold; it's just a rock road, get over it. The streets of gold are inside the city of Heaven. Just wait, have a little patience, you'll see."

We fly along the rock road a few more miles and finally hit the ground; I mean literally hit the ground. Allayer and Nipper lit down like a couple giant eagles, and I crashed and tumbled for a hundred feet. As I finally stop tumbling I reach up, a bit embarrassed, digging a wad of grass and dirt out of my mouth. *Yes, laugh it up guys, you could have warned me and given me a few helpful tips on landing.*

I take a sip of Tabula Rasa wine, swishing the dirt out of my mouth as we continue up the road.

Nipper had to stop every few feet, still laughing at my landing. "That was so awesome, I can't believe you didn't let off and lean back...," he had to wipe tears from his eyes before he continued; "I hope I'm around for your next landing."

Allayer tells Nipper, "Give him a break; I seem to remember the first time you tried to land, you hit the ground pretty hard yourself."

Nipper, a bit embarrassed instantly stops laughing. Allayer and I burst out and have to bend over in the middle of the cobblestone road with tears of laughter running down our faces. Then suddenly the laughter ceases when Allayer says, "Chado we are going to miss you, you've been the most fun we've had in a long time."

I look up, "You guys aren't going inside the city with me?"

"No, our journey with you is almost over. We have to get back to our regular job, sorry bud."

"Dang. I understand. Well, who's going to guide me the rest of the way?"

"Not sure, it could be anyone. If I had to guess, it would probably be your Guardian Angel."

We continue walking another mile or so admiring the beautiful landscape when Allayer stops, "Listen for a second..."

I hear a deep rumbling coming from over the next hill. It sounds a lot like my horses back home when I would call them in for their evening feed.

But the sound of my three horses running full out didn't compare to the sound coming from over the hill. I look over at Nipper and his smile tells me this is going to be a sight to see.

As the sound gets closer and closer, my heart races... I'm overwhelmed with anticipation, thinking, *this has to be the mighty horses of Heaven with a great stallion leading the herd.*

Our eyes fixed at the crest of the hill, I can now see the tops of their heads bobbing up and down as they gallop toward us, but something was different. It wasn't the mighty horses of Heaven at all. It was miniature donkeys, "What the heck guys?"

They looked to be only a couple feet tall. I hear Allayer and Nipper chuckling, "Hey Chado, you have to understand, we are standing on the planet of Heaven. Always expect the unexpected."

I look back at this herd of little donkeys, "My goodness, it must be at least two or three hundred."

As we continue in their direction, they all slow down to a walk. I don't know if it's their curiosity or they just wanted to love up on us. We were now surrounded by a huge herd of donkeys. Some were nudging and licking our hands. Memories of home flashing through my mind as I rubbed the forehead of several of the cutest little animals I had ever seen. After only a short time with our new friends they all scattered into the surrounding clover fields and started grazing.

We continue up and over the hill, my excitement growing with every step.

Nipper asks, "So what did you think about the herd of donkeys?"

"Well, they weren't what I expected. I just knew when I heard the sounds of their hooves, I was about to see wild mustangs coming over this hill."

"Don't worry, you'll get to see thousands of horses, they are scattered all over the pastures of Heaven."

"Wow Nipper, pastures of Heaven? That sounds like the name of a song or a really cool book."

"Yep, sure does."

When we walk over the crest of the small foothill, my eyes widen with surprise. I can't believe what I'm looking at. I feel weak-kneed as I plop down in ankle deep crimson clover. In the far distance, I see a tall flat top mountain with the shining city of Heaven perched on its back. The city's great wall continues from my left and to my right what looks like over a thousand miles. The wall glitters, being adorned with different kinds of precious stones. The height of the wall reaches the clouds hovering over the city. From our location, I can see a gate, its doors glowing pearl white, having the same appearance and color as a full moon.

There's a certain glow around the city that reminds me of scripture. *For the glory of God illuminated it and the Lamb is its light.*

I stand up and start heading in the direction of the city and I notice Allayer and Nipper aren't following.

"Hey guys are y'all ready? Let's get cracking."

Allayer stands up and walks over very slowly with a sad look on his face.

"What's wrong Allayer, did I do something wrong?"

"Of course not, it's just that..., well this is where God wanted us to drop you off."

"What do you mean drop me off?"

"He wanted us to bring you to this very spot so you could get a better picture of what Heaven looks like. At least from this overlook."

"Nipper, you can tell him."

"Chado, everyone else goes through a portal that drops them right in front of the gate and they can't see what you're seeing because they're so close to the wall. God wanted you to get a different view for some reason. Oh yeah, just a little heads up; there are twelve gates and they have the same names as the planets, which are the same as the twelve tribes of Israel. One other thing, the wall is around fifteen hundred miles long and the city is square, so do the math."

"So it's six thousand miles around Heaven?"

"Yes, that's about right."

"So do all the people on the planet of Heaven live inside the city?"

"Absolutely not, God allows His people to live anywhere they want. Someone like you living your entire life in the country probably wouldn't feel at home living in a city."

"Never thought of it like that. Well, will I ever see you guys again?"

"We are almost certain that will happen."

"I feel like we've become really good friends over this journey, and I hate to say good bye."

Nipper looks down as he takes one foot and lightly brushes the tops of the clover with his sandal mumbling, "Yeah I know, we haven't been able to spend this much time with anyone else we've ever transported. We both will miss you. But remember this, God knows our heart and He is the coolest, so I'm sure He will allow our paths to cross again."

Allayer and Nipper give me a big hug turning away and just like that, gone. Within a split second they both vanished.

19

Strange Critters

I turn back around setting my sights on the big pearly gate in the distance, then take a small sip of wine and tie the pouch that Samson gave me back to my side. I start my journey alone to the City of Heaven.

I walk for several hours enjoying the beauty of my surroundings, thinking of Allayer and Nipper, wishing they were here so I could pound them with a thousand more questions. Suddenly out of the corner of my eye, I catch a glimpse of something moving. My curiosity gets the best of me, so I change direction just a little to solve this mystery... then I see it again.

Other than the herd of donkeys, I haven't seen any other living creature.

I slowly walk over to a thick grove of trees near a small running stream, and whatever it was has gone. I'm thinking this would be a good place to kick back for the night. I look around and see all sorts of wild berries growing along the creek.

I'm thinking, *No one but me; a good cool creek; well why not.* I strip off my clothes down to my birthday suit and dive in.

So refreshing... I think back on my childhood when I would swim in Black Creek, our little piece of Heaven on Earth. You know, it's not much different than what I'm experiencing at this very moment.

I'm suddenly startled when I hear a twig snap.

"Hello, is anybody out there?" Nothing but silence, it must be my imagination. I dive back under the water and swim the width of the creek and when I surface I am face to face with

163

two little spider monkeys. After catching my breath I say, "Well hello there little fellows." They both just stare, and then at the same time turn around; one grabbing a sandal while the other takes my pants.

The chase is on. As I claw my way up the steep creek bank, I grab my other sandal and shirt. I run as fast as possible, ducking and dodging tree limbs, trying to keep both monkeys in sight. I start thinking, *what do I do if I can't get my pants back? Just walk up to Heaven's Gate nude and say, hey everybody I'm here on special assignment.*

Still chasing the two monkey thieves, we break out of the thick brush into an opening. I see both spider monkeys clearly now. They are both headed for what looks like an old timey barn. With every stride, I'm praying there won't be any people there. I'm gaining on them over the open terrain, and suddenly I have a funny thought that Allayer and Nipper would get a kick out of this scene.

Both monkeys stop right before going through the barn door and at the same time throw my clothes and sandal up in the air, turning and scurrying inside the barn.

At that point I change my gait from a full speed run to a slow, cautious walk. This has got to be the most ridiculous situation I've ever been in.

With the cool air hitting my lower parts reminding me I'm walking across an open pasture nude, I silently pray, *Please God, don't let anyone see me.*

I wonder if these two little rascals are setting me up for something. You would think from me chasing them, they would have quickly run up the nearest tree.

I finally get to my clothes, looking around to make sure no one saw this embarrassing moment. I hear a familiar sound; it was the whickering of a horse. Then again, I hear neighing.

After tying my sandals, I walk inside the barn and there they are. A pair of the finest horses I've ever seen. They both look like twins bred from the same stock. As I'm admiring each one, I notice they both have the rear ends and chests of quarter horses and the height and length of a thoroughbred with the long erect ears and head of a Tennessee Walker. I am looking at horses made in Heaven.

"I wonder who you guys belong to, and I wish y'all were mine. So awesome... oh well, I got to get going fellows; I've got a long way to go."

As I turn to head out of the barn, both horses neigh at me. I look back and they are both shaking their heads up and down as if trying to tell me something.

"Sorry friends, but you don't belong to me and I sure don't want to be labeled a horse thief right out of the batter's box."

I look up at the great wall of Heaven with the barn blocking part of my view. I try to guess how many miles away it is when I suddenly have a memory from my childhood. I was around eight or ten years old and our family went on vacation to the mountains. I had only seen pictures in books or watched Davy Crockett and Daniel Boone on our black and white TV, so I had no real idea of the grandeur of the mountains. When my dad said, "Hey, look at that kids, I can see the snowcapped mountains." My brother and I thought we would arrive in the next few minutes, but after a couple more long hours staring through the windshield we finally made it.

So I'm guessing I probably have at least a two or three day walk before I reach the base of Heaven's Gate. Looking back at the setting sun I'm thinking this barn is as good a place as any to camp. When I walk in the barn, both horses whicker almost to tell me, welcome stranger. I rub both on the head as I pass, heading for a pile of hay in the corner of the barn.

As I lie down, I look up at the two horses, both staring at me with their huge dark brown eyes. With feeling a sense of peace, I chuckle as I ask, "Hey guys, where did your little thieving monkey friends get off to?"

I close my eyes, still thinking back about our childhood vacation to the mountains, and a funny memory came to me. We were staying at a cool ski resort hotel with a beautiful river running right behind it. With my family being from Louisiana, we loved to fish. It didn't take long to figure out our fishing skills from the Deep South didn't work in the mountain streams. When we gave up on catching trout from the icy cold waters, we were all exhausted from the trip and turned in for the night. Well, except my older brother. I don't believe he had ever seen a fire alarm and was curious to what it would do if you pulled the red thingy down.

Jarred from our deep sleep, we all jumped out of bed and ran for the stairway. Yep, he found out what the red thingy was. Oh yeah, country came to town.

I open my eyes one more time before falling asleep and notice a beautiful sunset. The last few rays are shining through the open barn door, and I see dust particles hanging in the air from the occasional movement of the horses.

As I close my eyes, sinking further down into the soft hay, my mind drifts off into a dream. I see myself sitting by a small camp fire laid back with my head resting against a leather saddle. Out of the shadows of darkness, a great lion appears. Someone with me says, "Fear not, be still and know that He is God." The Lion has something in His mouth. As I turn to see who spoke to me, I'm suddenly at a different place, I can see millions of people all walking together, their path has a glow but they are surrounded by total darkness. The width of the line is six people across and the length is unending.

A bright light flashes and I'm now looking down from the sky at the barn. I hear a soft spoken voice, "*Take these animals, they will lead you.*" I ask, "Where will they lead me, where will they lead me?" over and over. As I wake and slowly open my eyes saying "Where will they lead me?" for the last time, I see the nose of one of the horses no more than an inch from my face. I feel the warm breath coming from his huge nostrils and suddenly he snorts and blasts my face with horse spittle.

"Thanks a lot for the morning wake up and a big double thank you for the shower." As I reach up and shove his head away, I notice I have a spider monkey still asleep wrapped halfway around my neck. As I stand up from my night's sleep, I look around and see the other horse standing, holding a saddle blanket in his teeth. I chuckle, "So my hairy friend, what are you doing with that?" He walks over just like he knows what I had asked and places the blanket on the back of the other horse.

Well, if that doesn't beat all! In all my years of owning horses I have never seen anything like that.

I suddenly remember my dream, "Take these animals they will lead you."

I just wonder if God set this whole thing up from the beginning. The monkeys stealing my clothes and leading me here to an old barn, with two of the finest horses in Heaven... what are the odds of something like this happening? Considering I'm way out here in the middle of nowhere... and come to think of it, Allayer and Nipper told me someone would show me the way, so I guess this is God showing me the way. Wow, not to mention providing transportation.

I re-adjust the blanket the other horse had placed on the back of his friend, sliding it forward a few inches. I grab an ole timey saddle from the floor of the barn and start getting my stallion ready to ride.

I hear something at the door of the barn, when I turn; I see the other spider monkey dragging a burlap sack with something in it. The little guy drops it at my feet, with both horses whickering at the same time sounding just like my horses at home when they knew it was time to be fed. The one already saddled nudges me from behind as if to tell me, "*Open the sack, dummy.*"

As I reach down to grab the sack, I could smell the strong fragrance of fresh apples. Another nudge now coming from both horses, "Okay, okay, hold on to your hooves." I reach in and pull out some of the largest apples I had ever laid my eyes on. After sharing the nice breakfast the little spider monkey had provided, I tie my wine pouch and the burlap sack with the remaining apples to the saddle horn.

I lead the saddled horse out of the barn over to a tree stump. With the height of these stallions, I need all the help I can get. As I climb up on the tree stump, I notice my new horse bows, almost touching his stomach to the ground. I laugh as I jump off the stump and easily hop in the saddle of this mighty

168

horse of Heaven without even using the stirrup. After he feels me settle into a riding position, he stands and we are now headed for Heaven's Gate.

* * *

With the other horse taking the lead, we pass underneath the shade of a great big cypress tree. Out of nowhere, the two spider monkeys drop down from the low hanging branches onto the back of the lead horse. They both turn and look at me as each one grabs a handful of mane. I smile, "I'm glad you guys decided to join us on our journey."

Both horses at the same time take off in a pretty fast gallop. I occasionally catch glimpses of the giant wall of Heaven as I look through the tall trees. The smooth gallop of my horse reminds me of riding my Tennessee Walker back home, as we dart in and out between scattered timbers. Through creek bottoms and foot hills we get closer with every stride.

Both horses slow down to a walk as we come around the side of a big ravine. The two spider monkeys bail off the lead horse, and then run over to the edge of the ravine cliff. My horse comes to a stop and does his bowing trick. I slide out of the saddle and walk over to the cliff to see what's going on.

As I peep over the edge, I see three old men fly fishing in a beautiful stream. Something catches my attention coming out of the brush behind them. As I watch for a bit, I see a giant grizzly. I immediately start hollering at them to watch out! They all three at the same time turn around and wave at me. I shout at them again and point at the grizzly. *Oh my God, they can't hear me for the sounds of the water rushing over the rocks!* I stand helpless on the cliff watching as three guys are about to be eaten.

The bear walks right up behind them, stands up on his back feet; *Oh no, this thing looks like he's twenty feet tall, maybe even taller.* I hear the two spider monkeys squealing, both jumping up and down.

One of the old men turns around, walks over to the bear and starts scratching his belly. I hear the bear letting out a huge roar, but it wasn't a roar of attack, it was more of a happy playful roar. Then the old man reaches in his wicker trout basket, pulls out a couple trophy size trout and gave them to this friendly bear.

The old man turns walks back to his spot on the river bank, and with the precision of a ballet dancer he takes his fly rod swinging it back and forth slowly releasing more and more line. The motion of his rod is perfect with the fly line circling, gleaming in the rays of the morning sun, enticing the trout underneath the crystal clear mountain water, to strike as the fly touches down.

I hear my horse whickering to tell me it's time to move on. After a few more hours in the saddle, we come to a split in the trail. The passage to our right is angled in the direction of the wall, or should I say the City of God.

The lead horse turns, heading down the narrow path to our left, with my steed continuing to follow. "Whoa, fellow, we need to go right!" I attempt to turn my horse in the direction of the city, "Come on now; get over there." I pull back on the reins, he starts prancing with a little pitching then starts to buck, finally he snorts one time then settles back down and continues down the trail to the left. "What's the matter with you, you crazy lug head?"

Both monkeys on the lead horse jump up and down chattering as if they're laughing at me in a foreign monkey language.

I start to think, *if God set this whole thing up, apparently they are bringing me somewhere special and I need to chill.*

I reach down and rub the side of my horse's neck, "Hey ole buddy, sorry for talking to you like I did. I understand you know where we're headed." And with a couple gentle pats on his neck we continue on.

Walking slowly through the narrow canyon I am now convinced God has more mysteries He wants me to see.

The clattering sounds coming from their hooves as they make contact against the loose rocks lying in our trail echo through the narrow canyon. The cliff walls on each side reach up for several hundred feet. As I admire all the different rock formations and colors, it reminds me of the old western movies.

My mind starts to drift off as the sound of the rocks clattering beneath the feet of the horses is almost hypnotizing. I have thoughts of the three fishermen. It would have been nice to have found a way down to the river so that I could have visited for a short spell. I could have asked about their huge friend the grizzly. The size of that thing was incredible.

I wonder if some of the animals here in Heaven are larger than what we had on Earth. Or maybe they were the same size and could have gone extinct before mankind could document their existence. Nevertheless, that bear was huge, and I can't get over that old man walking up and scratching that big sucker on the belly.

I just wish Allayer and Nipper had been with us; I really miss those two Angels.

This well used path led us through the narrow canyon, up to a rock gorge overlooking a beautiful valley that you could see for miles in any direction. As my eyes came into focus after leaving the shaded narrow pass, I could see herds of animals strung out across the plush green valley. The distance wouldn't allow me to make out what kind of animals they were.

As we turn to our right and start heading out of the canyon, the narrow trail has widened with a cliff wall only a couple feet to our right and to our left a bluff bank with a two hundred foot drop. The sure footed stallions go into a comfortable lope as we continued down the steep decline leading us to the valley.

As we gallop along, I can see layers of gold streaking across the cliff wall. I had the funny thought, "*I wonder if this is where the gold was mined for the pavement in Heaven?*" I chuckle inside and look back across the valley.

The horses slow down to make their way through a herd of elk feeding at the foot of the mountain. They all look up as we pass within a few feet, and without any fear, they drop their heads back down and continue munching on the tender grass.

On our journey across this wide valley, I see Heaven's wall more and more clearly as we continue to close the distance.

My amazement grows as we trot along; the different kinds of animals were so spectacular it would make a safari hunter go nuts. We were moving through giant herds of exotic animals that I have never seen before, even in books.

To my surprise, a large flock of lambs are grazing within a few feet of several Bengal tigers; neither is paying any attention to the other. Three tiger cubs just ran out from under one of the lambs, and then back under as to be playing inside the flock. I can remember Allayer and Nipper reminding me of the saying;

172

The Lion shall lay down with the Lamb. Well, it's not lions, but its sure close enough.

We travel another hand full of miles and the terrain changes from a flat plush valley to rolling green hills. Dandelions growing everywhere all nestled in tall bent grass. The smell of jasmine is in the air. Is that the dandelions giving off that fragrance? I actually don't know what a dandelion smells like. I guess it could be.

* * *

Hill after hill we gallop along, and I start thinking of this gift of being here and seeing these great wonders, that I am so undeserving, a vagabond, unworthy to even be in Heaven. I suddenly feel the overwhelming need to praise and worship God. I look toward the great wall, letting go of the reins I lift my hands toward the City of Heaven. I feel the rush of the Holy Spirit slowly coming up through my feet, the warmth filling every cell of my body and finally leaving through the tips of my fingers.

Yes I've felt this before, back on Earth several years ago. Was God allowing me way back then to have a taste of true worship like they have here in Heaven? It has to be. So I guess this will happen each time we worship? How cool is that!

Both horses slow down as we break over a hill; my mouth flies open without making a sound. Behold the great woolly mammoth; there must be a hundred, all feeding on dandelions. I can't believe my eyes; I'm actually looking at woolly mammoths.

My horse comes to a complete stop, and then bows for me to dismount. I grab the two sacks off the saddle horn, reach in and get both horses the last of the apples. I grab my wine pouch, lean my head back and squeeze a mouth full of wine, suddenly I feel both spider monkeys tapping me on the leg and reaching up. "What do you guys want? Surely not the wine?" They both start jumping up and down. I lean back for another swallow and they both start screeching. I laugh as I hand the pouch over to my impatient friends. As I turn and head in the direction of the giant mammoths, I point and shake my finger at both monkeys, "Not too much fellows and when y'all finish put the pouch back on the saddle horn."

As I walk toward this great herd of mammoths, I'm wishing I had some of my close friends back home with me to share this awesome experience. I bet my ole buddy Matt would believe in God if he could see what I'm seeing.

I slowly walk up to what looks like the bull of the herd. He's quite a bit larger than all the others. His tusks must be thirty feet in length. What a sight, the sun reflecting off of his beautiful white ivory tusk.

As I approach from his left side, I look into his big dark brown eyes, now staring back at me. I hold my hand out as a friendly gesture; I slowly walk closer, talking to him in a low soft tone. "It's okay buddy. I just want to make friends."

Of all things, at this very moment I suddenly remember a cartoon I saw as a kid. A little mouse runs out and scares the giant elephant causing a stampede. *"Dear God, please don't let a mouse around us right now, I'd hate to get run over by a herd of woolly mammoths."*

The great bull continues to munch on the dandelions and acts like he isn't bothered by my presence. I reach up and touch the long hair of his jawbone, while slowly forcing my hand through the thick fur. As I feel the bone structure of his jaw I notice the vibration as he grinds his teeth while chewing his cud.

After mowing down all the dandelions that he could reach with his long trunk he takes a couple steps forward. My hand slides away from his jaw as he moves; now I'm standing beside him. With his height I easily walk underneath his belly barely being able to reach his stomach standing on my tip toes.

Curiosity from the rest of the herd brings them all over to where I am admiring this giant. Now I'm surrounded, and if I were back on Earth, this would be one heck of a scary event.

Without any warning I felt something between my legs as a giant trunk scooped me off the ground. It was the bull- He picked me up, swung me around and before I knew it I was sitting on his back. I caught my breath and grabbed a hand full of hair making sure I wasn't going to fall off this two and a half story building.

I looked back at the horses, then back at the other mammoths and everything looked so peaceful as though this was all planned.

As I get over the shock of the giant trunk elevator, I crawl around on his back as he continues to graze.

Sitting on this giant reminds me of my horse back home, Ellie Mae. Sometimes a white crane would come and sit on her back while she grazed. The egret would wait on horseflies or other insects that would come flying around. I hope this bull mammoth didn't sit me up here to swat flies. I actually haven't seen any insects the whole time I've been in Heaven.

I feel the mammoth take a few more steps as he moves up for fresh dandelions. I don't know why but I lay down across his wide back with the right side of my face pressing down in the soft fur. As I lay still for a few seconds, I hear his heart slowly beating. It sounds like the slow rhythm of a distant bass drum.

With the mesmerizing, boom... boom... boom; like a soothing trance, I fall into a deep sleep and begin to dream.

A great lion walks out of the darkness, his eyes glistening from the reflection of a smoldering fire. I feel a hand on my shoulder, someone whispers, "Fear not Little Soul; fear not." The lion has two scrolls in his mouth as he walks closer and closer. "Who are you lion? Why do they call me Little Soul?" I'm suddenly alone and afraid, I hear the sounds of wings getting closer and closer. I try running as fast as I can, my legs are bogging down in black tar, I'm at the edge of darkness, I'm falling, I'm falling.

I suddenly open my eyes, *Oh no*! I reach to grab fur as I roll off this two story mammoth, bracing for impact. I splash down in belly deep water. As I stand up embarrassed, I reach up and pat the big bull mammoth on his front leg, "Thank you big guy for standing in water. Thank you."

Totally disorientated, I look around to get my bearings. Apparently, I must have slept for a while because the terrain looks different.

Wow, that was one crazy dream, it seemed familiar, a lot like the one I had last night back at the barn. God let me know in my dream that it was okay to take the horses, I wonder if there is something significant about the scrolls? Oh yeah, horses; where are the horses?

Okay, let me get my bearings, I see the wall, but no horses in sight, and where are those two little spider monkeys?

I pat the mammoth on his back leg as a gesture of thanks and friendship while wading out of the stream. Standing on the dry shore, I turn just in time to see the giant mammoth stick his huge trunk into the surface of this crystal clear creek and take in gallons and gallons of water. Reaching over his back and with the sound of a gushing waterfall he releases his payload, drenching his entire body. I can't help but laugh, "Hey ole friend, thanks for letting me get out of the way."

Now, where did my horses get off to? I hope they didn't head back to the barn.

I walk up the gentle slope leading out of the creek bottom, still no horses in sight. Well, I guess I can whistle like I use to for my horses back home. Taking in a deep breath I let out a long Louisiana whistle, wait for a few seconds, nothing. I walk a bit further up the hill, and let out another. I listen with my ear turned in the direction that I think they may be in, and suddenly I hear the familiar sounds of hooves pounding the ground, heading in my direction.

Now that's an awesome sight. As I witness one of the two horses breach the top of the hill in an all-out run heading right for me, not slowing down, I throw both arms in the air. "Whoa buddy! Whoa!" He tucks and locks both back legs underneath his long body, sliding up to me and stopping within inches of where I am standing.

"You lug head! You spooked me, and I was about ready to run for the creek. Where'd you leave your buddies?"

He quickly spins around and does his bowing trick allowing me to easily mount, and then we're off.

I can see the other horse grazing under a big pin oak tree, but no monkeys in sight. As we join back up with the other stallion I look around, still no sign of our little buddies. "Okay guys, I need to be going, maybe they'll catch up to us later. Let's go." I try to turn my horse in the direction of the wall and he won't move. "Okay, it's going to be like this." I lean my head back, look up as if to ask God for some help with my stubborn horse. As I look up, what do you know; I spot two monkeys asleep about twenty feet up, both sprawled out on a limb with my wine pouch hanging on a branch between the two. I start shouting, "Hey you guys wake up! Come on, we need to go!" Nothing, neither of the two move, they are completely out. Suddenly I remember how anxious they were for a drink of wine. "Are you kidding me? Are you guys drunk? That's all I need, a couple of stone drunk spider monkeys on my hands!"

My horse takes a few steps and stops directly beneath the lowest hanging tree branch. After an easy climb I retrieve both monkeys. I take their limp bodies and drop them in the empty apple sack. Before I tie it off to the saddle horn I peep in the burlap sack to make sure they're okay. They're both curled up and still sleeping soundly with what looks like smiles on their faces.

Both horses wheel around and get into a good smooth gait heading for the Great Wall.

* * *

As we put the dandelion meadows behind us, I can now see a road in the near distance. The entire thruway seems to have huge live oak and sycamore trees growing down both sides of the road. The horses slow to a trot for the last quarter mile. Both horses are now high stepping in a sort of prance on our last quarter mile before intersecting with the shaded road.

I feel movement on my left leg coming from the burlap apple sack. As I look down both spider monkeys poke their heads out. "Well hello little fellows, how are my hairy hung over friends feeling today?" They both give off a screech, and then climb out of the bag. One swings himself around to the back of the saddle, the other hangs onto the saddle horn with one hand, while rubbing his eyes with the other. "Well now, that will teach you not to drink too much wine."

To my surprise he reaches down and tries to untie the wine pouch. "You little rascal, no more wine for you. It says in the Bible to beware of strong drink. Nope, you're going to get me in trouble."

In an attempt to take the wine pouch away from my persistent hairy friend, I notice the lamb skin is bulging like it's full. How could this be? Samson, Nipper, Allayer, both monkeys and I have been drinking from this pouch, so how can it still be full? The story of Moses comes to mind. They walked in the wilderness for forty years and their sandals never wore out. God provided food, water and everything else they needed. Well I guess I've just witnessed a miracle. Come to mention it, I've been munching on the sweetest fruit that I have ever tasted. This all has to be the hand of God.

The sounds of my horse's hooves change as we step on the gold pavement. The beauty of the golden road leading under the mighty oaks is unbelievable. The limbs of the oaks and sycamores stretch out, almost touching the ground on all sides. Now with both horses walking side by side, the two monkeys jump over to the other horse. "Hey guys y'all feeling better?" They both stare ahead, as if to tell me in their own way; 'look!'

Through the shaded tunnel of trees, I can see a large group of people walking down this highway of gold. I feel excitement start to swell up inside me as I see what looks like a portal. Every few seconds someone walks out and they fall in behind the rest continuing toward the base of the mountain.

Before we reach the group of people, both horses stop. The one I'm riding bows down to let me know to dismount. As I slide out of the saddle continuing to stare at the portal, my

179

horse nudges me from behind. I turn, reach back and rub both horses behind their ears, "Well I guess this is where we say good bye, right?" One of the monkeys jumped over to my horse untied the wine pouch then tossed it on the ground. "Well I guess it is good bye. Thanks for showing me the way and providing me with such a smooth ride fellows." Both horses swing around and the click clock of their hooves on the golden road fades as they trot away.

I grab Samson's wine pouch off the ground, tie it to my side and start heading further on up the road.

As I walk past the portal, I can see the faces of the new arrivals. I remember what Allayer and Nipper told me about the folks just getting to Heaven with so many questions, and then their minds are opened and they have their answers. Yes, they were right, I can see their expressions changing from a dumfounded look to a nice smile as they realize all is well and they are now in God's hands. I remember Allayer also saying our minds would continue to expand with knowledge after a short time being in Heaven. I wonder if he meant after we're on the planet or inside the city of Heaven, *Oh well it doesn't matter. I'm just glad to be here.*

I continue to follow the scattered group of people slowly making their way up the golden road.

Coming up on the base of the mountain, the trees that were paralleling the road split off as to be growing around the base of the whole mountain. As far as the eye could see, in either direction the line of trees continued.

At the foot of the mountain, the golden road changed into a golden stairway. The stairway seemed to go for miles, right up through the low hanging clouds.

What I was witnessing reminds me of Moses in the Holy Scripture, Exodus 24:15-18,

"Then Moses went up into the mountain, and a cloud covered the mountain.

Now the glory of the Lord rested on Mount Sinai, and the cloud covered it six days. And on the seventh day He called to Moses out of the midst of the cloud.

The sight of the glory of the Lord was like a consuming fire on top of the mountain in the eyes of the children of Israel.

So Moses went up into the midst of the cloud and went up into the mountain."

It makes me wonder if the way I feel right now is how Moses must have felt a few thousand years ago. With each step, we are getting closer and closer to the dwelling place of the Almighty God!

As I look back at the portal, the people coming through now look like ants as we are almost at cloud level.

I can hear a few people having conversation as we move along. I chuckle inside as it seems they are asking some of the same questions that I pounded Allayer and Nipper with.

As I think back over my journey I know God is so good. He gave me Allayer and Nipper for the first part, then the two little spider monkeys. Then the two wonderful stallions; Yes God is good.

Just before we get into the clouds, I step aside as to allow everyone behind me to easily walk by. I have the sudden urge to look back over the distant landscape, and the beauty can't be put into words. I had been at several mountain overlooks where tourists would stop and look in awe at God's creation. It was no doubt something to see back on Earth, but this was much more. It looks like a thousand rivers and lakes scattered through

181

colorful rolling hills with the rivers all intersecting. Tops of distant snowcapped mountains line up on each side of the golden highway. The light reflecting off the golden road gives the appearance of glass. I see thousands of large birds flying near the wall. The wall glitters as to have different kinds of stone; could that be jasper?

Yes, I remember somewhere in Revelation, I believe around chapter 21. John the Revelator wrote, *"And he carried me away in the Spirit to a great and high mountain, and showed me the great city, the holy Jerusalem, descending out of Heaven from God, having the glory of God. Her light was like a most precious stone, like a jasper stone, clear as crystal."*

I count twelve layered foundations at the bottom of the wall, at the top of each foundation it looks like several hundred feet to each edge. Each foundation glitters with all sorts of precious stones. The first is jasper, the second sapphire, the third agate, the fourth emerald, the fifth onyx, the sixth ruby, the seventh chrysolite, the eighth beryl, the ninth topaz, the tenth turquoise, the eleventh jacinth, and the twelfth amethyst. John the Revelator saw this very thing in his vision. He also said, *"Now the wall of the city had twelve foundations, and on them were the names of the twelve apostles of the Lamb."*

As I continue trying to soak in the beauty of my surroundings and focus on the giant wall, I hear the sound of wings. This really sounded familiar. As I turn to look, oh my goodness! Those aren't large birds, they are Angels! Thousands of Angels; I wonder what they're doing? Maybe this is just a normal day around the kingdom.

I turn and make my way back in the slow moving line, continuing to hear the chatter and excitement in the voices of God's redeemed.

The clouds feel refreshing to my face and as I breathe in I catch the same fragrance of jasmine that I did back near the dandelion fields. How can this get any better? Blessing after blessing!

I see old and young in line and I'm wondering how the old people are making this hike. We have to be at least two or three miles up this stairway. I feel great. As a matter of fact I haven't been tired the whole time I've been here. But I felt the need to sleep the last two nights. I wish Allayer and Nipper was here, I could ask them.

I step aside again and let a few people by until I spot an elderly gentleman. "Excuse me sir, do you mind if I join you?"

He looks up and with a big smile, "Sure young fellow, I would love the company."

"Thanks, ole buddy." I reach out to shake his hand and join in the walk. "So what's your name and where do you come from, ole timer?"

He laughs, "I might look like an ole timer but I feel like I'm twenty-one again."

"I know what you mean. Isn't it great?"

"Yes indeed, I've been lying in bed helpless for the last fifteen years. My poor lovely wife has waited on me hand and foot every minute of it."

"My goodness, bless yawls' hearts. I know that had to be tough on both you and your wife."

"Yes it was. We both prayed every day that God would just bring me home and He did! Glory! I made it to be ninety-six and we spent all those years in Douglas, Arizona. Everyone around Douglas called me Ole Chet. My real name is Sheppard."

He stuck his hand back out for a second greeting. I chuckled as I shook his hand, "Pleased to meet you Ole Chet, my name is Chado Cole." We both start laughing.

"I know I know... my nick name sounds a lot like O Shet. Well I got stuck with that name by my best friend, you see he was tongue-tied and every time he would talk to anyone else about me, he would say, 'You know O Shet.' Do you get the picture?"

"Sure I do, I can see how someone would have a bit of fun with that. Don't feel bad, I got the nickname Codzs when I got hit you know where with a baseball when I was playing short stop during a tournament, and the name stuck. I hated it at first, but it didn't bother me after a few years. So Mr. Chet, is your tongue-tied friend still back at home?"

"No sir, he passed last year; he was ninety-seven and I'll be looking for him the first chance I get after we pass through the gate."

"I understand. I've got a few friends I can't wait to see also. Okay ole buddy, maybe we'll cross paths again." The ole man tips his head as I step back out of line.

I look back down the stairway and I see people scattered for miles. This visual makes you stop and think, if the lost back on Earth could only catch a glimpse of what I'm seeing, they would humble themselves and cry out for God. Come to think of it, if they could see into the Realm and know the darkness that surrounds them with the demons and power of the fallen angels that patiently wait on their passing, they would run to Christ!

I lift my voice to God, "Please surround my family with your love, Lord, that none will perish, Amen."

I slip back in line and continue my ascent up the golden stairway. Every so often I catch a glimpse of Heaven's Gate through the scattered clouds. I step to the left then as far to the right trying to see around the slow moving line of saints. The swirling clouds hovering over this mountain seem to be getting denser as we move along.

I can see what looks like the end of our line up ahead, but I don't think it's the end at all. It's just they are disappearing as they walk through the mass of clouds. This is so cool; we have to be near the gate, my stomach feels like a thousand butterflies are floating around. I wonder if everyone is feeling the same heart-pounding excitement as I am.

As I get to the thick grayish white clouds where the people seem to be disappearing, it reminds me of a foggy Louisiana morning.

When I begin to walk through the heavy vapor, goose bumps flood over my entire body. I have an overwhelming need to shout with joy and happiness. Almost embarrassed inside, I look over at a lady to my right and ask her, "Excuse me Miss, but I have to ask, how are you feeling, right now?"

She looks at me with a growing smile and suddenly starts shouting and jumping up and down hollering to the top of her lungs, "Glory is to God, and His Kingdom, hallelujah, hallelujah!" And before I know it, all the people in the mist of the cloud are shouting and praising God, including me. I am so glad to know I'm not the only one experiencing this strange feeling when we entered the mist of the cloud.

As we walked through this mist I noticed our clothing had instantly changed into a brilliant white cloth. The lady standing beside me was feeling of her sleeve, she rubbed the cloth with her thumb and index finger, and then held it up to smell. She looked over at me, "It's pure white cotton and has my favorite smell of roses." I immediately lifted my sleeve and pressed it against my face and I could smell jasmine, Could this be my favorite smell? I never knew I had a favorite smell, but as I think of it, I believe it is.

I burst out laughing, "God has thought of everything to give his children the desires of their hearts." As I think back over my journey I remember catching the fragrance of jasmine several times. The blessings of God are unending.

After the excited group of saints settled back down from the infilling of the Holy Spirit and our new clothes, I notice a change in the mist. It was thinning, I could see further and further ahead.

20

A City in Heaven

The Gate was slowly coming into full view as we walked completely out of the mist. We stepped off the stairway onto the flat surface of a giant courtyard. The courtyard has gold tile from one end to the other and between the joints of tile it seemed to be laced together with silver. The floor of the courtyard to my left had the appearance of pure glass, but when I looked to my right it seem to change, the floor almost looked like it was moving and had the impression of water. The glistening reflections of the pearl gate bouncing off the courtyard floor, has to be one of the most beautiful sights in Heaven.

From a long distance away, the gate looked like it was built with two pearls, but as I see it up close I can tell it's only one. The giant pearl looks like it was carefully split into two pieces to create this massive gate.

In the Book of Revelation, John talked about Heaven having twelve gates and each individual gate was of one pearl.

I stepped back out of line, just to get a better picture of what I was witnessing. I can see twelve Angels, six standing on each side of the open gate. The Angels have the appearance of my Guardian Angel, with the same type of armor. Their shields and swords are strapped across their backs. The tips of their wings are resting on the gold tile.

When I continue to admire every detail of the entrance, I notice above the gate a giant golden beam that stretches across the entire width of the opening. Across the beam the name *Holy Jerusalem* is inscribed at the center. As I see past the gate, the street of the city was pure gold, like transparent glass.

The long line of people that had already entered was being greeted by loved ones. I see childlike Angels scattered throughout the crowd reminding me of Allayer and Nipper as they first appeared so childlike when we first met. I remember they said their childlike appearance was intended to be gentle and comforting to make the transition easier.

I continue to watch the little Angels taking children out of the line and holding their hands as they lead them along the golden path. This picture magnifies the depth of God's love for His children.

Briefly looking back over the clouds hovering below us, I take a deep breath, turn and head across the courtyard toward the gate.

Walking in between the twelve Angels, I look to see if by chance my Guardian might be in the mix. Their faces all fixed staring straight ahead, almost as if looking right through me. I don't see my Angel; I guess I'll run into him later on.

As I slowly move along with the line of saints, I'm wondering, *if there are twelve gates and each gate has this many people walking through, there must be a lot of people dying or getting killed every minute.* I suddenly remember reading an article one time that said fifty-six million people die each year so that would mean about 153,424 on an average would die every day.

Wow, I have always been terrible at math. God is truly opening my mind!

So if over 153,000 are dying every day, I wonder what the average is between the saved and the lost. Okay, twelve gates divided by 153,424 people would mean that 12,785.3 would be here walking through if they were all saved. My goodness, that surely isn't the case because when I looked back down the stairway earlier, I could only see maybe a thousand people. Could my estimate be close? Where are the other eleven thousand? A scripture came to me from Matthew, 7:13-14,

"Enter by the narrow gate; for wide is the gate and broad is the way that leads to destruction, and there are many who go by in it.

Because narrow is the gate and difficult is the way which leads to life, and there are few who find it."

Wow, it must be a lot of lost souls walking the dark road into Hell every day. Man, what a scary and sad thought!

Maybe that was what my dream or should I say my nightmare was about when I fell off the mammoth. I saw thousands walking in darkness. My God, I shake my head and look down at the gold pavement, as I get rid of this dark vision of my dream.

Looking down each side of the street as I move along I don't see any familiar faces. I'm wondering, maybe my folks didn't get the memo. I chuckle inside as I continue.

Moving through small groups of people standing in the street, I stretch to see over their heads standing on my tiptoes. Still nobody in sight, and suddenly, I feel someone tug on my garment. It's one of the little Angels smiling up at me. He grabs my hand and leads me through the groups of saints. As we make our way out of the crowd and into an opening, I have a clear view of the street up ahead. He stops, let's go of my hand and points, and after giving me direction, he smiles and disappears back into the crowd.

After staring up the road, and still not making out exactly what he was pointing at, I continue walking in the general direction.

As I walk along this beautiful golden street, I have thoughts of seeing Jesus standing in a white robe with his arms spread open like I've seen in pictures, or my ole papa waving, "Over here Son!" or maybe even my sweet daughter, "Hey Dad, over here, over here!" My hope fades as I can see clearly up the street with no evidence of anyone familiar. The few people I pass smile and wave or nod their heads in loving gestures as I move along.

* * *

I see an odd sight further up the street, a tall stranger standing on the side of the road with two dogs sitting right beside him. When I get closer both dogs start running in my direction. "Are they coming to me?" The closer they get I noticed something familiar with both animals. "This can't be!" I kneel down in the street as I see the happiness in their faces; they run full speed heading directly at me. Both dogs tackle me and gently bring me down to where I am now laying on my back. Whining and whimpering, they lick my whole face. What a welcoming committee; it was two of my favorite dogs from childhood, Rex and Moushie.

I roll around on my back, right in the middle of the golden streets of Heaven, loving on my two best friends. What a blessing for God to have allowed my two favorite childhood dogs to make it into Heaven.

After a ton of dog kisses and laughter, I sit up and the stranger is standing at my feet. Actually he isn't a stranger at all. I could recognize those scars from anywhere, it was my Guardian Angel. He looked different, no wings, no armor, no sword. He was dressed like me.

He reaches his hand out to help me up. After I'm standing I see both dogs start running and darting in circles around us tucking their tails underneath their bellies as they did as pups when they were overwhelmed with happiness.

I hear the Angel speak, "They are sure happy to see you."

"I'm happy to see them too, and I'm also happy to see you again. This is actually the first time you've spoken to me and I've wanted to ask you your name ever since we were on Earth. Do you mind telling me?"

"Of course not, my name is Uriel, and I am one of many Guardian Angels."

"Uriel, that sounds familiar, I read somewhere that Uriel was an Archangel. Are you an Archangel?"

"No, God named me after Uriel the mighty Archangel."

"Wow, what a cool name. What does the name Uriel mean?"

"It means God is my light."

"Now that's awesome. So how did you get stuck with me, Uriel? Allayer and Nipper told me you've been watching over me ever since my birth."

"Yes, I've been with you throughout your whole life. Actually the Master assigned me to you years before you were even conceived."

"Why so early on, I mean before I was born?"

"Do you remember on God's mountain when Lucifer asked you about his coming to you as a child, and when he stood at the foot of your bed?"

"Yes, how could I forget? I sure didn't like having to talk with that evil rascal on the mountain! By the way, were you there in my room the night Satan came?"

"Yes I was there. I stood with two other Guardians in your room. Lucifer wanted to kill you. The demons that were assigned to your dad had informed Lucifer of Jesus appearing in your vision the year before. From this small piece of information he knew that if Christ had come to you in a vision, that God surely had big plans for you. He even went before the Lord God and asked permission to take your life."

"What the heck, Satan wanted to kill me? Were you there when he met with God?"

"No, I was watching over you. I got the news from one of God's messengers."

"What kind of messenger brought you the news? Was he like Allayer and Nipper, a messenger Angel?"

"Yes, exactly."

"What did he tell you, I mean, what did God tell Lucifer when he asked for my life?"

Uriel reached down as we walked along and gently patted Moushie on the head. "Well Chado, I'm not sure of the exact conversation, I only received bits and pieces and this is what I was told from the messenger: He said, it was a day when the sons of God came to present themselves before the Lord, and Lucifer also came among them. And the Lord said to Satan, 'Lucifer why are you walking in the midst of the sons of God?'

'I seek the soul of a child from a lost bloodline. He has no purpose in life or to you; he will eventually perish as the cursed bloodline of his father's father.'

'Woe to you, prince of darkness, I know the child you seek, but I hear his mother's prayers and the groaning from her fasting and I am faithful to bless her and her family. You have no right to this Little Soul. The curse of generations will be broken with his father. My protection will stand.' "

"My goodness, I can't believe God and Satan were having a conversation about me back when I was a kid, and especially the part about Satan wanting to kill me. Good Lord! So now I understand why you've been with me all these years. Uriel, thank God, and thank you!"

I stop in the middle of the street, take my wine pouch and have a small refreshing sip of wine. I held it up and to my surprise; Uriel takes the pouch and squeezes himself a mouthful.

"You know Uriel, thinking about that conversation between God and Satan, you mentioned where God called me Little Soul. Satan called me that back when we were on Tabula Rasa. Then I fell asleep lying on the back of a bull mammoth yesterday, I had a dream and in my dream, someone called me Little Soul. Apparently that's where it came from. So Uriel, I don't understand why God would use me. I'm just a regular guy, a nobody."

"Well let me explain something, God does his best work with the nobodies, remember the old lady that gave a penny and Jesus told everyone that this lady gave more than anyone there. God loves to do big things with little people."

"Can you tell me His plan for me?"

"I can tell you this; you're going to play a part in rescuing millions from the hands of Lucifer."

"Millions? How in Heaven's name can I do that? I'm no longer on Earth."

"You know the dreams you've been having?"

"Oh yeah, every detail, they just didn't make any sense."

"Did you dream about scrolls?"

"Yes, three different times."

"Do you remember everything you've seen thus far on your journey?"

"Yes, I remember everything, like it just happened, but I still don't understand what the dreams meant or what I'm supposed to do."

Uriel smiles, "Have patience, Little Soul."

We both chuckle as we move along.

"Chado, have you thought about where you want to go or who you might want to visit?"

"Well, I kind of thought Jesus would be here to meet us at the gate, can we go see Him?"

"Not yet, Jesus is seated at the right hand of the Father and He's on the throne in the center of Heaven right now. You'll know when it's time to see Him."

"Does He ever go anywhere or does He stay pretty much around the throne room?"

"He goes anywhere He pleases, and sometimes He stands at the entrance of one of the twelve gates and loves on the new arrivals as they come in. But He is Lord of Heaven not greeter of Heaven."

"Okay, I think I understand. Uriel, you say I'll know when it's time to see Jesus, how do you mean?"

"Sometimes but not very often, you'll hear what everyone calls the Trumpets of Gathering. There will be three long blasts from the trumpets and when you hear these trumpets you'll have three days to get to the center of Heaven."

"Why three days and three trumpet blasts?"

"If you haven't noticed, God uses numbers to represent different things, like the twelve gates, twelve tribes, God created the Heavens and Earth in seven days, number of completion seven; Christ's death and resurrection three days, Trumpets of Gathering three days, and so on."

"Uriel, what if I'm so far away and I can't hear it, or maybe on the other side of the wall?"

"Don't worry, they can be heard even beyond the Great Wall, and you'll also see everyone else headed for the center of Heaven. So tell me Chado, where do you want to go first?"

"Well I would like to see my daughter and my dad. Heck, come to think of it, I wouldn't mind meeting all my ancestors. That would be so awesome."

"You have eternity to meet everyone your heart desires, but let's take it slow right now and work on just a few. Somewhere in the mix we have to complete your task, but we have time for a few visits."

21

The Search for Summer

"Okay Uriel, what direction does my daughter Summer live in?"

"I don't know. We need to find out."

"What do you mean, you don't know? I thought Angels knew everything."

"Hardly. You see, God knows where everyone is, but the Angels have to do a little foot work. If you would, follow me, we'll head over to the Hall of Records."

"The Hall of Records, you mean Heaven has a courthouse?"

"No, not exactly."

As I follow Uriel down the street, I begin to hear music, it is beautiful. This harmony of voices and instruments is something I've never heard before. I look over at Uriel, "Where's it coming from?" He points toward a building down the golden path.

I begin to have an overwhelming need to lift my hands in worship as we continue up the street. As we get closer to the Hall of Records, this soothing and wonderful music was now clear enough to make out the words.

"*Blessed are all who fear the Lord, who walk in obedience to him.*"

Suddenly I hear a change in tempo as they started a new song.

"*Those who wait on the Lord shall renew their strength;
They shall mount up with wings like eagles,*

They shall run and not be weary,
They shall walk and not faint."

We walk off the street onto a long walkway that leads to the entrance of a magnificent building. The front reminds me of our nation's capital back on Earth. It had giant pearl columns with the architectural design of something I had never seen.

Over its doors the words Hall of Records were written. This building has to be the size of the White House or maybe even larger.

The angelic stone structures on both sides of the building couldn't have been made from human hands. The granite marvels seem to be moving, changing form and color as I watch in amazement. It looks like the stone angels are worshiping with the instruments they hold as they slowly move.

They are the source of this beautiful music. This scene reminded me of the scripture when Jesus told the Pharisees,

"I tell you that if these should keep silent, the stones would immediately cry out."

Uriel stepped in front of me and as he passed, he softly whispered, "This is only the beginning of the mysteries of God."

I couldn't seem to stop staring at this masterpiece as I slowly made my way toward the gold and silver laced doors that led inside.

Something caught my eye that I thought was odd. Before we entered the Hall of Records, I noticed there's no glass in the windows. As I look around at the other buildings they all have openings for windows but they don't have glass either. After giving it some thought, it occurred to me, I'm standing in Heaven, the temperature is perfect and there are no insects, and no thieves, so why would you need windows other than to feel the fresh air of Heaven. What a cool place to live.

Uriel smiles as he turns and opens the doors.

I look down at a floor that has the appearance of glass. The floor has streaks of pearl running like water that were inset in the gold tiles. The inside structure is a huge dome. I look up at the ceiling and it's covered in beautiful paintings.

"Wow that looks like it was painted by Michelangelo. He was the guy who painted the ceiling of the Sistine Chapel back in the early 1500's."

Uriel grins real big, "How do you think he got his talent?"

"Well God blessed him with it I guess."

"That's right; and he is the one that created this masterpiece."

"You mean I'm looking at the work of Michelangelo?"

"That's right. Isn't it beautiful? He and others with the same talent have paintings all over Heaven."

"This is truly amazing."

I look back across this massive domed building, and several hundred feet away, in the center of the room, a lady is standing behind a round desk.

I touch both dogs on their heads as we take off in her direction. I hear the clicking sounds of their claws against the beautiful floor causing an echo across this vast dome.

She sees us and waves to welcome us to the dome room.

As we head in her direction, I notice doors on the edge of this giant circled shaped room. Above each door is a single letter, and the number of doors are twenty six. I am too far away to make out what the letters are. So I guess that has to be the alphabet, A-Z.

Before I have time to ask Uriel, we step up to the counter. "What can I help you with on this lovely day, gentlemen?"

Uriel takes a step forward, "We need information on the whereabouts of Summer Allyce Cole. Can you help us?"

"Yes, what year did she arrive?" Being a bit choked up and having a hard time telling the lady what year my daughter passed, Uriel mumbles, "December of 2008."

"Okay gentlemen, if you would, follow me."

We walk back across the enormous room toward one particular door. As we get closer I can make out the letter on the door facing, it's the letter C.

I feel the butterflies rising in my stomach, *What if we can't find her name? No, she has to be here, I know she had to have made it.*

I feel Uriel's hand on my shoulder and at the same time Moushie and Rex reach up and touch their cold noses to my hands. Suddenly I feel a sense of total comfort as I watch the lady open the door.

When we enter the room, to my surprise it is totally empty except for a round stone table in the center. The room has no corners it is completely round just like the one outside. I whisper to Uriel, "There's nothing here." He holds his index finger to his lips and points to the table, then smiles.

The table looks like it's ten thousand years old. It has two handles, one on each side. The lady says, "If you don't mind, gentlemen." Then she points at the table. I'm wondering if she wants us to sit down. Heck there are no chairs.

Uriel shakes his head, smiles and then takes hold of one of the handles and starts spinning the table very slowly. I jump in to help and after a couple rounds the walls light up with thousands of names dating back as far as 33AD.

The lady motions with her hand for us to continue. We both push a little harder and faster and like a time machine the years are flashing by.

She looks over at us, "Okay guys, you can slow it back down." As we slow the rock wheel, the names come back into focus, I could see dates, we were around the 1600's.

Walking around this table, leaning against the wooden handles reminds me of the way they ground corn or sugar cane in ancient days, and here we were using it as a giant rolodex.

She motions again for us to speed back up, we make several more fast rounds and we hear, "Okay fellows, we should be close." After slowing down I look up just in time to see my birth year fly by, and finally we were looking at names in 2008. "Slow down guys, slower, okay you can stop. There she is." The lady points to my little girl's name.

The excitement overwhelms me, "Uriel, I see it! There's my daughter's name right there on the wall, Summer Allyce Cole!"

Suddenly Rex and Moushie both start barking at the same time. They are as excited as I am. I wheel around, kneel and grab both my dogs around their necks. "Guys, we're going to see Summer!"

After calming back down, I stand to read her information. The lady had us stop the wheel directly at a point beside her name and the entire wall was covered with just her information.

I asked the lady, "Is this normal to have that much information on one person?"

"Yes, fairly normal, some people have more, others have less. It's according to how often you ask for forgiveness of your sins. When someone dies and they haven't asked for forgiveness in a while, their sins are documented and they show up here. The sins you've asked God to forgive, He casts them as far as the East is to the West. In other words they are erased. It looks like your daughter hadn't asked for forgiveness for some time.

Let me show you something. If you would, move the wheel around a couple times. Okay, a little further, okay... stop. You see, here is a lady that was ninety-four years old when she passed and she has pretty much a blank page other than her location. So, on her death bed she was probably talking to God up to the time of her passing, and was continually asking for forgiveness."

"Yeah, my daughter was killed after a night out on the town with her buddies Christmas shopping. God was probably the last thing on her mind before she passed."

"Well the happy part of this is you know she made it and you're going to see her."

"Yes... thank you Jesus for your saving grace! Heck yeah, that's the good part, and thank you so much for the short lesson on how all this works."

We roll the wheel back to Summer's name and location and the lady reads it off, "Records show she is a volunteer in the Valley of the Children, and lives on site."

I turn and ask Uriel if he knew of this location? He shakes his head yes, and smiles.

The lady asks if we have anyone else we need to find before leaving? "Yes, my dad and my grandparents, if you don't mind."

After spending a while in the Hall of Records, I have locations for several family members and friends. Plenty to keep us busy for a while.

I look over at Moushie and Rex, "Well ole friends are y'all ready? Come on, let's go."

* * *

We all four leave the Hall of Records and make our way to the outskirts of the city.

"Uriel you say there are cities like this at all twelve gates?"

"Yes all twelve, and they are pretty much the same, God set them up to make everyone's entry into Heaven to have the same pleasantries that you're experiencing."

"So the city where the throne is located, is it the same as the gate cities?"

"No, not by any means, the place where the Holy Trinity is located is beyond belief. Have patience, you'll see in good time."

After we walk several miles passing mansion after mansion I see both dogs turn off the golden path and head down a narrow cobblestone trail. I whistle, "Come on Moushie; where are y'all going? Come on, this way fellows."

"Chado, just follow the dogs. I told them where to go."

"So Uriel, you can speak to animals?"

"Sure I can, and you can to if you would just let your mind go and quit asking so many questions."

I start laughing as I apologize, "I know, I know, I'll ease up."

We make several more miles disappear as we continue down the trail. I start thinking about how long the day has become. I've been inside the walls of Heaven for what has to be over twelve hours and I don't seem to know what part of the day or evening it is. I remember camping in the barn and it was night and the length of day seemed to be close to what it was back on Earth.

"Okay, I can't help myself Uriel, what time of the day is it?"

He chuckles, "Well Chado, there's no such thing as time in Heaven, or at least like it is on Earth or outside the walls of Heaven. God has a timeline, but it's not like anything you would understand. You see, inside the walls of Heaven, *The city had no need of the sun or of the moon to shine in it, for the glory of God illuminated it. The Lamb is its light. And the nations of those who are saved shall walk in its light.*"

"Yeah, Allayer and Nipper tried to explain this to me, and I wasn't real clear on it then and I'm still not real clear now. Like for example, do we sleep inside Heaven?"

"Sure, if you want to, you can sleep anytime."

"I'm not tired but I really like a good nap every now and then."

"I'll tell you this, when the people of Heaven sleep, God always gives His children pleasant dreams and a refreshed spirit."

"Uriel I'm still a bit confused, if God illuminates Heaven and we can't tell if it's day or night, will I miss seeing the stars and the moons?"

"What do you mean miss seeing the stars and the moons? You can go outside the gates of Heaven anytime you like and experience everything this solar system has to offer."

"Oh, I get it. So God is the unending light inside the walls of Heaven. Now that's a relief, because I do enjoy the night sky."

"Chado, God enjoys the night sky also, that's why He designed it like He did. He travels all over Heaven, inside and outside the walls. Someday you might be standing right beside Him and not even realize it. Chado this is something you might want to know, He can appear in different forms."

"What do you mean?"

"Well if He wants, He can take the form of an eagle, a giant bear, a mammoth or maybe just a little old lady. In other words, anything He desires."

"Wow that is so cool. You know Uriel; it would be such a blessing to meet The Almighty in person."

"Well Chado, how do you know that you haven't already?"

"I guess I don't know."

As we continue down the stone path, I start thinking back over my journey so far. All the animals and people I met, their faces etched in my mind like a photograph. Wow, any one of those could have been God.

"Oh my goodness, hey Uriel, I remember hearing a preacher quote a scripture that relates to this."

"Okay Chado, let's hear it."

"He said, '*Do not forget to show hospitality to strangers, for in doing so some have entertained Angels without knowing it.*' "

Uriel grins from ear to ear. "That's right, not only the people you met on your journey to Heaven, but all the faces you've seen on Earth, even from your childhood, could have been Angels or God himself."

"My goodness, when you think of it like that, it makes me wonder if I've always shown enough kindness to strangers."

"Chado Cole, can you imagine walking past a homeless person begging for food and find out later that it was the God of all creation?"

"No, I couldn't imagine, and I hope I never have. Uriel, do you know what panhandlers are?"

"Yes, those are the people who have a deceitful mind and use poverty as a tool to swindle folks out of their money."

"Yep, they are the ones that hurt the people that really need it."

"I know; that is so sad."

"You know people that have a spirit of giving get burned one time by someone like that and they stop giving to the homeless all together."

"Hey Uriel where did Moushie and Rex get off to?"

We walk a bit further, "There they are." I see both dogs darting in and out of sight as we follow our narrow cobblestone path. Our smooth rock path winds around rolling hills and plush green meadows that are filled with wild flowers and dogwood trees. Uriel spots a couple fruit trees near a creek up ahead.

"Hey Chado, would you like to sit for a while?"

"Sure bud that would be great."

Before we find a comfortable place to sit, Uriel plucks a handful of tangerines, tosses a couple over to me as we plop down at the edge of the stream. We both take our sandals off and ease our feet over into the frigid water.

"Oh, this feels good Uriel. You know this reminds me of Black Creek."

"Yes it does resemble the creek of your childhood."

"Well, duh, I guess you would know about Black Creek, if you've been assigned to me before birth."

"Yes, I followed you up and down those creek banks for years."

I chuckle, "Uriel, I wish I could have seen into the spiritual realm back then and got to meet you. I believe we would have been close friends."

"Chado, we've always been close friends, you just didn't know it."

"Well, I'm glad to finally meet you Uriel." I held my hand out when my Guardian Angel reached over with a firm grip and shook my hand.

I ask Uriel, "Hey bud do we have time for a quick dip in the creek?"

"Sure, I believe I'll join in."

We both strip down to the linen cloth covering our privates, and splash.

I was amazed at how clear and cold the water is. The depth from the shore only looked to be a few feet deep, but after heading for the bottom I realized the water was at least twenty to thirty feet depth.

As I surfaced, I see both dogs had already joined in the fun. I start laughing out loud, "God I can't believe I'm in Heaven, swimming with my two favorite dogs and my Guardian Angel in a creek just like the one I swam in as a kid. Hallelujah, thank you Lord!"

After we sloshed around for a while and got our fill of this amazing blessing, we all felt the need to move on.

As I got dressed into my white cotton clothes that had the awesome smell of jasmine, I watched Moushie and Rex shake as much water out of their thick fur as they could.

I glance over at Uriel to ask if he is about ready to head out, and I can't believe what I'm seeing. Uriel is facing away from me and hasn't put his shirt back on. His entire back is scarred, like he has been whipped by someone with no mercy.

22

Battle Scars

I had already noticed his face and arms were scarred but I never imagined his entire body had received this much damage. I turn looking the other direction, hoping he didn't see me observing his battle wounds.

"Chado, it's okay bud. You forget I can hear what you're thinking."

"Man, you got me. I'm so sorry Uriel. I couldn't help but notice your wounds and wonder how you got cut up like that. Do you mind telling me?"

"Sure I can tell you. We have a few more miles to go before our first stop. Chado, I'm going to remind you of an event that happened in your past life and then I want you to tell me the story about what happened. Is that okay?"

"I guess so, but what's that got to do with your scars?"

"Everything, you'll see what I'm talking about. Do you remember when your dog Buck got shot while you were on a project over in the state of Mississippi?"

"Yes."

"Okay, tell me from the beginning exactly what happened."

"It's been a long time ago, but I'll try."

* * *

"When I got the job as night watchman for the pipeline company, it didn't take me long to figure out that I needed a companion. The long twelve hour nights babysitting heavy equipment that was used to install steel pipelines cross country made me realize I needed a dog. So in my search for the perfect canine, I happened to stop at a general store for my nightly snacks and there was an ole female Catahoula Cur standing in front of the store. I petted her as I came in and also as I left. She hung around the storefront for several days, and each time I started to leave, she would try to let me know she wanted to go with me by raring up with her front feet on the tailgate of my truck. I had to ask the store manager who she belonged to. The manager claimed that she didn't belong to anyone and insisted that I take her. So I dropped the tailgate and without any persuasion she jumped right in.

After several nights of having her around, I knew I had definitely made the right choice. Sometime later, I bred her with my brother's Bull Mastiff and she had a litter of puppies. Before she gave birth to our new family of pups, I built a cypress dog house for the back of my truck. It was a thing of beauty, the craftsmanship of the aerodynamic roof would have made any dog owner sin with envy.

The proud mom gave birth to seven beautiful pups that were born on the pipeline in the back of my truck.

After they were around eight to ten weeks old, the guys on the pipeline would get a kick out of watching me arrive and dropping the tailgate, seeing pup after pup stick their heads out.

As time passed, I gave away all but one, and kept my favorite. He was the pick of the litter; Buck.

I guess if you compared him to Moushie and Rex, Buck would have to be one of my top three dogs ever.

In that season of my life, I managed to get married in between projects, and it seemed like every time I came home my wife would announce, 'I'm pregnant'. Wow, back to back, two girls and a boy.

Trying to send my wife through nursing school and facing a whole other type of expense with three babies, I had to figure out how to cut costs. So I started eating a lot more beanie weenies and sardines. Still struggling, I decided no more motel expense for me. I got permission from the owner of the company to camp along the pipeline. So Buck and I slept during the day anywhere there was a source of fresh water near the pipeline right-of-way. I truly believe the old man that owned the company liked my being out there.

On the larger jobs where we were spread too thin, they would hire another watchman. This is where I met Marvin; he was a preacher that really loved the Lord. He worked with us on several projects and became a dear friend.

I was finally able to afford a six hundred dollar camper. It looked like something from a comedy show, but it did keep the rain out. We had no running water or electricity, but it was definitely a step up from tents or sleeping in the back of my truck curled up with my furry friend. I remember using a twenty gallon water cooler in the winter time to bathe out of. This was only after the water in the creeks would get so cold it would hurt my scalp when I would try to wash my hair, and at that point I would start using the igloo cooler.

No, I couldn't crawl in a twenty gallon cooler. I would take the lid off each day and let the sun warm it up as much as possible. I would then take a big towel stick it down in the water, take a deep breath then squeeze it out over my head, soap up, shampoo up and then rinse right off. For a quick shave, I would twist the mirror around and before I knew it, I was as clean as could be.

As the days passed, Marvin and I would read and study the Bible. Uriel, as I think back, I truly believe being around ole Marvin really impacted my whole life.

Well anyway, one day after we awoke and were getting ready to head to our designated locations on the line, I told Marvin that I had an awful nightmare about Buck. I dreamed that he had come running up to me and his face was covered with bright red blood. We didn't think much of it at the time, but that was about to change.

My crew had shut down for the day on the side of a hill overlooking a land owner's home and property. As I was sitting in my truck before dark reading the scripture, I looked around for Buck and I saw he had made friends with the land owner's German Shepherd and they were both playing about half way between his house and my equipment. I remember smiling as I watched them harmlessly chase each other and I had the thought, the shepherd must be a female and Buck has a new girlfriend.

Suddenly the owner came out of his house and with a very hard tone started hollering at his dog to come home. I immediately got out of the truck and called Buck back up the hill. The land owner went back in his house like everything was okay.

After Buck came up to me I petted him for a few seconds, 'Buck, don't go back down there, you hang around here.' I stepped back in my truck, grabbed my Bible and continued to read, when suddenly I hear gun fire. POW, POW, POW, I look up to see where it's coming from and it's the landowner shooting a rifle, and he's pointing in our direction. I look back over and see Buck standing beside a Cat side boom that's parked in front of my truck. The shots continue: POW, POW, and I hear the bullet hit Buck with a thump.

Buck doesn't go down; he runs around and leaps up in the back of my truck. I quickly threw my Bible on the seat then grabbed my Colt 45 pistol. I jumped out of my truck and ran to my wounded dog. I could see the entry and exit hole from this maniac's bullet. It looked like a perfect heart shot, the entry wound was right behind the front shoulder. Suddenly Buck starts spitting up blood and with tears swelling and my heart pounding, I was getting ready for Buck to take his last breath.

With sudden overwhelming anger, I turn and start running down the hill with my pistol cursing and shouting, 'I am going to kill you, you sorry no good SOB!' Suddenly from out of nowhere something stopped me. I turned and walked past the open door of my truck, tossed my weapon on the seat, and slowly made my way to the back of the truck, dreading that I might find my best friend lying dead.

To my surprise he was still breathing. I could hear a gurgling sound coming from his chest. The look in Buck's face was something I had never seen before. I placed my arms around him and lightly hugged him as I whispered, 'Hang in there buddy, I'll get you some help.'

I slammed the tailgate and we tore out of there, heading for the nearest town. I called the other watchmen on the CB radio informing him of what just took place. Only by divine appointment we found a vet that was still at his office. I explained Buck had been shot and needed emergency care. The kind veterinarian brought him straight in and told me they would do everything they could to save him.

By this time the other watchman, Mr. Marvin, had already contacted the police. On my arrival back at the crime scene, the cops were on site talking with the shooter.

I parked my truck right behind the equipment and through the night air, I could hear them having conversation with the land owner. I actually heard them all laughing and joking like close friends.

It wasn't long until the two officers drove up to my location on the hill. They get out of their squad car with a cocky look, 'Sir after questioning the land owner, he claims your dog was attacking his cows and there is nothing we can do about him defending his livestock.'

I instantly start defending my dog, 'That's a big fat lie! Buck was standing in front of that Cat side boom right there. Besides that, Buck was raised around livestock and has never ever chased or harmed any cows. That guy is lying through his teeth!'

'Well sir, there is nothing you can do.' Both cops get back in their squad car and drive off.

As I sit in the dark thinking about what had just happened. The horrible scene plays over and over in my mind like a broken record. I can still hear their laughter, then echoes from the gunfire; finally seeing the face of my dog as he coughed up blood. Speaking of blood, mine now boils with anger.

There has to be something I can do; this is so wrong!

It finally broke daylight and when the first pipeline operator arrived, I took off in search of the local courthouse, not realizing it wouldn't be open that early in the morning. After that I drove back to the animal clinic and found that Buck was stable. The kind doctor told me it was a slim chance that he might pull through. Upon receiving this grave report, I headed back over to the courthouse and patiently waited until it was open. After a multitude of people went through the doors, I felt confident that at least one had to be a judge.

Since I had never set foot in a courthouse, I was lost as a goose. A lady at one of the many counters asked me what I was looking for. 'Ma'am, I would like to see a judge.' She grinned real big and said, 'Let me see young man, you stand right there and I'll check.' She was gone for a couple minutes and on her return, 'If you would, please follow me.'

To my surprise, she walked up to the chamber door of a lady judge, lightly knocked and I hear, 'Come on in'. Upon my entry I was greeted by a beautiful black lady with a warm smile. 'Come on in young man, and tell me what's troubling you to the point of wanting to see a judge in person. This has to be something special.'

I told her about everything that had occurred, even about the cops laughing with the land owner and how it gave me the impression they were all cousins or somehow related.

After explaining my story, she turns around and pulls a big thick law book off the wall. She plops it down on her desk with the sound of a deep thud. 'Come around here where you can see and help me find the laws that have been broken.' I walk around to her side of the desk as she drags her finger back and forth across the print. 'Okay, it says right here, cruelty to a dumb brute; it carries a fine from 60 dollars up to 10,000 dollars and or time in jail. Well young man, what would you like to do?'

'I'm not sure, I mean I don't really know how all this works, what would be your advice?'

'I can't give you advice on what you should do, but I can give you options on what we can do inside the guidelines of this law book and the final ruling would be done in a court room.

Saying that, if you want to press charges we will have him arrested or you can drop it and move on.'

'I would like to press charges and have him arrested.'

'Okay, I'll get it all started, and it was a pleasure meeting you sir.'

I gave her my humble thanks as I left her chambers. Walking back across the parking lot I was thinking, *Man how lucky was that, walking straight in and seeing a judge.*

On my drive back to check on Buck I prayed, *'Lord please let my buddy make it, he's such a good dog.'*

As I walked in the vet's office, surprisingly the kind doctor almost met me at the door and was eager to give me an update. I could tell he had a true heart for animals and took a special interest in this case. This man had stayed with Buck all night watching over his patient.

The vet explained to me that only time will tell if Buck makes it. The bullet went completely through his body, barely missing his heart and struck a part of his lung and he had quite a bit of internal bleeding. He informed me that they would monitor him closely and there is no sense in me having to sit and wait.

I praised the kind doctor and thanked him with great compassion as I left. I went back to our campsite and sought council from Marvin. I knew he had to have wisdom from the spiritual side of life, due to his many years of studying the Bible and being a preacher.

I gave him an update on Buck's condition and then told him about getting to see the lady judge and how I pressed charges on the land owner. She told me they were going to have him arrested.

The old preacher leaned back in his chair grinning from ear to ear, 'Well Chado, sounds like you just kicked a hornets' nest wide open.' His smile turned into a pretty good laugh. 'You just had an official judge write out an arrest warrant for a land owner that owns the property our pipeline is crossing.'

'Yes sir, I guess I did. What do you think is going to happen?'

'Well, I would imagine Mr. Fred, the owner of the company is going to fly hot, and then the gas company we're laying the line for will get involved also. It's going to turn into a mess. Chado, I wonder if the cops have picked him up yet.'

'I don't know, but I hope it's the same cops that were laughing at me and my dog, and they are the very ones that have to arrest that nut job.'

Marvin looks over at me with an odd expression, 'Chado, you know that weird dream you had about seeing Buck's face covered with blood? Don't you think that's a bit strange, the very same day you have the dream he gets shot? You said Buck was spitting up blood; right?'

'Yes, bright red blood, just like my dream.'

'Well, it might be more going on with this whole scene than we can understand.'

'What do you mean Marvin?'

'Who knows, God might be up to something in your life or maybe He's trying to get that land owner's attention. I know this, in the Bible it says,

'*And it shall come to pass in the last days, says God, That I will pour out my spirit on all flesh, your sons and daughters shall prophesy, Your young men shall see visions, Your old men shall dream dreams.*'

'Well I thought what I had was a dream and I'm a young man.'

'Chado, how do you know the difference if you were dreaming or was simply having a vision in a sleep state?'

'Maybe so, I just hope Buck makes it through this and I don't lose my job. We are barely above the water level financially.'

As evening fell, I arrived at my designated location on the line and I was met by a foreman telling me that I needed to head over to our field office. On my drive to the office, I was preparing myself to face the facts of being fired from my much needed job.

When I drove in the parking lot, I noticed several vehicles that were unfamiliar. They really stood out because normally everyone had gone home by this time of evening.

As I walked through the door, I was faced with several people from the gas company, the owners of the construction company and three land agents. They all stared at me without saying anything with a look of anger in their eyes.

I slowly make my way to an empty seat at the end of a long shiny table that had blueprints and note pads scattered in front of the men.

As soon as my butt touched the chair, old man Fred, my boss and owner of our company, lit in on me like a mad bulldog. His face got so red I could see the blood vessels swell across his forehead.

'You can't have a land owner arrested; do you realize what you've done? When you leave here you go drop the charges. I mean now!' He pulls out his wallet. 'How much is that dammed dog worth?' He grabs several hundred dollar bills out of his wallet and started shaking the money at me. 'Here take it;

I'll pay your vet bill and whatever it costs to drop the charges. Here, I said take it!'

The whole group of men started mumbling among themselves as Fred continued to shake his money at me and rave about what I did could shut the whole pipeline down.

At first, I felt like I didn't have a friend in the world. Not knowing what to say or do, I felt my face and scalp start to tingle as a fire started in my heart. Anger rose up through my whole body as I thought of my best friend Buck lying in the animal hospital struggling for his life. I quickly stood up and the room went silent. I slowly looked into each one of the men's faces, as their curiosity of what my reply would be kept them silent.

'Let me tell you this, it's pretty simple. That crazy land owner shot my dog out of pure hatred and I could care less if this pipeline ever gets laid. Buck was born on the pipeline and he has helped me watch over your equipment and helped protect your pipe from vandals and thieves. So, you can fire me or whatever seems fitting in your hearts, but I'm not dropping any charges. Mr. Fred, you can stick that money back in your wallet where it belongs, because there is no price you can put on my dog!'

The room exploded with everyone talking over each other trying to figure out what they should do.

I spoke back up and informed them that I would be in the parking lot waiting on their decision about my termination. I walked out to my truck, dropped the tailgate then hopped up. As I was sitting on my tailgate slowly swinging my feet back and forth I noticed my hands were shaking. *I need to calm down, I'll get another job somewhere; this has to be the right decision.*

The door to the office flies open with the owner's son, Mr. Jerry heading straight for me. I noticed he was smiling. 'Hey Chado, this is quite the situation we're in, wouldn't you say?'

'Yes sir, I believe it is.'

'Look, everything is going to be okay. Truth be known, the land owner can't kick us off his property. The land agents have already paid him for access. So with that being said, the pipeline will not be affected at all. We will lay right through and he can't do anything.'

'Mr. Jerry, will I lose my job over all this?'

He chuckles, 'No you're not losing your job. Chado, we all love Buck and when I heard what happened I knew he was lying about Buck attacking his cows. I've seen the way Buck acts around livestock many times in the past. Know this, I am behind you 100 percent on whatever direction you want to take this. I tell you what I would like to do, is to help you with the vet bill. I also would hope you might consider dropping the charges on this guy. I believe this would help keep the peace with the other land owners in our path. You've already stung him pretty good with his arrest. I heard from a pretty good source down at the police station that the ole fart's wife is out of town for the weekend. It looks like he doesn't have anyone to bail him out, so that means he has to sit in jail till Monday.'

'Mr. Jerry, I think that will serve him right. He wasn't only shooting at Buck; he was pointing his rifle right at the equipment.'

'I didn't know that Chado. If that's the case, he could have shot you or damaged the equipment. My goodness!'

During our conversation I felt a peace, now that I knew Mr. Jerry had my back and I wasn't going to lose my job.

'Mr. Jerry, I guess I'll go and see if I can get those charges dropped.'

'Ok Chado, I'll let daddy Fred know and inform that room full of company men. You get back out to the equipment and first thing Monday morning run over to the courthouse and take care of that. Oh yeah, keep up with the cost of the vet bill and whatever the court cost might be for dropping charges, and I'll refund you every dime; and Chado, I'll be praying that Buck pulls through.'

Monday came and went and our prayers were being answered. I was able to pick Buck up from the hospital and within days he was as right as rain.

My crews and equipment had moved farther up the pipeline away from the location where Buck was shot and everything seemed to be back to normal. I was back to reading God's Word daily and I felt led to scripture about forgiveness, because I hadn't forgiven this cruel man that shot my dog. I felt that God led me straight to: II Corinthians 2:9-11,

'For to this end I also wrote that I might put you to the test, whether you are obedient in all things.

Now whom you forgive anything, I also forgive. For if indeed I have forgiven anything, I have forgiven that one for your sakes in the presence of Christ,

Lest Satan should take advantage of us; for we are not ignorant of his devices.'

As I pondered over this scripture, it was easy to realize that I was falling into one of Satan's devices and my only escape would be to go and see this hateful man face to face.

After much prayer I felt that I was ready to look him in the eyes and tell him that I forgive him.

The following evening before my shift started, I drove to the crime scene. I boldly walked up to his door, lightly knocked several times and suddenly the door swung open, 'What do you want?'

'Sir, I have come here to tell you that I forgive you for shooting my dog and hold no animosity toward you.'

'I shot your dog because he was attacking my cows!'

'No sir. You can tell everyone else that lie but you are forgetting one thing.'

'And what could that be?'

'I was there and I watched as you shot your rifle multiple times and finally hit my dog that was standing only a few feet in front of my truck and the equipment.'

He immediately slammed the door in my face. So I headed back down his driveway, thanking God that he didn't shoot me. Suddenly I had a sense of peace that I had done the will of God and it was now completely over. I had truly forgiven the man from the bottom of my heart.

That very night a violent storm came through the area and I sat in the truck all night with my trusted friend Buck resting his head in my lap. We both dozed off as the driving rain pounded the metal roof of the pickup.

I woke up to the sound of my CB radio, it was Marvin. 'Breaker breaker, come in Chado Cole, you got a copy?'

'10-4 Marvin I read you, what's up on your end, did you make it through the storm okay?'

'Yeah, 10-4, that's what I need to tell you about.'

'Roger that. Did our camper make it through all the wind?'

'10-4 camper is fine, but you need to drive by the guy's house that shot your dog.'

'What's going on? What happened?'

'A tornado came through there and wiped his barns completely out. His home was spared, but the barns are totally disintegrated.'

'Wow, I was just there before dark yesterday.'

'You went over there? You crazy rascal, you're braver than I am. Why were you there?'

'I didn't tell you, but I felt led to go and tell him to his face that I forgave him for shooting Buck.'

'How did he act when you told him?'

'He slammed the door in my face.'

Marvin keyed the mike and I could hear him laughing, 'Man that's powerful. He didn't realize that he slammed the door in the face of one of God's children that had just humbled himself before God with a forgiving heart. Chado Cole, I truly believe that storm was sent for a special purpose.'

'Roger that Marvin, roger that.' "

* * *

"Well Uriel, what do you think? Was I pretty accurate on the details?"

"Yes, you have an excellent memory, good job Chado."

"Okay Uriel, with you being my Guardian Angel, would you mind telling me how your scars play in to all this?"

"Chado, you know each night when you sat in your truck on his property and you were reading the Word of God?"

"Yeah, I sure do."

"Well this guy and his land were under a generational curse and had two fallen angels and several demons that were assigned to him and his family. When you rolled up every

222

evening and opened your Bible, Lucifer was immediately informed of your presence. The fallen angels and those demons wanted you gone. Chado you have to remember Lucifer has always known that God was going to use you somehow later in life. So he saw an opportunity and tried to push you to a point of falling in one of his traps. In other words he wanted you dead, and he almost prevailed. The trick he used that night to bring you to the point of being out of control was that he knew how much you loved Buck and he also knew that was your weak spot. You know when you threw your Bible on the seat of your truck, grabbed the pistol and took off running down the hill?"

"Yes, I was so upset and out of control."

"That's right Chado; you were cursing and had killing that man in your heart. At that very moment you had two demons with their claws on your back pushing you toward your death."

"What do you mean toward my death?"

"That land owner was standing in the shadows of his home behind a patch of dead flowers with you in the scope of his rifle. He had just clicked off the safety and was squeezing the trigger when I attacked and killed the two demons that were pushing you. I then stood in front of you with my hands raised to Heaven asking God to stop you from going any further. While my hands were lifted toward Heaven one of the fallen angels struck me several times in the back, and at the same time another demon from out of the darkness reached up with his nasty claws and scarred the left side of my face. At the point when you turned around heading back for your truck, I lowered my hands of praise and defended myself against the dark forces. In only a matter of a few seconds, they fled back into the shadows."

"My goodness Uriel, I am so sorry I was out of control."

"That's okay Chado, I survived and here we are standing in Heaven. Hey, you want to hear something else about the ordeal?"

"Sure Uriel, I would love to."

"You know that lady judge you went to?"

"Yes, she was so nice to me, not to mention how pretty she was."

"Well Chado, what do you think the odds were of you walking off the street and getting to see a judge?"

"I guess pretty slim."

"That's right. God gave her a vision about the same time He gave you your vision of Buck's face covered in blood. The vision she received was of you coming to her for help. So when the receptionist came and told her there is a young man at my desk asking to see a judge, she knew that her vision was from God, and your arrival was divine appointment."

"I never imagined God was so involved. I knew the dream was a bit odd and after talking with Marvin, I felt it was something strange happening. Not to mention the storm that hit the guy's place. Uriel, can you tell me the reason all this happened? What was God up to?"

"Chado, over the years God has given this man many opportunities to humble himself and submit his life to Christ. But this was his last warning, God used you and Buck in his life, and when you humbled yourself and told him that you had forgiven him for such a hateful act, he slammed the door in your face.

At that very second God turned him over to a reprobate mind, being filled with all unrighteousness, immorality, wickedness deserving of death and Hell.

224

He blasphemed the Holy Spirit several times in the past and Chado, he walks the Earth condemned and will never see the inside of Heaven."

"My goodness, that's pretty scary Uriel, so a person can reject God to the point of Him turning away and allowing them to live the rest of their lives lost and apart from God?"

"That's right, and you witnessed the man's last chance. He will live the rest of his life on Earth with the company of demons and eventually face the judgment of God.

One other thing Chado, everything that happened those few days had a positive effect on everyone involved. The lady judge, Marvin, Mr. Fred, several of the guys working on the line and you'll love this, Mr. Jerry, the owner's son; well he still uses that story as he teaches Bible school. Even to this day he sometimes brings it up and teaches about seeing the power of God used through a dog named Buck."

I burst out laughing, "That is so cool; Mr. Jerry teaching Sunday school, who would have thought back in those days. You know, I always liked Jerry. You could just tell he had a good heart."

* * *

I pat the side of my leg and Moushie comes running up to me, barely brushing my fingertips as he catches back up with Rex, who's leading the way down the cobblestone path.

As I glanced over at Uriel, I noticed the deep scar on the left side of his face looked like it had faded and wasn't as visible as before. It must be the shadows of the tall red oak trees we were walking under that masked his injuries.

I see both dogs ears perk up as if they seem to be hearing something coming from up ahead. They both suddenly take off in a fast run.

"Uriel, what do you think, did they hear something in the distance?"

Uriel stops and holds his hand up. "Listen Chado, can you hear that?"

I turn my ear in the direction up ahead. I hear a breeze blowing through the giant Sequoia trees and I look up to admire their beauty. "Yes that's nice, what a sound."

"No, I'm not talking about the wind, just listen."

I turn my head again and in between the gentle gusts of wind, I suddenly hear the sounds of a cello accompanied by a mandolin and guitars.

"Uriel, what the heck? That sounds like a piece of home!"

"Yes, we are almost to our first location."

I start walking a bit faster, "Hey bud, you haven't told me who we were visiting first. Who is it Uriel?"

"Slow down Chado, that's a surprise. I can tell you this much, it's not the Valley of the Children where your daughter lives."

As we continue up the trail, my mind is racing. *Who all plays instruments in my family? Heck, there were several on my mom's side of the family. Well I did have a lot of friends that played also. Shoot it could be anyone!*

"Chado, give it a rest, we'll be there shortly and you'll find out."

"Okay, okay, I'll chill out."

We start up a gradual incline through the mighty redwoods, and the sounds of gospel bluegrass echoing through the timber were becoming clearer.

I suddenly see Rex and Moushie dart over the top of the hill and the looks on their faces was telling me to hurry up. They both wheel around and vanish back over the hill.

I look over at Uriel and we both start grinning, the overwhelming joy was filling my heart to the point of bursting as we made it to the top of the crest.

23

Guitars & Mandolins

I burst out laughing, when to my surprise, instead of the giant mansion I was expecting, I saw an ole time frame house that looked exactly like my granny's old home. The only difference, it was a larger version.

She even has a stream that resembles Black Creek, but this is way beyond our old home place. The giant trees in the background with her home nestled near a bend in the creek surrounded with fruit trees and flowers of many colors. Yes, this was way beyond everything I can remember about our childhood stomping ground.

"Uriel, this is definitely my granny's home place, but I thought everyone got a mansion!"

"Chado she didn't want a mansion, she chose this home. She actually didn't have to ask God, He knew exactly what was in her heart and, there it is."

My granny's old home place had a big porch all the way around, with a wide breezeway through the center on the inside. Back in those days, there was no such thing as air conditioning, so they built the houses with a wide breezeway through the center and totally open on each end. It was sort of like an extra wide hallway, and it worked really well. All the rooms were located on each side of the breezeway allowing the fresh air in.

Something else I remember, granny's house had a steep metal roof with a fireplace on each end and a pipe that stuck out of the kitchen wall that was connected to a wood burning stove. I can't believe I am looking at the mirror image of her earthly home.

I notice several people walking around outside and from the sound of music they must be celebrating something. From our distance it's hard to make out who the musicians are on the porch, but I can't wait to find out.

As we make our way across the small meadow in front of the home place, I see Moushie and Rex wagging their tails as they walk and mingle with the folks sitting in chairs out in the front yard. I still can't make out who they are, when suddenly two of the people petting my dogs stand and start pointing in our direction. The music stops and then I hear several people from the small crowd start shouting, "They're here, everyone they're here!"

I look over at Uriel, "Well I guess they knew we were coming."

Uriel smiles as he pats me on the shoulder, "Take off Chado, I'll be there in a bit."

I take off in a fast trot toward the house and see several people walking toward me that I don't recognize. As I get closer, the first familiar face is my cousin Bob. He had lost his life five years ago down in Texas when he was robbed and murdered. Right behind him is his son who drowned a year before in the Gulf of Mexico in a Jet Ski accident. After a few yards, I can make out one of my favorite uncles. I should have recognized the sound of his mandolin and know it was my Uncle Buddy. Right beside him sat Uncle Patrick. Everyone back home called him Dobber.

Bob and his son ran up grabbing me and shaking me, each taking turns giving me hugs with both of my uncles doing the same.

Bob grabbed me with both hands, one on each shoulder, "Chado Cole, you are going to love it here. I arrived a little over five earth years ago and right now, in this season, it's as exciting as when I first set foot inside the gate!"

As I gaze at my cousins and uncles, "Guys I can't believe we are all standing together here in Heaven, this is so amazing!"

"Chado they told us you were coming, so we put together a little welcome home jam session. Oh, did you happen to bring your guitar?"

We all burst out laughing, "Uncle Buddy I sure didn't but I did bring a friend." We all turn around as Uriel walks up. "Everyone, I want y'all to meet my Guardian Angel, Uriel."

They all introduce themselves as we head for the house. Bob taps me on the back and whispers, "Chado, you mind me asking, why do you need a Guardian Angel here in Heaven?"

"I know, it is an odd situation. Why don't you wait and I'll tell the whole group, I'm sure you won't be the only one that's curious."

"Sure, no problem, just don't forget. I would really like to know because I've been here five earth years and haven't ever heard of such."

"You got it Cuz."

As I make my way through all the warm welcomes from cousins, uncles and aunts from long ago, I am in search of the old lady that cooked the best sweet potato and coconut pies in American history, my Granny Tressie.

I carefully walk past the musicians' chairs on the porch with several instruments leaning against them. As I head through the open doors down the breezeway, I begin to smell my granny's cooking.

Suddenly she jumps out from behind a bedroom door with her hands in the air, growling like a bear and then bursts out in a contagious laugh. She runs straight up to me and wraps her arms around me, then reaches up and gives me a big kiss on each cheek. She then turns, grabs my hand, leads me into the kitchen, pulls out a chair and shoves two freshly cooked pies in front of me and says, "They are all yours, eat up child." I stare at the tops of both pies as I think back in time.

"Granny I never told you this, but after you were gone, each time I would have pie at just about any gathering, I would tell the story of you."

"Child, what story would that be?"

"Well Granny, do you remember how poor we were when I was a kid? At Christmas you would tell me, 'Child, I don't have enough money to get you anything, but I can bake you some pies.' To the day I died, I would always tell people that out of all the gifts I ever received, the only ones I could remember were your pies. That meant more to me than if you had given me silver or gold. Now that we are in Heaven sitting here together, I can let you know face to face how much that meant to me. Granny, thank you so much for all our wonderful childhood memories and especially the best pies ever made."

"Land sakes, child, you need to hush and get busy eating before they get cold!"

Uriel walks in and after I introduced him to Tressie Brooks, my granny, I cut a big wedge out of both pies, slide it over to him and we both sit back enjoying some delicious home cooking.

Uriel starts smiling, "Hey Chado, I've known your Granny Tressie longer than you have."

"Well I guess you have." Chuckling I said, "Especially if you followed me up and down Black Creek during my childhood."

I hear the sounds of my Uncle Buddy tuning his mandolin, and then suddenly my uncles and cousins cut loose playing a melody. I stop chewing and sit straight up in my chair. "Hey Granny, that song sounds familiar. Heck, that's a song I wrote just a couple years ago! It's called "Lamb's Book of Life"."

Granny and Uriel start laughing and I'm grinning from ear to ear. "How in Heaven's name did they get a hold of one of my songs?"

Granny spurts off a scripture:

"*Therefore we also, since we are surrounded by so great a cloud of witnesses, let us lay aside every weight, and the sin which so easily ensnares us, and let us run with endurance the race that is set before us looking unto Jesus, the author and finisher of our faith, who for the joy that was set before Him endured the cross, despising the shame, and has sat down at the right hand of the throne of God.*"

"Okay Granny, I still don't know how they could know my song."

"Well Chado, what your granny is trying to say with that scripture, is a cloud of witnesses are allowed to see out of the spiritual realm with a front row seat as they watch over their loved ones back on Earth; well, at least when God permits it."

"Child, your Uncle Buddy and Dobber watched you write all thirteen of your songs and they apparently like them because they play them all the time. They went as far as getting a cello and learning how to play it, just for the two songs that you said needed it. They heard you tell someone that both songs needed a cello to give it that special sound you were looking for. I believe one is "Reach Down" and the other is "Find My Way." My favorite between the two is "Reach Down"."

"I don't know what to say, all I know is the blessings are unending. I can't believe my kin are on the front porch playing songs that God blessed me with. It is truly wonderful to be here in Heaven. 'Thank you Lord.' And Granny, thank you for such a sweet homecoming."

"Ah child, we knew you were coming and were all excited waiting for you. Have you thought about where you might end up living? There's plenty of room on this ole creek and we would all love for you to nest down somewhere close."

"I probably will Granny, but I have a special job God wants me to take care of before I settle."

"I know. The Lord has given me dreams about that. You go ahead and tend to it, then you get on back over here and we can wait together for the rest of our family to get to Heaven. Chado Cole? One other thing..."

"Yes Granny."

"You better go spend a little time with your kin. You remember how anxious you and your brother were, waiting on your cousins to come home for the reunions? Well that's all I been hearing ever since I told them you were on your way here, Chado Cole, Chado Cole, Chado Cole, is on his way to Heaven. So go sit in with your kin for a spell."

"Yes Ma'am, I will."

* * *

As soon as I stepped out on the porch, Bob handed me a guitar and we cut loose like a professional band straight out of Nashville. We played every gospel song that anyone knew and twelve of the thirteen I wrote.

My Uncle Dewey would take a lead run while playing the upright bass. He would twirl the bass fiddle around just like he did when we watched him back on Black Creek. Those were such good memories of the reunions when I was a kid. I couldn't help but laugh with tears of happiness as I looked in the faces of each one of my relatives, realizing the joy they were experiencing was truly a gift from God. I was witnessing the perfection of talent, and happiness that could only be possible here in Heaven.

The perfect harmony of my granny's sisters' voices was echoing through the creek bottom, blending with Uncle Slug's harmonica and the sweet sound of Uncle Buddy's mandolin playing the song "Wayfaring Stranger". It caused me to stop strumming my guitar and just sit back in awe raising my hands in Heaven, praising God.

After we stop for a short break, I'm able to ask about other relatives that I didn't see at our gathering. Before anyone answered, I notice Bob set his guitar to the side, reached over and picked up a cello out of its case. My two uncles, Buddy and Dobber, move their chairs and place them one on each side of Bob, to be in a half circle facing me.

I'm thinking they must have a special song they want to share. So I set my guitar to the side, leaned back with a smile, waiting to hear how well Bob has learned to play the cello.

Right before starting their song I notice a small framed gentleman that looked to be in his mid-thirties walking with my granny. They made their way through the small group of relatives and I could tell they were heading in our direction. For the life of me, I couldn't make out who this guy was. I'm wondering if they've invited some special singer just for my homecoming.

Walking up behind Bob and my uncles, Granny sat down in the nearest chair available, and the man stepped up ready to sing.

As I look around at the group, it looks like everyone there has grins pasted to their faces as if this was to be something really special.

Bob slowly starts dragging the bow across the strings with my uncles joining in; I immediately recognize the song, its number thirteen, "Reach Down". Oh my goodness, they were about to do one of my favorite songs that I had written a few years back.

The instrumental at the beginning was like I had never imagined. Their timing is perfect as the man begins the familiar lyrics with a voice made in Heaven.

I leaned over in my chair and place my elbows on my knees with my chin resting in the palms of my hands. I hadn't noticed, but Granny had made her way behind me and I felt her hand on my shoulder. As I continue to admire the voice of this man and the beautiful instrumentals, I feel the warm tears run between my fingers down my forearms. I'm experiencing the most beautiful, soothing music I've ever heard.

When they were almost finished with the song, I look around at my relatives; their grins have vanished and they all have their hands raised praising God.

I reach up and touch my granny's hand that is still resting on my shoulder. I slowly turn looking back whispering, "Granny, who is that man, is he a relative?"

She starts giggling like she's thirteen years old, leans over with her lips almost touching my ear and whispers back "Oh child, that's your Granddad Patrick Brooks."

From the homemade wooden chair where I sat, I turned and stared at my grandfather. Since I had only seen him in old black and white photos in our family album, his young appearance left me shocked and speechless.

As the last chords were strummed on the guitar and mandolin, Bob slowly drug the horse hair bow across the strings of the cello for the final note; I'm thinking how God's blessings are truly immeasurable.

Suddenly as the instruments silenced, the whole group started rejoicing, continuing to raise their hands and voices to God in worship.

As my two uncles cut loose playing an old song, "Sugar Foot Rag", my granny grabs my hand, pulls me out of the chair and starts dancing. We both burst out laughing as she twirls me around like we were really dancing with the stars.

As I look in her glistening bright eyes, I can't help but remember the last time I saw her, she was on her deathbed. Now I'm dancing with my Granny in Heaven!

While we are still twirling and spinning around, I ask her if she remembered the scripture:

"Oh Death, where is your sting? O, Hades, where is your victory?"

As the song ended, she reached up and gave me another kiss on each cheek.

"Granny, how is it that Grandpa looks like he's in his early to mid-thirties?"

Before she could answer, my Grandfather Patrick walked over with his arm extended, and as he shook my hand he pulled me closer in, turning a hand shake into a great big warm hug.

"Chado Cole, I know we've never met but from time to time the Lord would allow me to peek in at you and I'm sorry your life on Earth got cut a little short, but we're so glad you made it."

"Grandpa, Mom told me so many great stories about you and how so dearly she loved you. I always regretted never getting to see you, with your passing before I was born."

"Yes, He took me pretty early in life, but I didn't mind at all. God let me know that He would watch over my family and would eventually allow us all to be reunited."

Grandpa smiled as he pointed across the group of family members standing around the porch. "See there, He is true to His promises. What else did Millie tell you about me?"

"She said you were a Godly man, and you would walk around your old home place and talk to the Lord like He was standing right beside you. She also said you were super smart and even designed and helped build a naval base somewhere down in Florida."

"Son, any accomplishment in my short life on Earth was only by the hand of God leading me through it. I can truly say it wasn't me."

"Awe, come on Grandpa, from what Mom told me I've always considered you to be the smartest person in our whole family."

He grins as we slowly head for the back porch. "Chado, you know I've been here enjoying the blessings of Heaven for a long time now and those hard years on Earth don't compare to the constant joy we have here. I can't wait until your mom gets here. She is going to absolutely love it, especially the way I remember her as a little girl always wanting to sing."

"Yeah Grandpa, could you always sing like that, I mean when you were back on Earth?"

Chuckling, "Heck no, Chado, I couldn't carry a tune around in a bucket. You've only just begun to see the many blessings God gives us here in Heaven. Did you notice how well Bob played that cello? He just found that thing sitting in a case right over there on that rock and suddenly he sounds like he had been with an orchestra all his life. Chado, I'm telling you the mysteries and blessings of God are unending."

"Grandpa how is it you're so young? From what I read in the Bible, I thought everyone would instantly be young when they became immortal, but since I arrived, I've seen a lot of folks that are still old. Just here at this gathering, my uncles and aunts all seem to still look close to the age they were when they passed. Even Granny looks about the same. Well, I have to admit they all have a certain glow and appear to look a bit younger, but not by much!"

"Chado you're going to love this. You see your relatives standing around out there?"

"Yes Sir."

"Look at your Uncle Loy; he arrived here about twenty five years ago, now that's going by earth years, because time doesn't mean a whole lot here in Heaven. Okay, saying that, he was in his eighties when he passed, so how old would you say, he looks to be now?"

"I don't know, maybe around sixty, or sixty five?"

"Yes, that's about right. Are you catching on?"

"I guess, Grandpa."

"Well heck, I'll give you an example. Just say someone dies and they're a hundred years old. As soon as they arrive in Heaven their age clock starts going backward and doesn't stop until they are around the age of thirty three-years old. Remember now, that's how old Jesus was at his resurrection, and we believe God chose that age for us here in Heaven. Wouldn't you say the age of thirty-three would have been the prime age of our lives when we were mortal?"

"Yes, I've never thought of it like that, and it must be so cool for an old person with each passing hour, knowing they're becoming younger. It's the total opposite of the dread we felt as we looked in the mirror year after year and seeing old age creep into our faces. God is so cool Grandpa."

I hear Granny, "Chado Cole! You run down to the creek and fetch that big black diamond watermelon. It should be chilled down and ready to cut."

After we share a few more memories and have our fill of watermelon, I let everyone know that Uriel and I have to be moving on. I want to see Dad and Summer before we focus on our mission.

A handful of my cousins follow us for a few miles, but before turning back, Bob wanted me to promise him, "Chado, you are going to settle down around here somewhere, right?"

"I probably will, but I would like to see where Dad's place is and what it looks like around the Valley of the Children before I make up my mind."

"Cuz, you do know your dad and Uncle Spike live only a few miles from here, don't you?"

"No, I didn't. Well, that's good news."

Bob smiles as he takes a sackcloth pouch off his shoulder, and hands it over, "Here Chado, Granny wanted you to have this."

As I open the pouch, I can smell a mixture of homemade cornbread, biscuits and I see a couple jars of figs. We both laugh, "Granny hasn't changed a bit, has she?"

"Godspeed, Cousin."

* * *

Uriel and I head back in the direction of the cobblestone road with Rex and Moushie still leading the way.

I hear Uriel mumble, "Chado, you have a wonderful family that has loved you dearly on Earth and also here in Heaven."

"I know... I hated to leave. I truly believe I could have stayed right there on that creek bank for eternity."

"Yes, your family chose well when they made a decision on where to live. When it's time, God will give you a certain desire for where He wants you to call home. Right now isn't the time for settling down."

Uriel reaches over and pats me on the shoulder. "Little Soul, after we visit the rest of your family, at some point God will instruct you with more detail about your mission."

"Uriel, you think He might tell me in person?"

"Maybe, but often He gives dreams and visions while you sleep. Oh, by the way he might just send a messenger."

"A messenger; like Allayer and Nipper?"

Uriel chuckles, "Maybe."

"Wow, Uriel that sounds pretty exciting, but I'm still a little uneasy on what the mission is about."

"Have no fear; God will lead you through it."

As we make it back to the cobblestone road, I reach in the pouch Granny gave us and broke off a couple chunks of cornbread and shared it with Uriel and our two pups. We passed Samson's wine pouch back and forth, washing down some of the best cornbread ever cooked as we continue to admire the unending beauty of Heaven.

"Hey Uriel, I've been meaning to ask you, when Nipper and Allayer were transporting me here and we were entering into the atmosphere of Heaven, they were trying to teach me how to fly. As a matter of fact I crashed and burned on my landing. Allayer and Nipper got a big laugh out of that. Well anyway, after I got here, I don't seem to know how, or maybe it's just I haven't had the desire to fly."

"Chado, God takes away the desire because He wants everyone to slow down and enjoy every blessing He has to offer. Just think, if everyone here was zooming around, you wouldn't have the peace and tranquility He has provided. I can tell you this; He has portals set up in certain areas that everyone can use when He allows it."

Before I could ask any more questions about the portals, I happen to look over at Uriel and noticed the deep scars on the left side of his face had completely disappeared and his skin was now clear and smooth.

"Uriel, your face, the scars are gone where the demon clawed you!"

He slowly reaches up and rubs his fingertips across where the scars had been. "Chado, I guess God decided I had that particular scar long enough."

I reach over and pick up part of his garment that was covering his back, "Uriel, you still have quite a few scars remaining on your back, but it looks like the ones you said the fallen angels gave you are gone also."

241

Uriel smiles as he pulls his garment down and holds his hands up, "Thank you Lord."

I could still see several scars remaining on Uriel's arms, his forehead and back. I can't help but wonder why God didn't just remove them all.

"Chado, it's not His timing for all to be removed. Listen, we have a little while before we see your father, I want you to tell me another story of your past and leave out nothing."

"What story?"

"Remember when you were sitting on the bayou in central Louisiana all night watching for the pipeline company? There were two different nights that you were under attack from the darkness."

"Are you talking about the night when the guy drowned in the bayou or the guy that wanted to rob me? Come to think of it, there was another one that I caught stealing batteries out of a bull dozer. That was a rough area I was in!"

"The two I want you to tell me about is the guy that drowned and the one you thought was going to rob and kill you."

"Sure, well how do I start this?"

* * *

"Okay, our pipeline right-of-way was down on the inside levee of Rapides Bayou and that meant we had to lay through some of the most crime ridden areas of Alexandria.

Every evening before dark, after the crews all went home for the night; I would pull out a couple fishing poles and catch catfish out of the bayou. One particular evening, just as soon as the last employee had just driven away, a tall black man came walking up, what seemed like out of nowhere. It really frightened me and Buck, with this surprise visit from a total stranger especially at our dismal location.

It was almost dark, but the distant streetlights were enough to make out the friendly expression on his face. This abnormally tall man, wearing a long black leather jacket, walked straight up to me with his hand out as to greet me with a hand shake. I slowly reach out and shake his hand. The whole time I'm thinking, '*My pistol is lying on the seat of my truck, what if he attacks me?*'

His hand is so big his fingers completely wrap around my whole hand. I nervously ask him what can I help him with and he starts looking around as if to see if we were alone. Noticing his curiosity only added to my concern of being totally vulnerable for an attack. My mind still racing, '*With his size he could easily kill me, throw me in the bayou and drive off, and no one would know anything for at least twelve hours.*'

To my surprise, he asked me if I would be willing to trade a bucket of worms for a bottle of wine. I didn't see any bucket of worms, but just so I could get him off my work site I told him, 'Sure, bring me your bucket of worms tomorrow evening before dark and I'll buy you a bottle of wine.'

He turned and walked back into the darkness, and since I had been caught off guard, I decided my pistol would be in my belt every minute from now on.

The following evening he must have been watching from the shadows, because as soon as the last employee left, he showed up with a five gallon bucket of worms. There were so many red worms in his bucket I could have fished for a month and not used them all.

Being a man of my word, I drove over the levee to a nearby store and I bought him two fifths of strawberry wine.

On my return, when he saw I had bought him two bottles instead of just one he was so happy, he was acting like a kid with candy. Apparently he was an alcoholic.

He didn't know it, but my reason for buying two was my hope that he would move on. My idea backfired; he spotted my extra fishing pole and asked if he could join me.

At this point I felt a little more at ease. This giant of a man seemed to be harmless. So I pulled out another lawn chair about the time my wife drove up on the levee with a surprise dinner she had cooked for me. It was one of my favorites, green bean casserole. Noticing it was almost dark; I thanked her and sternly let her know she needed to get out of this part of town right quick.

After she left, I found myself sitting beside Tall Man on the edge of Rapides Bayou, sharing my extra fishing pole and a large helping of casserole.

The evening rolled on, but we weren't catching anything, because there had been heavy rain over the last several days. This was causing the bayou to have way too much current and fresh water in it as the small tributary gushed toward Red River.

I noticed Tall Man's countenance rapidly changing as he was almost through with his second bottle of wine. He was repeating over and over, 'When the man upstairs says it's your time, it's your time.' Over and over, then he would ask, 'You believe me? You better believe me!' Then he started telling me about how many people he had killed in bar room fights. 'You believe me, you better believe me.' Then he started reaching over every time he would repeat himself and shove me really hard on my shoulder.

I finally stood up and stepped back a few feet with my hand behind me with my Colt 45 at the ready and told him, 'It's time you get down the bayou, ole buddy.'

He stood up, 'You get in that truck and you go get me some more damned wine! You do what I say, you hear me?'

At this point, I'm checking to make sure my safety is off and ready to light him up if he starts coming at me. I reach in my pocket and I pulled out six dollars. This was the change I had left over from buying his wine earlier. I slowly reached out and handed him the wadded up money, then I took a couple steps back. 'You need to get out of here and I mean right now!'

He suddenly started talking nice again as he was walking back and forth in front of the lawn chairs that were sitting only a few feet from the edge of the bayou. His feet got tangled on the small honeysuckle vines growing at the edge of the water.

As he twisted around facing Buck and me, with the bayou directly behind him, he fell almost in slow motion, comically reminding me of the 'Ice Tea Plunge' commercial. I couldn't help myself; it was totally funny to see this giant fall like a huge tree without any expression on his face or movement with his arms, just plainly falling.

I stuffed my pistol back in my belt, quickly grabbing my handheld light, I ran over to the edge expecting to see him swimming back to shore. This wasn't the case.

Tall Man went down like he had bricks in his pockets. I shined the spotlight back and forth across the water. Finally, I saw one hand come up, he was grabbing at thin air... then it disappeared. Realizing he was drowning, I threw down the light and my pistol, slid down the bank and was just about to dive in.

But then... total fear gripped me, with a sudden memory of when I had seen my older brother try to save my cousin from an overflowing canal down in Lake Charles. My cousin almost drowned my brother and himself by clawing and climbing on top of my brother's head holding him under. If it hadn't been for the help of a couple of adults that jumped in, my brother and cousin would have both perished.

I knew if I jumped in, there was no way I could have saved this guy. Especially from his enormous size and the way he clawed and thrashed the top of the water when his hand broke the surface. He would have surely pulled me down with him.

I hurried back up the bank, grabbed one of my fishing reels, and with the river weight and bare hook, I started casting to the location I had last seen his hands come up. After many attempts trying to snag a piece of his clothing, the small sliver of hope I had to save him, quickly faded. Tall Man had now been under for several minutes. He had to be dead by now.

I loaded Buck in my truck and drove back to the same store I had bought the guy's wine at. I used a pay phone to alert the police, and within a few minutes it seemed like the whole police force showed up. It actually turned into a circus with cop cars sliding down the levee and each one running up to me asking what happened. After telling my story over and over, finally the genius of the group starts accusing me of murder. He sarcastically asked me, 'Where is the wooden two by four you used to kill him with?' Yes, some real screwballs.

After I finally explained just what happened to one detective that actually had a little common sense, everything was resolved.

They eventually got a crew down the levee, launched a flat-bottom boat and used a long bar with hooks as they drug the bottom. They finally hooked his long black jacket, bringing him to the surface. It was a ghastly sight!

After they saw the bucket of worms, the two empty bottles of wine and found the six dollars that I told them I gave the guy, the lynch mob had finally all accepted my innocence.

After he found out the true identity of Tall Man, the one detective who seemed to be pretty level headed shared information with me that really bothered me. He informed me I was very lucky because this guy had in fact killed several men in his past, some were bar fights and others that were still under investigation. He said during a fight he would get his big arms around their heads and snap their necks and each time he would somehow get out of it claiming self-defense."

* * *

"Okay Chado, now tell me about the one that you thought was going to rob and kill you."

"Well, that's a much shorter story and I didn't think much about it until after it was over."

"Just give me the quick version; we're not far from your dad's place."

"Sure, it was pretty much the same area, just down the levee and a little closer to the bad part of town."

* * *

"Well Uriel, as I remember, it was pretty cold and had been raining off and on for several days. None of the crews had worked very much the last couple weeks, and we had to babysit the equipment night and day. I remember one evening I was

247

sitting in my truck on top of the levee reading, and every few minutes I would glance up to see if everything was okay. One of the times I happened to look up, there was a black guy standing about fifty feet away from me, straight out in front of my truck. At first glimpse he looked very suspicious. I thought, *why would anyone be standing around in drizzling rain this time of evening?* I'm sure he was up to no good.

This guy was acting very strange, as he would stare at the equipment and then out of the corner of his eye look over at me. He finally starts heading in my direction and without showing much movement on my part, I quickly grabbed my pistol, then I tossed the holster over on the floorboard of the passenger side.

I rolled my window down as he walked straight up within inches of my door. It was like he was trying to see inside my truck. I asked him, 'What can I help you with?'

With a very cocky attitude, he started asking me stupid questions, 'What you doing by yourself out here boy? When yo people coming back?'

I lied and told him the whole crew were on their way back and my boss will be here any minute.

'Ain't nobody coming back here, you all by yo self Mista.'

At this stage of our conversation, I figured we were about to do business. I stopped answering his foolish questions and started concentrating on his movements as if I was sitting in a funny car watching for the green light and whoever leaves the line first wins the race; and in this case whoever draws first gets to live. His words faded as I zoned in on everything about him. I noticed he had two small scars above his left eye and a look on his face that was very easy to read; he was about to either rob me or kill me. I also noticed with his right hand still in the pocket of his army jacket, that it was more than just his hand. He was holding a gun, partially concealed.

I slowly cocked the Colt 45 auto without making a sound and had it pointing at him through the door. At this point I had decided if this guy makes a move, I won't stop shooting until I blow him to the bottom of the levee.

He kept edging even closer, looking over in my truck. I noticed a sudden change in his face when apparently he must have seen the empty holster lying on the passenger side. I believe he knew that I had the drop on him and he wouldn't have a chance. He suddenly backed off, turning and heading back down the levee toward the hood.

For the next several nights, sitting in my truck was like being behind enemy lines. I even went as far as taking an old quilt and stuffing it into a jacket and placing a ball cap over the make believe head. My thoughts were, if this guy or someone like him tries to ambush me they would take out the dummy instead of me. I would sit it up in the driver's seat, then I would hunker down on the passenger side. For a bit more insurance, I brought my Browning 12 gauge short barrel shotgun with the plug out. I guess I was as ready as could be for his retaliation that never came. Thank God."

* * *

"Uriel, I was so glad when the crews finally moved completely out of that area. That was definitely a scary place! So why did you want to hear those two particular stories?"

"Chado, what I'm about to tell you will probably make the hair stand up on the back of your neck. You know when

249

Allayer and Nipper brought you through New Orleans, Chicago and the other cities and you witnessed the presence of darkness with the legions of demons and fallen angels?"

"Yes, how could I forget? I was really glad you were with us; that was truly a spooky sight around those cities."

"Well Chado, you better be glad I was with you on the levee. You see, that section of Alexandria was as bad as, or maybe even worse than, some of the other cities. Lucifer again was notified of your presence in one of his dark zones, and he set several traps that you almost fell in."

"What kind of traps?"

"He knew you were under the protection of God and he had no right to take your life. His plan was to try and get you to kill the thief or Tall Man and have murder in your heart. By doing this, it would be just enough that God would take away your protection. Remember, Lucifer has always known that God has a plan for you; he just doesn't know what it is. So another attempt was made on your life by his dark forces."

"So tell me, what happened in the Spiritual Realm?"

"That gun holster you tossed over on the passenger side of your truck was actually the first step in keeping you out of trouble. When you pulled your gun out and tossed the holster, I gave it a little nudge and made sure it landed far enough over that it would be visible to the guy you were about to kill."

"Wow, I was sure that's exactly the reason why he backed off; he saw the holster. So if you hadn't given it that extra little nudge, my goodness, I would've had to shoot the guy. Uriel, it would have been self-defense, right?"

"This is true, and the courts would have seen it exactly that way. And God knew you would have been right to defend yourself. But here's where Lucifer would use it against you.

250

When you first saw this guy up close, the way he looked at you and talked to you in a disrespectful way, you immediately hated him. You then wanted to do battle, and finally had visions of blasting him to the bottom of the levee. God knows you were only human to react this way. If you had been walking closer to the Lord at that time, you may have witnessed to this fellow, even while pointing a pistol at him through the door of your truck insuring your protection. However, you wouldn't have looked at him with hate, but the love of Christ and Satan's little snare wouldn't have worked."

"I totally understand; you know I've always had a problem with any confrontation. Without thinking clearly, I seem to jump head first into a fight. So what ever happened to that guy? I just knew he would have come back and tried to ambush me."

"He did have plans, and he was going to bring his gang with him. But that same night, the police had a raid on a local drug den and he and his crew were all arrested and eventually served several years in Angola State Prison for drug trafficking."

"So what about Tall Man, you know, the guy that drowned?"

"Well, that's where it got a little nasty. Tall Man as you call him had a history of sending several men to their grave. He actually was possessed by three demons and they were very powerful and cunning. Tall Man had tormented so many people, and the Christians in his family had come to a point where they would avoid him like a plague. For years they prayed and fasted for his deliverance, but Lucifer had such a stronghold on his soul that anyone who approached him with the Word of God, he would curse them and threaten them with their lives."

"So I was actually fishing with this guy? Good Lord!"

Uriel chuckles, "That's right you were sitting beside a man possessed with demons and didn't know it. Chado, listen to this: Lucifer summoned the demons that possessed Tall Man, with orders to kill you. And from every dark corner of that city, the night sky overhead was filled with fallen angels. They were floating like vultures, circling that whole area. Yes, you were in grave danger that night. God even sent six other Warrior Angels to help me at the hour of need and I welcomed the additional protection!"

"Goodness gracious, all this was going on just because I wanted to kill that guy?"

"No Chado, because Lucifer wanted to kill you. He sent a wolf in sheep's clothing and he was carrying a bucket of worms."

"Wow, I had no idea I was dealing with a crazy man, not to mention demons."

When you saw his countenance change and he started repeating himself, that was no longer Tall Man talking, it was those demons that dwelled inside him. At the moment you stood, reached around and had your hand on the pistol, there were demons swarming you like bees, lightly brushing your hand trying to prompt you into pulling your gun. You couldn't hear them but they were repeating over and over, "Kill the bastard, kill him!"

"Where were you Uriel? Well I mean, what were you and the other Angels doing?"

"At that time the other Angels were just a couple hundred feet overhead, they had a made a small circle around us and the fallen knew if they dared to cross, they would have been destroyed. I stood beside you and at that very second I reminded you of the six dollars in your pocket, and instead of pulling your gun you pulled the money out and handed it to Tall Man. This action infuriated the demons, so they decided to try something else. They confused Tall Man, and that's when he started pacing back and forth in front of the lawn chairs. He finally tangled his feet in the vines, and all at once the demons shoved him backward into the bayou."

"They actually had the physical power to be able to push him over the edge?"

"Yes and when you threw down your spotlight while sliding down the bank with intensions of saving Tall Man, that's when they attacked us both. I stood in front of you with my hands raised to God, praying for Him to stop you from diving in, knowing it would have meant sure death for you. At that point, several demons came out of the darkness, two were behind you pushing and whispering in your ear, 'Dive in hero, save him, you can do it, save him!' The rest were climbing all over me while I was continuing to raise my hands, pleading with God to stop you. Somehow, one of the fallen angels got past the Guardians and struck me multiple times, finally penetrating my armor and wounding me in several places. That's when God gave you the memory of your cousin and brother almost drowning, and seeing this vision frightened you enough that you froze in your tracks and realized, if you dove in you would surely die. The demons and the fallen angels saw my hands drop to take hold of my sword; they retreated only to run straight into the swords of the other Guardians that were now coming to defend us. They were destroyed along with Tall Man and the three demons that had possessed him for so many years. They were now trapped inside his corpse as he lay motionless on the muddy bottom of Rapides Bayou."

* * *

I hear Moushie and Rex barking in the distance, "Uriel, you know back when Moushie or Rex would tree a squirrel or bay up a hog they both had a certain bark but that sounds like their happy bark. I think they are trying to tell us something."

"Yes, they are. We're almost to your dad's place."

"Awesome, I wonder if he knows we're coming. Granny knew, so maybe Dad knows also. I kind of wish we could surprise him and see the look on his face. Pop really knew how to kid around. He would have the construction crews in tears with the silly jokes he told... and they loved it."

Suddenly I see both dogs trotting back in our direction, yep, we must be close. We top a small hill and behold, I see a huge lake, it must be twenty miles across and the length goes out of sight. It's just as beautiful as everything else I've seen so far. There are homes scattered up the shoreline as far as I could see, each one spaced out at least a mile or two from the other. Some look like mansions and others are smaller but just as beautiful.

As we head down the long egress toward the lake, I have a memory where in the Bible it talks about having mansions when we get to Heaven. I look back across the beautiful homes, comparing each with the design of my Granny's house. I come to realize, they are all mansions, just different styles with each fitting the hearts of who live there. What a cool thought. I look over at Uriel and catch him smiling.

"Chado, you're starting to catch on."

"So which one is Dad's place, can we see it from here?"

Uriel points off to the left at a great big stone house that's partially covered by a hill.

"I wonder why they built it like that, I hope Dad's not worried about tornadoes here in Heaven."

"You're right, that is a bit odd. Chado, you'll just have to ask him."

24

Cuddles

As we get closer, I see a huge pasture behind Dad's house, with at least forty head of horses grazing on the greenest river bottom grass you've ever seen. My dad's house is sitting right at the mouth of a river that feeds straight into this crystal clear lake. It is truly gorgeous.

I see Rex and Moushie dart around the side of the home facing the river and both were wagging their tails as if greeting someone. Only a few seconds pass and I see two old gentlemen appear. Both start waving with one tossing his straw hat in the air. Moushie, not wasting any time, picks up the hat and runs straight for me.

As we approach both men, I could tell right away it was Dad and Uncle Spike. Without saying anything, I reach out handing my dad his hat while shaking Uncle Spike's hand. And the first thing Dad says to me, as he gives me his ole stern look, "Boy, I thought sure you would have busted Hell wide open."

His comment takes me off guard and suddenly I remember how funny Pop was back on Earth, and realize God allowed him to bring his funny sense of humor along with him to Heaven. We all burst out laughing as we head back around the house toward a huge pin oak tree right at the water's edge.

Dad and Uncle Spike had built all kinds of chairs and tables. Some were out of wood, some were stone and the craftsmanship was unbelievable. I didn't say anything, but my dad was not a very good carpenter back on Earth. So apparently God has gifted them both with some new skills.

As we each found a comfortable chair to sit in, they both wanted to know how Mom and Aunt Sis were doing. I let them know they were fine, their lifestyles hadn't changed much and they had the normal aches and pains that come with their age. They get out of the house for church and the usual trips to the grocery store, and Mom's still planting rose bushes everywhere she can.

"Well Chado, who's this big fellow you got traveling with you?"

"Dad, Uncle Spike, meet my Guardian Angel, Uriel."

"Hello, Mr. Uriel, why in heaven's name would Chado need a Guardian here? This is the most peaceful place in all God's creation."

"Well Dad, God has something special He wants me to do for Him and before you ask, neither one of us really knows exactly what it is. But if I survive it, I'll tell y'all everything after it's over."

My dad looks over at Uriel and I'm thinking, *here we go, Dad is about to embarrass me or crack a joke.*

"Ole friend, you know Spike and I are brothers and we married sisters so that meant Spike's two boys were my two son's double first cousins. You know I never thought about it, but if either of the two of us would've had daughters instead of sons and they ended up getting married, our grandkids might have ended up playing a banjo."

I look over at Uriel shaking my head and we all start laughing at Dad's corny joke. Uriel shakes his finger at Dad, "Travis, you know that's borderline sin."

"Yeah Dad that's right, you better watch it, you might get in trouble up here."

As our happy conversation continued, I felt a gentle touch of something on my side. Without looking, I reach over to feel what's touching me, while still focusing on a story Uncle Spike was sharing. I notice my wine pouch is missing. I quickly turn just in time to see a hairy little critter dart around the corner of Dad's home, with Moushie and Rex close behind.

"Hey Dad, what was that? It stole my wine pouch that Samson gave me."

Uncle Spike gets excited, "Samson from the Bible, that Samson gave you the pouch?"

"Yes sir, I met him on Tabula Rasa. So what kind of critter just stole my pouch?"

"That was probably Benny."

"Who the heck is Benny?"

"Y'all come on and I show you, as a matter of fact we'll let you meet all our critters."

As we follow Dad I'm thinking this will be great; Dad always loved to have a few barnyard animals around back on Earth.

"Chado, I got something I want to show y'all before we go out to the barn."

He turns and walks through a huge door to his home, as my curiosity gets the best of me. I want to ask, why in the world anyone would need a door that big, but I'll hold my questions, I don't want to spoil any of Dad's surprises.

Just like baby ducklings following their mom, we continued on. I was really surprised how neat the inside looked. Back home Dad was satisfied without having all the bells and whistles, but this was definitely nice. We passed in front of a beautiful fireplace and I had to ask, "Hey Uncle Spike, why would you need a fireplace if the temperature is always perfect in Heaven?"

"You know, I asked the same question when I saw your granny's wood heater when I first arrived. Well Chado, let me see if I can explain how it all works. You see, if a person desires to have all four seasons like we had back on Earth, they can."

"Well that's cool, but what if your neighbor doesn't like the cool weather?"

"God knows the desires of everyone's heart, so the people that are likeminded about the seasons settle in the same areas. And you know almost everyone that comes to Heaven still loves the seasons."

"Yeah, I understand, and as I think about it I would really miss seeing the fall colors or a beautiful white frost. What about in the cities at the twelve gates?"

"God keeps it at a perfect temperature around each city and the seasons everywhere else are mild and comfortable. You might have a snow in the winter and before you know it flowers are blooming. Chado it's nothing like you've ever experienced. I'm telling you, it is perfection."

Still following Dad admiring the woodwork and the interior of his home, we're led to a huge rock wall with another great big door. It appeared that through this door was a hidden room in the side of the hill.

I look over at Uriel," Hey bud, there is no telling what my Pop is about to show us."

* * *

Uriel smiles as we both turn and watch my dad on one side and Spike on the other, both grab hold of two big handles of the double doors. As they start pulling I hear the screeching sound of the hinges as they swing open. The room is so dark I could only see a couple feet inside the threshold.

"Chado, go on in there."

"I'm not going in there, Dad. This is your house, you go in there."

"Awe... don't be a scaredy-cat, go on in there."

"I'm telling you Dad, I'm not going in there."

Dad and Uncle Spike burst out laughing with Uriel joining in on the fun, when I hear Dad, "Cuddles, wakey wake. Cuddles, come on boy, wake up."

We wait for a few seconds, nothing.

"Come on Cuddles, wakey wake. If you get up I'll bring you fishing."

I hear a deep growling yawn coming from inside the dark room. As we continue to wait, I hear the clicking sounds of claws against the rock floor and the sound is getting closer.

At this point, we all take several steps back away from the door. The sounds of his claws stops just inside door with this giant creature still hidden in the darkness.

"Come on Cuddles, don't be afraid. It's my son and his friend Uriel. Come on little buddy." Dad looks over at us, "He's a bit shy, but he'll warm up to you."

He edges a few more inches closer and I see his black nose barely showing through at the edge of the dark room.

Uncle Spike tells me, "Go pet him Chado, I promise he won't hurt you."

Uriel, standing behind me gives me a gentle nudge, "Go on and make another friend."

I stand frozen in my tracks, thinking, *there's nothing to be afraid of, and anything with the name Cuddles has to be a sweet little cuddly animal of some sort, right? It's just the whole dark cave thing that's kind of strange.*

As I take a few steps forward, the black nose disappears back into the dark room. In a friendly gesture, I hold my hand out in front of me as I slowly move in his direction. Now my hand completely disappears through the shadows of the dark cave. I start to feel the warm breath of whatever kind of animal that's in front of me. Suddenly, I feel a huge warm wet tongue completely wrap around my hand. His tongue feels like it's the width of a medium size bath towel. I knew at this moment this was definitely not something small and cuddly.

I step a little closer reaching up with my other hand to feel the side of his face. The tips of my fingers slide through cool silky hair. I softly whisper, "What are you big fellow?" Without the animal resisting, I take another step forward, shoving my hand deeper into his fur. The thickness of his pelt reminded me of the giant woolly mammoth I had befriended in the dandelion fields on the other side of the wall. Surely this isn't a mammoth, what the heck; I'm standing in total darkness with some kind of giant animal.

I hear Dad, "Come on Chado, he'll follow you out now. Let's go get your wine pouch back from Benny."

As I turn, I feel his warm breath on my neck as we head out of the dark room and I'm thinking, *this is so cool, I've made another friend, just don't know exactly what it is yet, but got a friend.*

When we broke out into the light I couldn't believe my eyes, it was another huge bear, just like I saw back where the three old men were fishing. He looked as big as or maybe even larger than the other one. This sucker was standing on all four feet and his back was as tall as a big Clydesdale horse, my goodness, this is so cool!

"Dad, where did you get this big rascal?"

"Well, the dark room back there was his original home. You see in the back of that room is a huge cave. When I got here to Heaven and was looking for a place to live, I stopped off and was fishing right over there at the mouth of that river. I was catching trout as fast as I could bait my hook, when Cuddles walked up. I shared my fish with him and made a friend. After he finished his dinner of fresh trout, I saw him head back to his den. And Chado, at about that same time I felt the presence of God tell me this will be my home." Dad points, "I laid down right over there underneath that apple tree and fell into a deep sleep and when I woke up, the house you just walked through had appeared in the side of that hill. I guess you could say Cuddles and I are roommates."

"Dad that is the wildest story I've ever heard. I can't wait for my brother Gerald to get here; he will get a kick out of this. My dad living with a giant bear! Who would have ever thought?"

"Yeah, your big brother will love this. By the way how's he doing?"

"Oh, he's okay. Stays busy, always building stuff and he's got his place really looking good. Hey Uncle Spike, I bet you can't get Gerald to walk in that dark room with Cuddles yawning."

Uncle starts laughing, "No he wouldn't go in there; I didn't either when your dad showed me."

"Chado, Benny is probably hanging out at the barn, and if that little rascal figured out how to get that cork out, he's probably hid out and drinking your wine."

On our short walk to the barn, Cuddles heads over toward the river. I'm guessing he's either thirsty or wanting to go fishing. When he sees we aren't following him, he stops, sits down on his butt, and gives out a huge moaning sound.

"Hey Dad, what's the matter with Cuddles?"

Dad starts laughing, "I got him pretty spoiled. That rascal will sit right there and pout like a three thousand pound baby. He's trying to con me into bringing him fishing."

"Pop, you never spoiled me and brother, how is it you got so soft hearted?"

"Well... I guess you could say, Heaven will just do that to you."

Rex and Moushie appear from the barn running out to greet us. After they say their hello, they run straight over to Cuddles.

As they approach the giant bear, both dogs are shaking their tails showing that their intentions are friendly. Cuddles suddenly stops his moaning, rolls over on his back wanting to play with Moushie and Rex. Both dogs start rubbing against the giant bear with their bodies and finally Moushie leaps up on the stomach of Cuddles and all at once, all three get up and head for the river.

"Chado, you do know they've been friends for quite some time now."

"No, I didn't. Is this where Rex and Moushie have been the whole time?

"Yep, this is their home and you're welcome to stay here too Son, if you want. We really love it here. Now, let's see if we can find that monkey."

"So Benny is a monkey?"

"Yes, he's a spider monkey and he is mischievous as they come. I believe the Lord truly has a sense of humor because Benny will tickle your funny bone. And he has a brother that's just about as bad."

"Yeah, I ran into a couple spider monkeys on my way here and they were a hoot also."

Dad heads through the barnyard with chickens, ducks, and turkeys all running up to him begging for his attention. He squats down and they seem to love on him by rubbing their heads against his hand like a house cat would do. He stands back up, walks over to a wooden shelf at the barn, grabs a few handfuls of grain and tosses it in the air. "Here you go fellows, enjoy."

As we walk through the barn with no sign of Benny in sight, Dad tells me to watch this. He opens the double doors in the back of the barn, unveiling the most beautiful green pastures I'd ever seen, stretched out alongside the river as far as the eye could see.

"Dad, I don't know what to say, this is beyond words."

"Well that is a pretty piece of land for sure and certain, but you just wait and watch this."

He reaches over and grabs an ole timey bull horn that was hanging looped over a wooden peg. This ancient bugle looked like it was made from the horn of some kind of mountain goat. It looks about three feet in length and has an odd twist from the mouthpiece all the way to the big end.

I look over at Uncle Spike and he's smiling with his index fingers stuffed in both ears. With a loud voice he tells me "It's called a Shofar horn!" Suddenly I hear Dad take a huge breath, press the horn to his mouth and my goodness, he blows into it. That thing is so loud I bet Mom can hear it back on

Earth. The chickens and ducks scattered, all heading toward the river. I even caught a glimpse of both spider monkeys as they bail out of the loft, and Dad finally runs out of air.

"Good Lord Pop! Where did you get that thing and how could it be that loud? Goodness!"

"When the Lord gave me this barn, it was hanging right there on that peg and I started using it."

"Using it for what, to scare all your critters away?"

"Nope, just wait and listen."

* * *

Within a few seconds I hear a rumbling in the distance, and over the horizon I see at least a hundred head of horses heading straight for us in full gallop.

"Guys, this is one heck of a sight. Hey Dad are they all yours?"

"No indeed not, they're just like Cuddles the bear. They're just our friends living here in Heaven with us and we all enjoy their beauty and friendship. You see that herd; it's just a handful that stays around here. The rest roam all over Heaven. And Son, you see those two stallions in the lead?"

"Yes sir."

"Well, they are my favorite and I believe God sent them to me because there's something special about both of them."

"Yes sir, they are mighty fine."

As they get closer to the barn, the main herd peels off and heads straight for the river. Dad's two favorite stallions run straight up to where we are standing. They both slide their back feet as they come to an abrupt stop only a few feet away. They stand side by side like they have been trained in a circus and are showing their God-given talents.

Suddenly I catch a glimpse of something running between our legs heading for the horses. It's the two spider monkeys and one is dragging Samson's wine pouch.

"Hey Dad, there's something very familiar about this whole scene."

I walk over to the horses and as I looked in their eyes, it occurs to me this is definitely the same horses and the same spider monkeys that brought me to Heaven's Gate. Dad and Uncle Spike break out laughing.

"So... the three old men that were fly fishing with the bear. That was you guys?"

"Yep that was us."

"Well Dad, who was the third man?"

"Would you believe if I told you it was Theodore Roosevelt?"

"No way, you're pulling my leg!"

"Nope it was him, the 26th president of the United States. He was an outdoorsman back in the early 1900's and that hasn't changed; he really loves to fly fish."

"Now that is truly amazing! Pop, how in the world did y'all end up meeting a President?"

"Chado we met Teddy right there on that same river you saw us fishing on."

Uncle Spike chuckles, "Come to think of it, we've met a lot of Presidents, Kings, Queens, Princes, you name it. But you know what? Everyone in Heaven is equal. There is only one King here and His name is above all names, Jehovah God!"

"Amen, Uncle Spike, Amen!" I see Uriel shaking his head in agreement.

"Hey Dad, how did you and Unc know where I was that day, I mean when you sent the horses and the monkeys to show me the way?"

"Well Son that was a God thing. He gave Spike a vision, and let me tell you, it was pretty detailed. You know the Lord does that from time to time. Well anyway, He wanted us to give you a little help after Allayer and Nipper dropped you off. When Spike told me the Lord wanted to have a little fun with the monkeys snatching your clothes, and you having to run bare-naked through the woods across that meadow, I was all in!"

They all started laughing.

"Go ahead fellows, laugh it up, no one saw me but the monkeys!"

"Hey Chado, to top off having a little fun that day with you, the Lord showed us a new fishing hole on that river. Spike and I had been fly fishing in the same area several times but that day; He put us right on top of a honey hole. We fed Cuddles so many trout he could hardly walk."

"Yeah, I got to see you feed Cuddles, but I actually thought he was going to eat you instead of the fish." Dad and Uncle Spike chuckle.

"So when we first got to the river, God sent the horses and those two little monkeys to give you a tour. I tell you Chado, you would never have seen the mammoths or known how to find your way through that mountain pass if He hadn't. Well anyway, after the horses dropped you at the portal, they turned back, came here and after a bit more fishing, we all went back home... and of course Cuddles followed us the whole way. You know, I feel really bad if I go fishing and don't bring Cuddles with me."

"Why's that Dad?"

"I left him one time when we went to visit your Granny and he was sitting on his butt moaning, and would you believe when we got back he hadn't moved an inch. He was still right where I left him, and yes he was still crying. So I've never left him since."

I couldn't help but laugh, "Dad I always knew you were an old softy."

I see Uncle Spike turn and point at a knotted rope swing hanging from a big cypress tree at the edge of the river bank. "Hey Chado, you and Uriel want to have a little fun?"

I look over at Uriel, "Hey bud, we got time for a swim?"

He smiles, "Chado you sure love to swim."

Dad pops off, "Yeah he does, and I told him that deep sea diving was going to get him killed, and it did."

"But Dad, that was all meant to be, remember God numbers our days, and if it hadn't been on the bottom of the Gulf, it would have been somewhere else."

"I reckon so, but I did tell you."

"I know, I know Pop."

We all head over to the rope swing and as we step up to the edge of the tall bank overlooking the deep end of Dad's swimming hole, I see a funny sight. It's Cuddles, and he's standing on all fours in about six feet of water with Moushie and Rex both lying across his back. They all three notice our presence, with Moushie and Rex bailing off the giant's back, swimming for the shallow end where several horses are pawing and playing in the clear cool water.

As we strip down to our linen clothes, preparing to try out Dad's rope swing I'm thinking; *"Could this be where I would want to spend eternity? I love everything about this place, all of Dad's animals, this beautiful river, the lake, mountains on both sides of this grand valley with rolling hills. Yes, this would be awesome, it's even pretty close to Granny's; but I wonder how far it is to the Valley of the Children? I would surely want to be close to my daughter."*

Suddenly with Uriel hearing my thoughts, he glides past me being the first off the swing, "It's about a two day ride on horseback..."

I laugh as I see Uriel cut several flips and then hardly making a splash cutting through the surface of the water like an Olympic diver.

Uncle Spike laughed, "Can you match that Chado?"

"I don't know Unc; I'll give it a shot."

I pull the rope as far back as I can, feeling the soft sand of the river bank with my toes, I lean forward and take off running as fast as I can go. Right before swinging away from the edge I'm thinking, *"What in the world am I doing?"* The knotted rope sends me up at least thirty feet in the air. Giving it my best shot, I tuck my body and try to flip as many times as possible. Midway through my fancy flips I lose track of how I was going to land, when suddenly I manage to do a perfect belly flop. Striking the surface of the water feels like I had landed on concrete. Embarrassed at my belly buster, I swim underwater for the next few seconds heading for the shallow end, and yes, everyone is still laughing as I surface.

I look at the guys and they all give me a round of applause and I bow as I walk through the small herd of horses standing in the shallows.

Dad, trying to protect his son's last small remnant of ego, changed the subject as I walked up the bank. "Hey guys! Y'all want to see something really neat?"

"Sure Dad, what you got?"

"Come here Cuddles, come on buddy." Dad slaps the side of his leg a couple times, "Come on Cuddles, come to Poppa."

Cuddles and both dogs were on the other side of the river when Dad started calling. Without any delay this big grizzly jumped off the bank reminding me of a Labrador retriever going to fetch a duck. This three thousand pound fur ball hits the water, sending a huge wave toward four horses that were still standing belly deep in the river. The horses being spooked from the wave, came running out of the water along with Cuddles and my two dogs. What a sight, "Dad that was pretty cool. Is that what you were talking about, Cuddles causing the horses to stampede out of the river?"

"No, watch this: Cuddles, go feed the horses, go on, you know what to do."

I look at Uncle Spike, "You know, back on Earth it would be the other way around, the horses would be the food for a grizzly."

I continue to watch as I see Cuddles mosey up the river bank toward a huge apple tree. I notice all the horses have now directed their attention to Cuddles and the entire herd starts moving in his direction.

I look over at Dad and he's grinning from ear to ear. He points back at Cuddles, I turn to see the giant grizzly rare up on his back feet, placing his front paws against the tree and with great force he starts violently shaking the apple tree and he's grunting with each shake. I see and hear the thump of hundreds of apples hitting the ground. My dad yells out; "That's good Cuddles, they have enough, don't want to give your buddies a tummy ache."

Just like that Cuddles stops shaking the tree. He turns around, sits down leaning against the trunk, with three of the wild horses walking up each having an apple in their mouths dropping them one by one into Cuddles' furry lap.

Still not believing what I had just witnessed with my own eyes, I ask Dad if he trained them to share and help each other out like that. "Chado, we haven't been here very long; this is just how neat Heaven is. God has everything living with harmony and love up here."

"I don't even know what to say."

"Don't say anything, just listen, learn and enjoy."

We all start getting dressed after our enjoyable swim when I hear Dad speaking with Uriel. "Hey friend, do you mind me asking how you got those scars?"

"Not at all Travis, they came from fighting demons and fallen angels."

* * *

As Dad and Uriel continued their conversation I couldn't help but notice that more of Uriel's scars had faded and some had completely disappeared. I want to ask Uriel what's going on, but I feel maybe now isn't the time. I think I'll wait until we're back on our journey.

Uriel and I hang around Dad and Uncle Spike with all their critters enjoying so many stories of what they had seen and done while they've been in Heaven, and finally Uriel gives me a nudge letting me know it was time to move on.

"Chado, I want you and Uriel to take Max and Hollywood, they are two of the finest horses in Heaven. This journey y'all are on; might be why God has always made me feel that they were very special."

"Uriel, you think we should take Dad up on his offer?"

"Saddle up, let's go Bud."

After we gear up, ready for our journey, I walk out to the river where Cuddles and the dogs are sitting. As I get closer, Cuddles stands up on his back feet and waddles over. I take this to mean he wants his belly scratched. So I oblige him with a nice long belly rub and when I stop he gently drops back down standing on all fours. And to my surprise he gives me a big slobbery lick right across my face. "Okay big guy, thanks for the sugar." He grunts a couple times in some kind of bear language as I scratch him behind his ears. "Cuddles, I'll be coming back and you and I will do a lot of fishing together." I give him a little short rub across his giant forehead as I head back to the barn.

"Moushie, Rex, are y'all coming or staying?"

I notice Uriel had already mounted and he seems to be ready to ride.

"Okay boys, you better make your mind up quick because we are about to go see Summer."

Almost back to the barn, I shout out to Dad, "Hey Pop, what's the name of the horse I'm riding?"

"The one you're riding is Hollywood and Uriel's on Max."

"Why did you name him Hollywood, Pop?"

Dad and Uncle Spike start laughing, "Because he thinks he's prettier than all the other horses."

As Uriel and I swing both horses around under the barn, Dad's two spider monkeys bail out of the hay loft landing on the backs of our horses, and to my surprise Benny had Samson's wine pouch with him.

I hear Dad and Uncle Spike both start laughing, "Hey Chado, I forgot to tell you, wherever Hollywood and Max go, so do Benny and Clyde."

"Okay Pop, we don't mind having passengers."

We take off in a slow gallop. And just a few yards out I twist around in the saddle looking back and I see Dad and Spike waving goodbye. I also see Moushie and Rex dart out from behind the barn heading in our direction.

"We'll be back when we get back, and thanks for the horses Dad!"

Uriel looks over at me, "I guess Rex and Moushie are coming after all."

"So Uriel, you say compared to Earth time it's about a two day ride to the Valley of the Children?"

"Yes, give or take."

25

Twelve Strongholds

"Hey Chado, I'd like to show you something pretty special that's not far out of our way, if you're interested."

"Sure, I'm interested, what is it?"

Uriel smiles, "Have patience, Little Soul, we'll be there soon enough."

We ride for what seems like several hours following the cobblestone road as it winds in and out of tall redwood trees growing alongside the lake. Over the sounds of the hooves striking the stone road and the squeaking of the leather saddles, I hear the roaring sound of a waterfall. Both horses slow down to a walk as we approach what looks like the edge of the world. The roaring sound of the water crashing on the rocks below is almost deafening.

I slide out of the saddle, quickly walking to the edge as I feel the cool spray from this magnificent waterfall. My curiosity grows as I edge closer and lean over to see the river below. This scene is breathtaking, and nothing compares to the ongoing beauty of Heaven.

As I look back at my traveling companions, I notice the cobblestone road splits just before the cliff, and before I could ask...

"Chado, if we go to the left, we cross a bridge that brings us to the other side of the river down below, and it leads us to the Valley of the Children. If we go right the trail leads up to Angel's Mountain."

"Angel's Mountain, that sounds cool."

"So are you still interested in a bit more adventure?"

"You know it bud. Let's get to getting."

After mounting back up, I see Moushie and Rex wanting to go left toward the bridge, now I'm wondering if I made the right choice.

I hear Uriel laugh, "Chado Cole, you've been turning left when you should have turned right all of your life. It has gotten you into trouble so many times making wrong decisions. As a matter of fact, I've received a lot of my scars defending and protecting you from your bad decisions."

"I'm so sorry Uriel."

"Hey it's okay, Chado. The pain of my scars could never compare to the suffering and shed blood that Christ endured for the sins of all humanity! His great sacrifice and unmeasured love was shown when he gave His life on the cross at Calvary!"

"Uriel, I don't even know what to say, all I know is that I am undeserving to even be here!"

"Little Soul, here's the good news; as you know, Jesus Christ rose from the dead, set the captives free and now sits at the right hand of God!"

"Hallelujah my tall friend, hallelujah!"

"Chado, something else we can both be thankful for; we survived, and now we're headed for Angel's Mountain!"

"Uriel I'm still not confident of my decision, should we have continued on to the Valley of the Children?"

"No, that's okay. It won't take us long, and we'll be seeing your daughter in no time. It's just that the Almighty wants you to see this and now is as good a time as any."

"You know Uriel, I've made some pretty big bloopers in my past."

"Hey, don't beat yourself up so bad. What I was referring to, when you were mortal and had an impulse or made

275

a quick decision, you had a bad habit of not seeking God's will and this caused you to stumble quite often."

"I totally understand, Uriel. I made a lot of stupid mistakes. Yep, I turned left and should've gone right, many times. Hey, Uriel, about your scars, I didn't want to say anything in front of Dad and Uncle Spike, but I have to ask; how is it that your scars are fading and some have disappeared completely? What's going on with that? I know God heals but I can't figure out why He doesn't just completely heal all of them at once."

"Chado, this adventure we're on is different than anything I've ever seen God set in motion. I feel God urging me to ask you about each event when Lucifer made attempts to either take your life or deceive you into thinking God's not real."

"Now that's a scary thought. I have doubted my faith a few times and wondered if God was truly real. I was foolish in those weak moments."

"You're weakness came from not reading God's Word enough. Remember your faith is strengthened as you read and hear God's Word daily. Don't you know while on Earth it was a daily battle against the powers and principalities of hell?"

"I know now, that's for sure and certain! Anyway, if you don't mind finish explaining about your battle scars."

"Well, I've noticed as you tell the stories of your past, the scars I received during those battles start to fade away. I'm guessing God wants to remind us of the ongoing battles fought in the spiritual realm protecting His children. But, I believe His main reason is He's refreshing your memory, and all this is somehow tied to the dreams about the scrolls and this mission."

"The mission, I can't wait to find out what that's all about. Uriel, if telling those stories will get you healed up, would you like me to tell you another? Maybe God will get rid of the rest of your scars right quick and snappy!"

Uriel chuckles, "Not right now, we're almost to Angel's Mountain."

* * *

I feel Benny the spider monkey as he reaches around me trying to untie the wine pouch hanging on my saddle. "Hey little buddy, are you thirsty?" I take a small sip before handing it over to Benny, and as soon as he gets a mouth full he jumps still holding the pouch, landing on the back of Max. I can't help but grin when I see Benny show his friendship by sharing our wine with his little buddy Clyde.

As I turn and look ahead over the horizon, two giant statues come into view. They are Angels and they have to be at least three hundred feet tall, one on each side of the road. They both are holding their swords straight up with the other hand holding giant shields. The tips of their wings touch in the center of the road, creating an archway over the entire entrance. The sight of these two statues tells me this has to be a very special place.

Uriel looks over at me, "Chado, it is a special place but there are eleven more just like this one, each facing one of the twelve gates of Heaven."

"So the center of Heaven where God's Throne is located would be behind all twelve?"

"Yes, the throne of God is seven hundred miles behind the Angel's stronghold, directly in the center of Heaven."

"Well, how far would it be to the nearest gate?"

"The gate this stronghold faces is seventy miles away. The other eleven are the same."

As we slowly walk our horses underneath the archway, I feel a sense of humility and reverence. I want to ask Uriel a thousand questions, but I know it is not the right time... This is a time to be quiet and humble myself in the presence of God's Warriors.

Uriel turns off the path onto a narrow trail leading up a steep incline. After riding a few hundred feet up, I notice the breath coming from both horses was creating vapor, telling me this thin cool mountain air isn't any different than it is in the high altitudes on Earth. Uriel looks over at me smiling, "Chado, you're catching on."

Right before reaching the top, we both dismount. As I slide off Hollywood tossing the reigns over the saddle, both horses head over to a patch of grass between several boulders.

We walk just a few more yards to an overlook, "Chado, this is as far as I can take you. It's not that it's totally off limits, but it's kind of the Warrior's private place and we like our solitude. God wanted me to bring you here and give you a glimpse of one of the Strongholds where the Guardians dwell."

"I understand, this is plenty close enough for me. Uriel, I've had a weird feeling ever since we rode underneath the statues that I don't belong here."

"Chado, God has only allowed a few outside of the Angels to come here. It's very private; remember God's ways are not our ways. But, He wanted you to see at least one of the twelve Angel Strongholds."

"Do they know we're up here?"

"Sure they do." Uriel points at several locations surrounding the entire area, "Look closely, can you see the Sentinels standing guard?"

"Yes, I can. They blend right in to the mountain. Uriel, are they worried about being attacked here inside Heaven?"

"No, Lucifer knows they would quickly be destroyed if they tried anything here. The Guardians have been ordered to stand guard from the time of the great rebellion. That's when a third of the angels were deceived by Lucifer and he convinced the fallen angels to follow him. From that single rebellion we honor God in this way. We will stand guard until the end of days on Earth."

Overlooking this valley that's hidden down inside of this beautiful mountain, I can see what looks like thousands upon thousands of Angels. This picture reminds me of vast armies marching, preparing for battle. I notice several hundred are gliding above the multitudes, and as they circle, several turn and fly away completely out of sight.

On the other side of the valley, I could see a giant herd of horses; some were saddled and appeared to be adorned with armor, ready for battle, others peacefully grazing.

In the center of this great valley stood a giant portal resembling the ones we've passed through. However, this one looks like it's ten times larger - large enough for legions of Angels to freely pass through at a moment's notice.

"Uriel, it looks like they're preparing for battle."

"Yes, they know not the hour, but they see the signs and know it draws near."

"What draws near, the final battle, THE Armageddon battle?"

"Yes, and the seven years of tribulation is about to begin. These Angels you see are patiently waiting on Gabriel and Michael to give them orders from God. They are listening for the sounds of the trumpets."

"You mean the trumpets that God had John the Revelator write about in the Bible?"

"Yes, there will be seven seals opened and seven trumpets will sound. This will signal these legions of Angels to ride through the portals preparing for the final battle. At the last trumpet God will separate the wheat from the tares, saving His children and allowing the ones who have rejected Christ to remain and drink from the cup of damnation and destruction. The Antichrist will deceive the Nations as he stands on the temple mount and claims to be god; I say woe to the inhabitants of the Earth. This is called the ABOMINATION OF DESOLATION!"

"Wow Uriel, when you put it like that, it really sounds like it's about to go down!"

"That's right, it seems we are in the final days, and I'm starting to believe God has a plan to use you somehow in the midst of all this for some kind of last warning."

"Well, I'll be glad when the big mystery is revealed!"

I look back over this awesome scene one last time before heading back down the path, thinking if folks back on Earth could see what I'm seeing and know what's coming in the near future they would tremble in fear!

As we mount back up, "Hey Uriel."

"Yeah bud, what's on your mind?"

"The Angels back there that were circling overhead, I noticed every so often you would see one or two head out in different directions away from the Stronghold. Where were they going?"

"I don't know, they could be headed anywhere, some bound for the city of God, or just decided to fly around enjoying Heaven. Chado, you do know the Angels have free rein and can travel anywhere they want. Well, as long as they're off duty."

"Do they ever go visit with the people, just say like my Granny or Pop?"

"Absolutely, we enjoy hanging out with the folks. We play sports, go fishing; actually God wants us to do all kinds of fun stuff with the people of Heaven. I went swimming with you twice."

We both chuckle, "That's right, I have to apologize Uriel. We've been together so long I don't even think of you as an Angel, but more like a best friend. You know Heaven just keeps getting better. It's nothing like palling around with my Guardian Angel. Hey, you know John the Baptist?"

"Sure, I know John."

"Well, I guess you would, my bad. Anyway when I first got to Tabula Rasa he hinted around about playing baseball. Allayer and Nipper said he was a strikeout king. You think we all might get to play a little hardball?"

"Chado, baseball needs to be the last thing on your mind right now, remember you have eternity for all that."

"Okay, got it."

* * *

We make it back to the bridge, taking in more beauty as we cross over. As usual, Moushie and Rex are still leading the way.

281

"Uriel, you think my two dogs know where they're going?"

"Yes, they've made this trip many times with your dad."

"You know, I didn't even ask Pop if he had seen Summer."

"Oh yeah, he makes that trip quite often. Your dad is pretty good with those kids. They love him to come and tell his silly stories."

"Wow, my pop telling stories to kids in Heaven, I wish my mom could see that, it would warm her heart."

"Not to scare you, but I believe she's scheduled to be here pretty soon."

"Well Uriel, that news makes me feel pretty good. Before I got killed she was always having heart problems, hip problems, well you get the picture. Knowing when she gets here, all her pain will be gone and her age clock starts going backward, getting younger by the second. That's going to be awesome!

"Hey Chado, I wonder if she'll like Cuddles the grizzly?"

We both laugh, as we finally reach the other side of the lake.

"Uriel, I wonder if Dad and Spike might try to get her to walk inside Cuddles den without any light."

"Probably not, but I wouldn't put it past your silly pop."

Both horses come to a stop as we hear singing coming from the woods to our left. Moushie and Rex turn, looking back to get permission to go investigate. "Go ahead, you can go." Like a flash they disappear into the forest.

With the sweet sounds of singing getting closer, I see a few glimpses of something white. To our surprise, three little girls appear from behind the redwoods, each one holding a lead rope attached to a sheep. The sheep had tiny bells hanging from their necks and the trotting and movement of each, caused the bells to chime. The beauty of this trio was that the bells seem to be in perfect time with the voices of this three part harmony. We continued to sit in our saddles and enjoy a concert as the forest turned white with hundreds of sheep all following the three precious little girls. We remained until they went out of hearing distance.

Uriel looks over at me, "Now wasn't that a treat."

"Unbelievable, I can't get over the constant blessings here in Heaven."

After our roadside entertainment had moved on, Moushie and Rex rejoin us as we make our way further down the road.

* * *

"Uriel, you ready for another story?"

"Sure why not, we probably have time."

"Okay, anything particular you have in mind?"

"Chado, I have three different stories and I want you to choose which of the three. The first to choose from is the time when you were on a pipeline project in Utah. The blasting crews were using dynamite to blow up the side of the mountain, and they didn't have barricades or warning signs up; you drove your ATV right in the mix just seconds before it went off."

"Oh yeah, I remember that day. I had just knocked off from work and was hauling butt on my four-wheeler back down the right-of-way. I was heading for my truck that was parked at the bottom of the mountain. It was so steep and rocky we had to use ATV's to access the pipeline right-of-way. Traveling at mach-1, I topped a steep ledge and had to slam on the brakes, sliding right up in the middle of a blasting area. Their fuses were laced across the rock, all leading to the drilled holes for the explosives. At that point I was thinking, '*I am about to die!*' The men in the blasting crew were shouting, 'Get out of there! It's about to blow!' Yep, that was a close call for sure."

"Chado, the second one, you were in Charlotte North Carolina at that all night diner when those two guys tried to kill you. The third story, you were working as a diver involved in setting a rig platform in three hundred feet of water when that big storm came in."

"Wow Uriel, those were some scary times!"

"Chado, you are aware that each event I mentioned, you would have been killed if God wouldn't have had me there protecting you."

"I would have died?"

"Yes, and here's the scary thing, the ones I mentioned are only a few, there have been many times."

"Uriel, I feel like stopping Hollywood jumping over and hugging you."

"That won't be necessary. I'm not what you would call a huggy kind of Warrior Angel, if you know what I mean."

"I understand, I just don't know how to thank someone for saving my life over and over."

"Hey bud, I was just doing my job, and yours was a little more complicated since Lucifer had a bull's-eye on your soul. Look, you just complete your mission and that will be thanks enough."

"Okay, well which one of the three incidents caused you to receive the most injuries?"

"In two of the three incidents, I didn't get injured at all. The one that I carry the scars from was number two, North Carolina. That was a rough night in Charlotte."

"Where do I begin?"

"You choose, it's your story."

* * *

"Okay. Well I guess I'll start with the date. It was August 26th 1992; I remember because it was the day after my birthday and Hurricane Andrew came right through Lafayette, Louisiana. This is where we were living at the time, and right in the midst of the storm I received a call from my boss, Bo Jangles. He wanted me in Charlotte, North Carolina immediately. I wouldn't have deserted my family in the middle of a hurricane, but we were almost dead broke and the brick home we lived in was on high ground and the winds were under a hundred miles an hour so my wife and I made the decision. I threw my duffel bag on the passenger side of the floorboard, kissed the wife and kids good bye and hit the road.

It seemed like the storm followed me all the way to the Carolinas. Bo gave me orders to go to the North side of Charlotte, call him when I got there and he would come meet me. He mentioned it was a secluded location and would be easier if he guided me in.

I drove straight through without stopping other than fueling and the occasional bathroom break. Not realizing what time I would arrive, I ended up rolling into Charlotte around three a.m.

Not wanting to call my boss that early, I pulled in at an all-night waffle house at the Sugar Creek exit. It looked like a nice area due to the major motels scattered on each side of the interstate, and I felt this would be a safe place to kill a couple hours. My plan was to call Bo around five a.m. and let him know I was in Charlotte.

As I got out of my truck, I noticed an elderly man was making his way to the door of the diner. 'Hello there young man, I see you have a bicycle in your truck.'

'Yes sir, I carry it along with me on my jobs, you know, trying to stay in shape.'

'Well young man, you better lock it up, this is a bad area and it might not be there when you come back out.'

I chuckle, 'Oh, nobody would want that ole thing.'

I held the door open for the old gentlemen and was thinking, *surely, it's not that bad around here.*

As I walked in, I chose a seat near the grill thinking I might save the waitress a few steps while they waited on me. After ordering a cup of coffee and looking over their menu, I couldn't help but hear the conversations between two waitresses and the cook. They were talking about drug deals openly going down in the parking lot, and one of the ladies that worked there had been molested.

I'm thinking, *there's no way it could be that bad here, surely not with the nice motels and everything so manicured and clean outside, they must be talking about another location.'*

After I order my food, a pretty young brown-skinned girl that was serving the old man at the far end of the diner, came over and started asking very strange questions. 'Hey mister, are you traveling by yourself?'

'Yep, right by myself.'

'You worried?'

'Worried, what do you mean worried? I drove in from Louisiana and I'm pretty tired, but I'm not worried about anything.'

I noticed she had a funny look on her face as she turned away making a humming sound, then telling the lead waitress that she needed to use the pay phone.

The waitress replied, 'There's the phone right there, go ahead.'

'It's long distance, I'll use the pay phone outside.'

Now I'm thinking something is a little fishy here. Even the lady waiting on me got quiet. My waitress reaches over, refilling my cup of coffee as I hear the cook, 'Order up.' She turned grabbed my food sliding the plate over without saying anything. At that point, I should have thrown a few bucks down and got the heck out of there, but I decided to go ahead and eat.

Right before I finished my meal, two black guys walked through the door. As they walked passed me I smiled and spoke, 'How you guys doing?' Their response was a cold stare. They both sat down in the booth directly behind me. I hear the waitress, 'What can I get for you fellows?'

'We don't want anything.'

'Well what about a nice hot cup of coffee?'

'I said we don't want anything; do you hear what I'm telling you?'

The kind waitress quickly walked away and headed to the other end of the grill.

I felt something telling me, *'Get out of here as fast as you can.'* That strong sense of fear drove me out of my chair. I stepped up to the register and as I waited on my change, out of the corner of my eye I could see both guys staring at me like an animal waiting on its prey.

As soon as I turned for the door, they both followed behind me. My truck was parked across the drive in front of the very pay phone that young waitress used to call these monsters. It's no doubt this is a set up, and they are going to rob me or maybe even kill me. Without wasting any time, I quickly walked across the drive, already having keys in hand ready to unlock my truck, with both guys about ten feet behind me.

'Hey boy, you a cop? You look like a cop.'

My truck was a 1991 single cab pickup, with no power door locks, the extra few seconds fumbling around with keys getting my door unlocked could be the end for me.

As they were getting closer, still talking trash, I suddenly remember my 10mm pistol is lying on top of my clothes inside the army duffle bag over on the passenger side.

I tricked both guys, acting like I was sticking the key in the driver's side lock. They got a bit closer and I darted like a rabbit around the front of my truck with both gangsters laughing. 'Where do you think you're going, you don't have anywhere to run boy.'

With much pride and being so sure of themselves, they didn't try to catch me; they just slowly walked around my truck still running their mouths.

That's all I needed, just a few extra seconds. I hit the key hole perfectly on the passenger door, twisted the key, I hear the lock pop. I yanked the door open, reached down, and unzipped the bag. There it was, my Colt auto 10mm lying right on top of the clothes, exactly where I placed it, as I said good bye to my family back home. I leaned back between the seat and door frame, as I quickly swung around at the same time pulling the slide back as I chambered a round.

They both recognized the sound as they were only a couple feet away on the opposite side of the door. I have now zeroed in on the chest of the louder, and probably the dominant one of the two bad guys. With this action and now having the upper hand, they both back away very angry, edging toward the diner entrance. They both continue their street slang cursing at me, 'You got yo blank-blank gun with you!'

Hearing them repeat this over and over I notice the one that I had in my sights, he pulls out what looked like a Berretta pistol. The outlaw tries to be cool and holds his weapon gangster-style off to the side. As I'm leaning against my truck holding my pistol with both hands one eye closed, and a fine bead on his chest, I break silence. 'You point that gun at me and I will kill you where you stand, you sorry sucker!'

At that very moment I almost pulled the trigger, and would have, if he had pointed his pistol in my direction. Something deep down inside was telling me, '*Chado, you're from another state, if you kill him you'll go to jail. Don't do it, it's not worth it.*'

As they continued talking trash I respond, 'That's just the way it is, that's just... the way it is.'

They both got real quiet for a few seconds, and then finally retreated to their car. They watched me scramble across the seat, drive out of the parking lot, and no sooner than when I pressed the throttle on my diesel truck, the chase was on. Not knowing where to go in this unfamiliar town, I just took off mashing the pedal to the floor trying to outrun these outlaws. Diesel trucks were made for pulling. not for running for your life.

As I see the sports car gaining on me, I knew if they got close enough, his passenger would surely try and get a shot through the window. I slid down in the seat as far as I could get to still see over the dash with my foot pressed as hard against the pedal as possible. In a short distance ahead I see a split in the road. This might be my only hope. If I can manage to force these guys to go left, I might make it out of this alive. With my position hunkered down in the seat I can't see out of my mirrors, but I can now hear the motor of their car through my open window. I position my pistol pointing in their direction, ready to at least shoot back if they open fire. They are gaining on me, out of the corner of my eye their front bumper appears, edging closer, now almost even with my door.

Our speed now is just under a hundred miles an hour as we bounce down through the back streets of Charlotte. As we get closer to the fork in the road, I slowly edge over, pushing their car as far to the left as possible. At the last second I whipped my truck over to the right missing the barricades only by inches. Taking no chances, I quickly made my way back to the safety of I-85.

A few days later, one of the older operators working on the pipeline invited me over for dinner. As we were enjoying each other's company, Mr. Miller's wife asked me if I had seen the news. 'No Ma'am, I haven't.' In her thick Tennessee drawl, Mrs. Miller responded, 'Well Chado, you know down there at that waffle house at the Sugar Creek exit? Well there was a man talking on that pay phone you told us about there in front of that diner. The news folks on TV claimed some thugs shot and killed him. They took his vehicle and everything he had. You reckon that might have been those same two guys that tried to get you?' "

"Uriel, I left the Miller's home that night thinking deeply and wondering if I had made the right choice. You know I've never wanted to do harm to anyone that didn't need it, but I have always regretted not pulling the trigger on those two guys. At the least, I should have alerted the cops and informed law enforcement about their little system with the witch that made the call. You know, even if I would have got into trouble and gone to jail, the guy Mrs. Miller told me about might still be alive."

"Chado, we are almost to the Valley of the Children and don't have a lot of time so I'll shorten this up. Charlotte, North Carolina; St. Louis, Missouri; Chicago, Illinois; and many other cities are run by people that have lost their way. Greed and pride rule their lives. They sell out to the highest bidder to advance themselves. They claim to help the helpless while they fill their own hearts with lies and find ways to justify their behavior to themselves. They live luxurious lifestyles and give false hope and encourage people to believe others are supposed to support them with their labor. They flock to the churches on Sunday and shout with joy, claiming to praise God and confessing Jesus as Lord. At the same time they support politicians that slaughter the unborn like cattle. They boldly claim the protection of women, and in the dark shadows allow the destruction of millions.

In all the wars, 1.1 million Americans have died in battle. But as a result of the slaughter of the unborn in abortion clinics and back rooms, over 58 million have perished. This measure of sin has given Lucifer and his fallen great power and now he has his own strongholds over these cities.

You were caught right in the middle of a fierce battle fought that night. We weren't alone, there were over a hundred of God's Angels fighting with me, and we prevailed. You have to understand, the dark legions that own those cities are coiled like snakes around the hearts of people that run cities just like Charlotte. Chado, I say woe to these people, because they will eventually drink from the cup of God's Wrath.

Little Soul, one other thing; you know the man Mrs. Miller told you about that was killed while talking on the payphone? As soon as his heart stopped beating he walked through one of the portals of Heaven."

"Uriel, were you injured during all that?"

"Yes, I received several scars that night." Uriel chuckles, "But, you should have seen the other guy."

* * *

I hear Moushie in the distance; he's cutting up barking his heart out. Rex joins in and at the same time both spider monkeys bail off Hollywood and Max. They hit the ground running full monkey speed in the same direction all the barking is coming from. I look over at Uriel and he's trying to be serious with his Marine Corps look, staring straight ahead. "Okay Uriel. What's over that next hill? Are we there yet? Hey bud, are we there yet?"

He can't help himself; I finally see a big smile start to appear.

"Give it a rest Little Soul, the Valley of the Children is just over that hill."

"Uriel is it just a valley or a small town? How big a place is it?"

"When we top that ridge you'll be able to see only a small part. I haven't told you but the Valley of the Children is 777 miles around the entire valley."

"Wow, now that's a big valley! I wonder how hard it's gonna be to find my daughter."

"That won't be a problem. I know right where she is."

I see Hollywood's ears perk up. He starts to prance like he did when we rode into Heaven's Gate. I reach down and pat him a couple times on his neck. "You big show off, I see why Dad named you Hollywood now."

I pull back on the reigns, "Calm down big boy, it's just Moushie and Rex barking, calm down."

"Chado, can you hear that?"

"Hear what?"

Both horses come to a complete stop.

"Uriel, you definitely have better hearing than I do. All I can hear is Moushie and Rex yapping."

"Just listen. It sounds like someone knew we were coming."

26

Valley of the Children

Staring at the crest of the hill with my head turned just a bit, I start to hear the happy sound of children singing. The words of the song sound like the twenty-third Psalms; yes, I believe it is.

Both horses begin to prance in perfect time as we trot up the hill. Their movements are so well timed; it was as if they were performing a dance they had trained for a thousand years.

The silhouette of children comes into view as they walk over the horizon. Hundreds more, following closely behind, all continuing to sing as they walk in our direction. I see several adults walking with what looks like a giant parade of kids. They seem to be all ages, from toddlers to teenagers.

Uriel points toward the center of this huge mass of kids and I see both dogs and the two spider monkeys walking with two young ladies. "Could that be Summer? It sure looks like her. Uriel, is that her?" He just smiles and sort of shrugged his shoulders.

As we get a bit closer, I can see the spider monkeys are holding the hands of both ladies. Max and Hollywood at the same time come to a stop just a few yards shy of reaching the line of kids. Both horses do their bowing trick and allow us to easily slide out of the saddle. Now standing on the ground at a lower altitude, I lose my view of the two women.

The kids all swarm around us, grabbing our hands leading us in the direction of the valley. Some are still singing with others laughing. Their faces all glowing with joy; I can't help myself, I reach down and pick up two toddlers, holding one in each arm pressed against my ribs. They both start kissing me on the cheeks, it feels like butterfly wings tickling my face.

One of the toddlers stops giving me sugar made in Heaven and with an ever so serious expression, stares at me with the greenest eyes I've ever seen, "Are you my Summer's daddy?"

"Yes Sweetie, I'm your Summer's daddy. Little one, do you know where she is?"

This precious little girl turns around and points through the crowd, "There's my Summer, right there."

Suddenly the kids hushed their singing as they all moved to the side, clearing the cobblestone path, creating a wall of children standing on each side.

With a clear view of my daughter, I slowly set both toddlers on the ground as I feel the overwhelming presence of the Holy Spirit. It's like a rushing wind filling my heart with a spiritual presence that floods over me, as I fall to my knees in humility and thanksgiving. "I lift my hands to you, O Lord!"

As I bow down on my knees thanking God, staring at the stones in the road, with my strength poured out I feel the touch of both toddlers as they kneel down and hold my hands. I look up as my daughter places her hand on my face. "Hello, Daddy."

The kids suddenly start singing and dancing filling the street with laughter. The toddlers pull at my hands, "Get up!"

As I stand, my sweet daughter jumps up in the air with me catching her, just like she did as a child. I embrace her as I hold her up for several seconds with her feet dangling off the ground. I'm thinking, this is the first time I've got to hug my sweet daughter since she took her heavenly journey.

"I've missed you so much, Daddy!"

"I've missed you too, Sweetie! Oh... how I've missed you!"

Both spider monkeys start jumping up and down then crawl up on our shoulders. "So, Daddy, I see you've met Benny and Clyde."

We both burst out laughing as they jump off our shoulders, disappearing in the crowd.

"Daddy, there's someone here I want you to meet."

Summer turns and gets the attention of a lady standing in the midst of the kids. As she's walking in our direction, "Hey, Summer, she looks a lot like you, as a matter of fact she could probably pass as your twin!"

This beautiful blonde-haired blue-eyed lady walks up.

"Lori, I want you to meet my Dad, and Dad I want you to meet your sister."

"My sister? I don't have a sister!"

Lori holds her hand out and smiles, "Chado, I've waited a long time to meet my older brother, so don't spoil it. You are my brother!"

I reach out to shake her hand and as I touched her fingers I pulled her in for a great big hug. "Lori, you know the strangest thing, I always wanted a sister."

"Well, Dad, looks like you finally got your wish."

"Summer, how did you guys meet?"

"Lori was waiting for me when I came out of the Hall of Records. I had just looked up everyone that I knew who had passed, and when I walked out of the building, I felt like I was looking at my older self. You know the Cole gene is pretty strong. I didn't know if she might have been a sister that I wasn't aware of."

"So have you guys been hanging together ever since you met each other?"

"Yes, I started to get a place near Pawpaw's, but Aunt Lori thought it would be a good idea to come here and help with the kids before I made a decision on where I wanted to settle. And I am so glad I did, because I love it here!"

"Well Sweetie, I am so proud of you! Knowing my daughter is working with kids here in Heaven just thrills my heart."

All the kids start heading back over the hill, and we turn and follow the crowd.

"Summer, I almost forgot, I want you and Lori to meet my friend Uriel."

They all chuckle, "Don't bother. We've known Uriel for quite some time, and we know he's been watching over you. But what we don't understand is why your Guardian Angel is still with you?"

"Well, Sweetie, I know it's a bit hard to believe but God has your dad on a special assignment."

"Not really, Pop, God does some really cool stuff, and you should hear some of the stories Lori has, she's been here even before birth."

"Now I'm confused, before birth, what do you mean?"

"Lori, you want to explain to your brother?"

"I sure will. Chado, a little more than a year after you were born, Mom had a miscarriage during her pregnancy with me, and I've been here ever since."

"Hey that's right; God says in His Word, *"In the womb I knew you."*

We make it to the top of the ridge looking over part of the valley, "Wow guys! I was thinking I was about to see a giant valley. This is a huge city!"

"Dad it's not just a city, I believe this is the most important place in Heaven, well other than the Throne of God."

I stand in awe as I gaze across this giant city. The buildings are the size of football fields strung out for miles on both sides of a super wide thruway. The road has to be at least a half mile wide and looks like it's made of gold. It glistens like still water with reflections from the brilliantly colored buildings. Beautiful paintings scattered on some of the smaller ones. "Let me guess, Leonardo Da Vinci's paintings?"

"Hey, that's pretty good Dad. Would you like to meet him?"

"Sure, maybe later on. Right now, I just can't get over what I'm seeing. This is totally amazing! Why are the buildings so huge? Okay, Summer, tell me what all goes on here."

"God calls this place the Valley of the Children because this is where we receive the aborted babies. And you ask why the buildings are so big, well, Pop, this will break your heart. In the United States alone there are around 2,500 to 3,000 unborn put to death daily. So if you factor in all the other countries with the USA, the numbers are unbelievable."

"Lori, what's the count worldwide since 1980?"

"A little fewer than 1.5 billion have been received and that's not counting miscarriages like Mom had with me."

"My goodness, now that's something you don't hear about in the news. Who takes care of that many kids, I mean how in heaven's name can anyone manage something like that?"

"God's got this covered."

"You know Dad, everyone here thinks it's about to come to a close; you know, final curtain time."

"I know, Sweetie, I've been getting the same vibes from the Angels I've met."

"Hey, Lori, can you tell me how and who takes care of all these kids?"

"Big brother, you will love this. God puts it in the hearts of the bloodline!"

"Okay. You lost me."

"Well just say a baby gets aborted today and somewhere down through that child's bloodline they have an ancestor that's here in Heaven. They might have died as far back as the 1600's or maybe even 50 AD. That person is told by God's messengers, or maybe even by the Almighty Himself, to come here and receive a child from their bloodline. God gives them a special desire to love and nurture the child until they become an adult. Some like Summer are volunteers that just have a heart for kids, they settle here and do God's work."

"So how old does a child get before they stop aging?"

"Dad, how old was Jesus when He died on the cross?"

"I believe he was around thirty-three years old, right?"

"Right, and how old were you when you were in your prime years?"

"I guess when I was thirty-three or so."

"Right, that's around the age God chose for everyone here in Heaven. Look at your sister; she looks not a day over thirty."

"This is so cool, the old get to Heaven and their age clock starts going backward becoming younger every day until they hit their prime. The young, their age clock allows them to grow up and have a normal childhood reaching their peak at thirty-three."

"Yes Dad, God really loves kids, and He makes Heaven even more special allowing these little ones to grow up here."

"Our God is an Awesome God!"

"Yes and He reigns on Heaven and Earth."

I chuckle, "Man how many times have we read that scripture?"

As we finally reach the giant thruway, I notice the kids start heading off in different directions.

"Hey Sweetie, where are they off to?"

"Some are going to classes, others off to the playground and some heading over there."

27

Hands of the Ancestors

I turn as I see Summer pointing in the direction of the largest building on the left side of the thruway.

"Dad, that's one of many receiving areas located here in the Valley."

"A receiving area, like a receiving area for babies, that kind of receiving?"

"Exactly, we can show you. It's the coolest thing Dad."

Lori waves over a couple teenagers, "Chado, let the kiddos take Max and Hollywood to the stables, the animals aren't allowed inside any of the buildings."

"Moushie, Rex, y'all go with them, and take Benny and Clyde along."

I can't help but laugh as I watch all six of our furry buddies head off following the two teenagers. "Chado, I hope Benny stays out of the wine pouch."

"Yeah, so do I, he is a little rascal."

Summer and Lori both smile as they make a hand gesture to keep following.

"Lead the way Sweetie, I'm coming."

As we get closer to the receiving area, I notice hundreds of people exiting the building and they are all carrying infants. Without having to ask, I can tell their destination is a row of building across the throughway.

The overhead walkway is filled with people coming and going from one building to the next like a giant assembly line. It's almost confusing seeing these lines and thinking over a period of time, how they must move thousands of kids in and out of here. Wow!

Before entering the building, I hesitate for just a second, admiring more beautiful stone work and the peculiar name written over the entry.

"Hey, Dad can you read what it says?"

"Sure, I can read Hebrew, it says, Hands of the Ancestors."

"That's right, follow us Pop, you're about to see a miracle."

We follow Lori through a side door, not interrupting the flow of people coming and going through the main entrance. As we step inside, Lori leads us up a short set of stairs onto a small balcony overlooking the entire open area.

I count twelve portals, two lines of people at each portal. One line walking in empty handed; the other walking out holding infants. As I look across the open area I count twenty-four lines total.

I see Summer point back at a giant balcony that almost reaches across the entire entryway. "Hey Dad, we're just in time for the changing of the choir."

There are hundreds of children of all ages standing at attention in the choir loft facing the portals getting ready to sing.

To my surprise, the toddler with the green eyes that I held earlier steps up in front of this massive choir and begins to sing. Her beautiful voice has a clarity and volume like I've never heard.

This two foot tall toddler begins to sing by herself the first part of Psalm: 67.

"God be merciful to us and bless us,
And cause His face to shine upon us,

That Your way may be known on Earth,
Your salvation among all nations."

Around verse three, the voices and instruments of this children's choir join in, creating an unbelievable heavenly sound.

I can't help myself as I'm overcome with joy. I turn around and look into the eyes of Summer and Lori as I start laughing, "This is so unbelievable!" I look back over the twelve portals with thousands of people coming and going and the sounds of this magnificent heavenly choir penetrates my soul.

"Sweetie, it just keeps getting better and I am totally blown away with the little toddler! Who is she?"

Summer and Lori starts grinning from ear to ear. "What's up, who is she, do we know some of her family?"

"Dad, her God given name is Roselyn, we call her Rosie. She only has a few people in her bloodline that made it to Heaven, and they're overwhelmed with the number of kids they have; so that's where we come in."

"What do you mean, where we come in?"

"Dad, I received Rosie and took her in as my own, along with several others. Do you remember her calling me, 'My Summer'?"

"Yeah, I thought that was pretty sweet."

"Well I guess she'll probably call you My Pawpaw Chado".

"You know, Sweetheart, I wouldn't mind that at all. As a matter of fact she can call me whatever she likes. I actually fell in love with her when I first picked her up and held her."

I see Lori heading back the way we came in.

"Follow us Dad, we'll get a bit closer; I want you to see the miracle."

* * *

We go back down the steps and make our way around the side until we're standing only a few feet away from one of the portals. I watch the most amazing thing happen, right before my very eyes.

The portal openings look like a sheet of water, favoring a thin membrane, and I can easily see through to the other side.

Suddenly a beautiful Angel appears at the threshold just on the other side of the portal. She's dressed in a brilliant white garment and there's a glow that radiates, hovering around her with the appearance of purity and total peace.

I feel the touch of Summer and Lori as they place their hands on my shoulder, with a soft whisper,

"Watch closely Dad."

As the Angel reaches her hands out, I can now see in the palm of her hand, she's holding a tiny unborn, undeveloped baby. Tears start to swell as I see the baby is in a fetal position as though to still be in the mother's womb; it's the size of a small bird and not moving.

My eyes widen as the ancestor of this child's bloodline reaches through the clear liquid with the Angel laying the tiny baby in her hands.

My God, My God, the miracle takes place!

Tears of joy fill my eyes as the ancestor very slowly pulls the undeveloped, aborted baby back through the portal, with almost the exact representation of natural birth.

Out of chaos, from an evil world, this unwanted child is now resting in the arms of a loving ancestor as a fully developed baby. As the child takes her first breath, filling her lungs with the air of Heaven, she cries out with new life under the protection and love of God.

I continue to watch as the ancestor walks past me, not looking up but staring into the face of her beautiful baby. This scene reminds me of when I gazed upon Summer as I held her for the first time. This special moment, seeing and holding new life and feeling a new love, and only at that very second really understanding that this gift of life was truly a gift from God.

As I turn and look back through the portal, the Angel disappears with another taking her place, this constant flow seems to be never ending.

"Come on Dad, we have something else you might like."

On our way out of the building, we walk past the hundreds of eager relatives lining up behind one another, and each time they hear the first cry of a newborn they lift their hands in praise and thanksgiving.

The sounds of newborns crying echoing across this grand auditorium from each portal seem to blend with children's choir creating an odd harmony that is completely soothing to the hearts of everyone here.

As we exit through the side door, I feel the hand of Uriel on my shoulder as he whispers: "Now you know why God calls this place, The Hands of the Ancestors."

We follow the line of people heading over the arched crosswalk, and I notice how busy everyone seems to be.

"Hey Summer, I see lots of people doing different jobs here in the Valley; what do you guys do to pass the time?"

Lori and Summer smile, "Oh, we stay pretty busy; Dad, we teach school."

"You're both teachers?"

"Well, not like teachers on Earth, we teach the little ones the ways of God. When they come here God gives them knowledge way beyond a normal kid back on Earth, and that alone makes our job pretty easy. I guess when it comes down to it, we help with decisions, where and what they desire and how to use their special skills that God blesses them with. This helps everyone to become more productive here in Heaven. This also helps getting them ready for their roles and duties when the thousand year reign of peace begins. You know Dad, the New Heaven and the New Earth! Pop, we just don't get to Heaven and sit around like kings and queens expecting everyone to wait on us."

"Summer, you're too funny!"

* * *

"Hey Uriel, the teens brought back Max and Hollywood: they're right on time! So what's next on the agenda guys?"

"Well Pop, that building right there has the portals where all these people are transporting to and from their homes, or at least to the nearest portal to their homes."

"Little Soul, you can call it God's super highway here inside Heaven. We can go in and let you see it, but it almost looks exactly like the portals across the street. It's your call."

"I guess we can skip it; I'll probably be using it someday in the future, yeah let's skip it. I'm curious to know what Summer was talking about, when she said there was something else I might like. So what's the surprise kiddo?"

Before she could answer, six toddlers come running up with Rosie leading the pack.

"Summer, Summer, did you hear us sing?"

"Yes, and so did your Pawpaw."

"My Pawpaw?"

"Yes your Pawpaw Chado."

Suddenly, I had six toddlers crawling all over me with Rosie asking, "Are you my Pawpaw Chado?"

"Yes Sweetie, I'm your Pawpaw Chado."

"Did you hear us sing?"

"Yes, and I thought I was hearing Angels singing, and I looked up and you know what?"

"What, Pawpaw?"

"I saw you and I was so proud of how beautiful y'all sounded."

"Thank you Pawpaw, God taught us how to sing like that."

"Well, He did a good job. Hey Rosie, would you like to ride Hollywood, that giant horse right there?"

She rolls her big beautiful green eyes with a funny little expression, "I'll have to ask my Summer if it's okay."

"Go ahead, but hold on tight."

Hollywood and Max do their bowing trick making it easy to place all six kids on their backs, and wasting no time both spider monkeys climb aboard.

"Okay Summer, where to?"

"How about, we take a camping trip to the most beautiful beach in all God's creation?"

I slowly look around and see mountain ranges on both sides of the valley, as the kids all start to giggle.

"No Pawpaw, we get to go through a portal, there's no beach around here silly willy."

I hear another toddler, "It's field trip day for the kids that live here in the Valley, and we get to go see the sea monsters."

They all start growling and giggling.

"Hey, Uriel, what do they mean, sea monsters?"

"Oh, it's harmless. They're talking about the sea creatures that live in the ocean below the planet."

"Yeah, I got to see that when Allayer and Nipper transported me in. It actually looked like the planet was sitting in the ocean."

"Not really, I guess you could say the planet of Heaven hovers above the waters; it just looks like that from space."

"What about the ring around the planet?"

"That's the beach they're talking about, Chado. Let me put it to you like this, God designed it especially for the kids and it is amazing. I'm a Warrior Angel and I love going there, so get ready for something pretty special."

We head for what looks like the center of town. "Hey Dad."

"Yeah Sweetie, what you got?"

She points toward a group of homes sitting on a little plateau overlooking the city.

"Pop can you see the house up there on the far right surrounded by that group of fruit trees?"

"Sure Sweetie, it looks very nice."

"Well, that's where 19 kids, Lori, and I all live together, right there in that home. And we have plenty of room if you want to live there with us."

"Thank you Sweetie, you know I haven't made my mind up yet. Granny, my cousins and your Pawpaw Travis have asked me the same thing. I tell you what, for now why don't you just keep me a cozy spot available for visits?"

"Sure, Dad."

I see a golden archway with what looks like a portal the same size as the one on Angel's Mountain. It's large enough to walk an army through. In this case hundreds of kids that are all patiently waiting in front of a closed portal.

"What's going on Uriel, why is it closed?"

"All portals that lead to the outside of Heaven are only open by the instruction of God. Just watch."

I see two Warrior Angels standing directly in front of the portal; they both jam their swords in the ground and then lift their hands in praise to God for only a few seconds when suddenly the face of the portal turns to liquid.

Both Angels sheath their swords as they walk through with a stampede of size four sandals running behind them headed for the open portal.

28

The Beach

As we stand in line behind several hundred kids all flowing through the open portal, I notice Moushie and Rex with both spider monkeys close behind disappear into the crowd.

"Hey Uriel, is it okay to bring our animals through the portal?"

"Sure it is; they love the beach."

"So I take it Max and Hollywood have made this trip before."

"Daddy, they've been here several times with Pawpaw Travis, and he even brings Cuddles the grizzly bear here lately. Pawpaw said he can't leave Cuddles at home anymore because he sits and pouts the whole time he's gone. And the kids love riding Cuddles, especially when he swims in the Sea of Glass. As a matter of fact, Dad, you're in for another treat."

"What, what kind a treat?"

I feel Lori tap me on the shoulder, and as I turn around she's pointing back behind us. I see two riders approaching on horseback, and wouldn't you know it, a great big grizzly walking in front of the riders. It's Dad, Uncle Spike, and Cuddles.

Lori takes off running, clearly excited to see Dad. I guess I can't get my head wrapped around her being my sister and that's her dad too.

"Hey Chado, you should have seen how excited she was when your dad came walking through the gate when they first met. Remember now, she was raised here in Heaven by your Grandfather Pat, and has been waiting on your mom and dad to get here. Your dad just made it here first."

As I turn and watch my sister running to greet Dad, I hear her shout with a loud voice, full of excitement.

"Hey, Daddy you made it!" She runs past Cuddles, giving him a quick scratch on the head. I watch Dad as he takes his foot out of the stirrup and Lori using it to launch herself up on his horse. As soon as she was seated behind the saddle, she wraps her arms around Dad placing her face against his back.

"I didn't know if you would make it in time, Daddy. I'm so glad you came."

"Oh, Sweetie, you know I wouldn't miss a chance to come see you and Summer. Chado's homecoming beach party was a good excuse to get out this way, and on top of that, you know how much Cuddles loves the beach!"

Both horses bow allowing everyone to dismount.

"Hey, Pop, did you train those horses to do that?"

"No, they came fully loaded like a high dollar luxury car you would buy: power steering, air, and also rising and lowering capabilities."

We all burst out laughing at my silly dad!

"Glad y'all came, Pop."

"Chado, we wouldn't miss out on this for nothing."

After he gives Summer a great big hug, he reaches up with his arms out toward Rosie. She stands up on the back of Hollywood and jumps, Dad catches her in the air, swings her around placing her on his shoulders, with her giggling the whole time.

The other five kids get Uncle Spike to help them out of the saddle, all wanting to ride on the back of Cuddles.

As I take in this happy scene, I look over at Uriel as we smile at each other, "I know Chado, God's blessings are unending..."

Walking through the portal holding on to the reigns of Hollywood, I quickly turn around mid-step through the opening, so I can watch his big beautiful face appear as he passes through this strange, liquid membrane of the portal.

Seeing these constant miracles of God's handiwork, I have a brief vision, or maybe just a thought of somehow sharing what I'm experiencing with the world. If they only knew the love, joy, peace and happiness that God has waiting here, they would turn from the wickedness of the world and seek His face.

I hear the thoughts of Uriel, *"Yes Chado! That's right! The generations have turned away from God's Word and think it's foolish. Lucifer has subtly fooled people for so long they have become their own gods. Hell will be expanded to make room for the wicked, unless they escape his trap."*

* * *

As we all step through the portal, I see hundreds of kids running in different directions across the white sand. Hollywood nudges me with his nose as he wants me to move along. "Okay big fellow, I'm going."

Dad heads over toward a stone table under several palm trees with Cuddles waddling along behind him, and kids still perched on his back.

Looking around as I stand in awe, the beauty of this place can't be real. *"How can this be?"* The Planet of Heaven looks like it's hovering several miles above the crystal clear Sea of Glass.

"Summer, can you pinch me and wake me out of this dream?"

"I can pinch you, but this is no dream, Dad."

As I continue to gaze at the unending beauty, I remember how it looked from space when Allayer and Nipper were bringing me in. This beach looked like it was a circle around the entire circumference of the planet. And the water beneath was like an ocean floating in space. It literally looked like a giant block of water, and the white ring was centered under the planet, with the water on both sides of the ring all hovering in space.

I feel Hollywood nudge me again, "What do you want bud?" He reaches around and grabs the leather strap on his saddle with his teeth, then letting go, he starts nickering.

"Oh, I'm sorry Hollywood; you want that ole saddle off!"

I take his bridle off and as I'm un-strapping the saddle, he turns and rubs his head against my back; I guess his way to say thanks. No sooner had I thrown his saddle on the ground than he and the other three horses trot off to the seashore.

"So what do you think Son, it's pretty nice wouldn't you say?"

"Oh my goodness, Pop, it's unbelievable."

As we all lay back under the palm trees taking in the beauty, I see several kids gathering huge seashells.

"Hey Dad those look like the ones we use to get down in Florida."

"Yeah, I remember that, you and your brother would run around the house irritating everybody. Y'all were constantly blowing in them, it was okay for a while, but good-night... after a while it would hit a nerve!"

We all chuckle and continued watching the kids. I notice they were carefully stacking the shells in small groups making sure the sizes were placed in a certain order and direction.

"Hey Summer, what's up with the kids stacking the seashells? I see other groups of kids doing the same thing down the beach."

"Oh, they're getting ready for the symphony."

"A symphony?"

"Yeah, later tonight God will change direction of the wind and as it blows perfectly through each seashell, the sound is like a musical symphony. The melody will penetrate the hearts of the children and they will each fall into a deep sleep. God then allows them to have unique dreams, each one designed special for each child."

"Wow! So it's kind of like a lullaby?"

"Yes, that's right."

"Well they must love it, because they sure are busy about their work."

I see the horses standing belly deep in the water with kids lined up, each taking turns jumping, cutting flips, and diving off their backs. Not far away, Cuddles is floating on his back with Moushie, Rex and several kids all laying across his big fat tummy.

"Uncle Spike, where did the spider monkeys get off to?"

Just as he points directly over us, Clyde drops a coconut hitting me right in the stomach!

"You little rascals, I'm going to shave your tails!"

They both let out a screech while scurrying down the tree, and then hide behind my dad.

"Pop, your monkeys are spoiled worse than Cuddles."

Lori gets up brushing the sand off her backside. "Well, would anyone care to go swimming with the kiddos?"

"I would! Come on Uriel; let's show these kids how to cut a proper flip from the back of a horse."

As we make our way over to the edge of the shoreline I ask, "Hey Summer, before I get in the water, what about the sea monsters the kids were talking about, where are they?"

"Oh Dad, you big baby; I thought you used to be a great and fearless deep-sea diver."

"Well I don't remember having to deal with sea monsters!"

"Big brother, the sea monsters are a lot like Cuddles, very large but harmless. You do know that God has endowed all creatures here in Heaven with a kind heart."

"Well Sis, but aren't we kind of on the outside of Heaven?"

"Trust me; this is definitely still a part of Heaven."

"Yeah, I have to agree, this is so awesome. But when will we get to see the sea creatures?"

"You'll see that tomorrow Dad; God's going to open the tunnel."

"A tunnel? Where could there be a tunnel? All I see is beach and water."

Uriel smiles, "Have patience Little Soul, have patience."

* * *

As we strip down to our linen clothes and head for the water, I notice something very different about Uriel. I hesitate to ask until I get a good look at his chest, shoulders, and back.

He climbs up on Hollywood and as he turns around getting ready to bail off, I'm absolutely positive now.

Uriel takes a normal little dive into the pristine water and as he surfaces he's smiling. "I know Chado, they're gone... All

315

my scars are gone. After your latest story, God removed the last of my scars. Hallelujah to the King! I am healed and renewed!"

I stand in ankle deep water, watching this mighty Warrior Angel gently help the toddlers, one by one, onto Hollywood's back. With each movement, Uriel's huge muscular back flexes, showing no sign of the deep lacerations that previously covered his skin. My heart is filled with joy as I acknowledge the love and healing power of God. Suddenly, without any warning I'm overwhelmed with sadness and humility. With this great heaviness pressing down I am forced to my knees. Now feeling the cool water flowing across my legs I bow in humility. With the sensation of hypnosis, I close my eyes as crystal clear visions start to play out.

I'm standing in the midst of each battle watching Uriel as he protected me from the dark principalities of hell. With each injury from the spears and swords of the demonic fallen angels, I feel a deeper sense of humility and sorrow; knowing my wrong choices had brought this pain upon my Guardian Angel.

I lift my hands toward Heaven, *"God, how can I ever repay Uriel for his pain, loyalty and love, as You, O Lord, had him watch over me?"* With my eyes still closed I feel the touch of someone as they grab my hands.

"Little Soul, stand up, let your heart be filled with joy." As I open my eyes, there's no one there; "Hey, who just touched me? Am I losing my mind?" All the kids and Uriel are still playing and swimming around the horses. Could that have been God? Was I just now touched by the Holy Spirit? *"Dear Lord, are you still here?"*

I suddenly feel a gentle breeze coming from behind me and I watch as it creates ripples on the still water. I hear the laughter of the children cease as they all stop playing and become silent with all eyes on the growing ripples. As I look up and down the beach, every kid has their attention on the wind that now seems to be going in circles just a few yards from shore.

"Hey Uriel, what's going on?"

He smiles as he points over at the swirling whirlpool of water. Summer and Lori walk up and stand beside me.

"Dad, you're going to love this."

"Love what; what's going on?

Lori whispers, "Chado, we thought God was going to wait until tomorrow to open the tunnel."

"You mean He's about to do it now?"

"Yep, God just showed up!"

* * *

As we continue to watch, a very small water spout appears in the center of the whirlpool. Now gathered behind us, hundreds of kids start cheering and clapping.

The small waterspout resembling a miniature tornado starts growing, getting taller and wider with each passing second. As I stand in awe looking up at this 500 foot pillar of water, "Hey guys this must be how the children of Israel felt when they witnessed the parting of the Red Sea."

"Yeah Dad, or maybe when they followed the pillar of fire by night and the pillar of clouds by day across the desert."

I feel someone grab my hand and as I look down it's the green eyed toddler, "Hey, my Pawpaw, would you hold me?"

"You bet Sweetie." I pick Rosie up and place her on my shoulders, with her letting out a cute little giggle.

"How's that Sweetie?"

"Thank you my Pawpaw, I can really see good from here." As I start feeling a strong wind coming from behind us, Rosie is now clinching onto the hair of my head.

"It will be over in a second Pawpaw, God's moving the water."

I notice the sea is receding; the wind is actually moving the water back, away from the sea shore.

Rosie points as the giant water spout moves offshore leaving a tunnel exposed. "There it is Pawpaw; we get to see the sea monsters today!"

I follow as everyone heads through and down the long tunnel. It appears to lay on the bottom just like the pipelines we use to lay in the Gulf of Mexico. The only difference, this pipeline is transparent and large enough to drive a semi-truck through. As we continue to descend deeper, fish of all species are swimming up to the children.

"Hey Pawpaw, you can put me down, I want to pet the fish."

"Pet the fish; Sweetie you can't pet the fish, they're on the other side of the tunnel."

I gently set Rosie down; she looks back at me grinning from ear to ear, turns running over to the side. A huge grouper that looked to be four or five hundred pounds sees Rosie and immediately swims up directly in front of her.

"Oh, so you mean you're going to play like you're petting the fish."

She lets out a funny little laugh, turns and sticks her hand through the transparent tunnel wall. The grouper acts like they're lifelong friends as he gets close enough for Rosie to start rubbing his head.

At this point I feel I've seen it all, until I catch a glimpse of a large shadow appearing in the distance.

"Hey Summer, what the heck is that?"

Before Summer can answer, I see several more giant shadows appear, and they all seem to be heading in our direction.

"Hey Rosie, could you pull your hand back in please, it's making Pawpaw nervous."

"Oh, Pawpaw, they're friends and there's nothing to be afraid of. They won't hurt us."

"Dad the one in the middle, well I think God calls that species the Leviathan."

"My goodness, he's huge!"

Summer and Lori start laughing. "What's so funny?"

"Dad, that's just a baby."

"What, you have got to be kidding; it's the size of a railroad tanker."

"Just wait, its mommy and daddy will be along soon."

The other large shadows come into view; it's a school of giant white whales. They swam straight up to a group of kids doing the same thing as Rosie. Their little arms dangling on the other side of the tunnel looking like fish bait.

"So what do you think Dad, ready to pet a fish?"

"Give me a second; I'm still trying to get a handle on the kid's safety."

The baby leviathan gets close enough for me to make out its features. Thinking back on memories of dinosaur pictures, I've never seen anything that even comes close to this animal. Its scales looks like a warrior's shield, all layered like tiles of a roof, fastened together in a way that could never be penetrated by a spear or sword. Its head shaped like a crocodile with two sets of jawbones overlapping one another. Several rows of teeth resemble those of a great white shark. Its tail is flat and wide like a whale allowing it to move with great speed.

This giant swims right up to Rosie, gently nudging her friend the grouper out of its way.

"Come on Pawpaw, come pet Tizzy."

"Okay Sweetie, is your friend Tizzy a boy or a girl?

Rosie turns cupping her hand and whispering, "She's a girl, silly willy."

I chuckle at Rosie, and slowly stick my hand through the side of the tunnel, peering into the fiery red eyes of this prehistoric beast.

Tizzy the sea monster, now becoming my new friend, moves closer and allows me to touch its mighty forehead. Just as I was getting used to the whole petting a sea monster thing, I swear Tizzy winked at me just before she swam off.

"Wasn't that fun my Pawpaw?"

"Yes Sweetie, that was awesome. Let's go catch up with Summer and Lori."

We continue several more fathoms deeper, (for you land lovers, one fathom is around six feet). At this point of our journey we seem to be a couple hundred feet down. The kids are having a blast running back and forth, some pointing out their favorite fish or sea monsters, others still reaching through petting whatever fish that comes along.

As we catch up to Summer, "Hey Dad, check out that family of sea turtles; isn't this beautiful?"

"Yes Sweetie, I could have never imagined anything as spectacular as this."

"Look, look, I see Tizzy's parents coming."

When I thought I've seen it all, Tizzy the leviathan swims out to meet her parents and she looks like a minnow swimming beside a shark.

I hear my Dad and Uncle Spike coming up behind us, "Now that's a full grown fish right there, wouldn't you think?"

We all are laughing while admiring the biggest fish in Heaven.

After spending some quality time with family and friends at fifty fathoms, we see the kids all start heading back up the tunnel.

"What do you think guys? Are y'all ready to head back up?"

"Sure Dad, but before we go I want to show you one other fish."

"Okay, where is it?"

"Hang on big brother. Okay, do it Summer."

Summer pulls out a small conch sea shell and starts to blow through it. She actually played sort of a melody that sounded pretty awesome.

"Okay, what now guys?"

I see Lori point, "There he is. Come on old timer, over here." A giant white whale slowly swims up, stopping just on the other side within arm's reach.

"Go ahead Dad, give him some love."

I reach through rubbing his side, and when he feels my touch he backs up until his left eye is within inches of my face. As I gaze into the eye of this whale, I sense a mysterious kindness coming from another one of God's special creatures.

He turns and slowly swims away disappearing into the dark blue depths.

"Okay Summer, why did you want me to meet this guy?"

"Daddy, do you remember Jonah being swallowed by the great fish?"

"Sure Sweetie, Jonah refused to preach in Nineveh so God used the fish to get his attention, I believe he stayed in his belly for three days and then the great fish spit him out on dry land. After his whale ride he journeyed for three more days to Nineveh, finally fulfilling God's command."

"Well Dad, the white whale you just petted, he was the mighty fish that swallowed Jonah."

"You mean God brought a whale from Earth."

"Yep, He brought a lot of creatures from Earth."

"Hey Chado, you know that horse you've been riding."

"Sure Pop, what about him?"

"His real name is Comanche and he was owned by the US army back in the year 1868. He actually survived the Battle of Little Bighorn. He was named for his bravery and loyalty in the fight with the Comanche. We believe God was disappointed with the wars between the American Indians and the horse soldiers, but He loved Hollywood enough to bring him to Heaven."

"So Hollywood was at the Battle of Little Bighorn, wow, and that's where Custer saw his last sunrise!"

Almost back to the beach I hear Rosie, "Who was Custer, Pawpaw?"

"Oh, he was just an ole arrogant soldier that let his pride get the best of him. He and his men were killed in one of the many foolish battles fought back on Earth."

* * *

As we walk out of the tunnel, kids scatter in ten different directions. Moushie and Rex run up to get a quick pet, then dash off to catch up with Dad.

"Hey Daddy, would you like to swim a bit more, go hang out with Pawpaw Travis or maybe get our campsite ready for the night?"

"Hey that's right, we're outside the wall and we get to see the night sky. Yeah, let's get our camp ready."

"Okay Pop, you want to help gather some firewood?"

"Firewood, we can have a fire in Heaven?"

Lori and Summer chuckle, "Brother, we can have or do just about anything we want, as long as it's pleasing to God."

I hadn't noticed before, but there is drift wood lying everywhere. As I happily start gathering the scattered wood I hear Lori, "Hey Chado, watch."

I turn and see the giant water spout moving back in our direction. As the last kid walks out of the tunnel the waterspout centers directly over the opening. I feel a breeze coming from across the great sea and at the same time the waterspout decreases in height getting smaller and smaller until it's completely gone. As the wind continues to blow in our direction, the dry land we had just walked across is now covered with water. We all watch this miracle of God as the entrance disappears.

"Hey Uriel, is it always like this?"

"What do you mean?"

"Well, it just seems like the miracles are constant, every time you turn around there is something cool happening."

"Let me put it like this, Heaven itself is a miracle. The little toddler, Rosie is a miracle. You're a miracle. So to answer your question, is it always like this? Yes, it's unending. Chado, you need to remember, when God loves someone, its depth, height or width can't be measured. He wants to continually please His children here in Heaven. So yes, Little Soul, it's unending."

"Thanks Uriel,"

"Hey Chado, hand me that last piece of driftwood. We need to hurry and get back before the concert starts."

"A concert, I thought it was going to be a symphony!"

"Well, the concert is first with the children's choir, and I don't want you to miss any of it. Well truth be known, I don't want to miss Rosie singing. I just love to hear that toddler sing!"

As we approach our campsite sheltered by the coconut and palm trees, I see Dad had already started the fire.

"Hey Uriel, what are those kids picking up out of the sand?"

"Remember how God fed the children of Israel with manna when they were in the wilderness?"

"Yeah sure. Is that manna they're picking up?"

"No I don't think so, it's probably sand shroons."

"Sand shroons, what the heck are sand shroons?"

Uriel starts laughing, "You will love this. God sends special food to His kids, I've been around from the beginning and He still surprises even the Angels with all sorts of delicacies. But I do believe those are sand shroons the kids are gathering."

"So what do they taste like?"

"That's the funny part."

"What do you mean?"

"Well just say your favorite taste is dark chocolate, oranges, or maybe like your dad the taste of fried quail. Whatever it might be, when you bite into a sand shroon that's what you taste. And get this, during your meal if you crave

324

something different, your next bite will explode your taste buds with whatever you're craving."

As I drop my arm load of fire wood, I can't help but laugh, thinking about this whole food thing.

"Hey Daddy, what's so funny."

"Ah nothing Sweetie, Uriel was just educating me on sand shroons and my funny bone got the best of me."

I was just about to find a comfortable spot to lay back when Cuddles, Moushie, Rex and the two spider monkeys plopped down right where I was about sit.

"Well guys, I hope I didn't trespass on your spot."

They all look up giving me some kind of silly animal grin. I walk up and give each one a good scratch, and as I observe Cuddles, I'm thinking bear skin rug, yeah, that could be comfortable. So I pat the giant bear on his wide forehead then slowly lie back against his thick soft fur.

AHHH, I could get use to this. "Cuddles I hope you don't mind if I use you as a pillow."

Summer and Lori walk up with a handful of sand shroons. "Here Dad, try this out."

Before I took a bite, "Let me see, what would be something I feel the desire to taste..."

"What's your favorite food, Dad?"

"I guess grilled steak and shrimp is my favorite."

"Well, take a bite and see what happens."

As I bite down and slowly start to chew, the bitter taste of olives fills my mouth. The two spider monkeys start screaming, jumping up and down on the back of Cuddles. The kids, Dad and everyone else burst out laughing.

"What the heck Summer, what did you just feed me?"

"Dad you forgot to give thanks."

"That's right, shame on me. Heavenly Father, forgive me for not remembering to give thanks. I pray you bless the kids that picked these sand shroons that you have provided. Amen."

"Okay Daddy, chill out, and try it again."

"Are you certain it's not going to be bitter?"

"Trust me Dad, down the hatch."

"Okay, just for you Summer."

As I tried it again, the awesome taste of steak and shrimp screamed from my taste buds. "Wow... double wow, this is unbelievable! Can I have another?"

"Sure Pop, eat as much as your heart desires, just leave room for desert."

Leaning back against Cuddles, we watch the evening sun set, as we enjoyed a delicious dinner provided by our Maker.

I notice a group of around a hundred children line up behind the conch seashells, preparing for the evening concert. The wind suddenly stops blowing, the stillness brings a complete silence over the whole area. You could hear a pin drop.

I notice the toddler Rosie, with a childlike elegance, walks over and stands directly in front of the choir. A puff of wind hits my face from a different direction, another, and then another, now a steady soft breeze.

Summer leans over and whispers, "Dad, keep your eyes on the sun. Something special is about to happen."

As I stare at the setting sun directly behind the choir, I notice the sea looks like a sheet of glass reflecting the bright red clouds and two distant moons that have now appeared.

With only a sliver of the setting sun remaining, the light and reflections from the sea create a bright white cross that expands its light throughout the heavenly skies.

I feel the wind getting stronger as I begin to hear a multitude of different tones coming from the seashells. At the very second Rosie starts to sing the cross slowly begins to disappear.

The voice of this special little girl blends with the breath of the Holy Spirit, as it swirls through each of the shells. This heavenly duo is now creating a harmony like no other.

Just as the children's choir joins in, the light of the cross fades away. Feeling a sense of total peace, I lean back against the thick fur of a giant grizzly bear named Cuddles. My two favorite dogs are now laying their heads in my lap. I feel my sweet daughter's touch as she leans over and places her head on my shoulder.

Starring out into space, admiring the many planets and the twin moons that light up the night sky, I think back and realize how foolishly I lived my life on Earth, and wasted so many years. I should have spent my time sharing the Gospel, and trying my best to help draw more people to God. If the lost souls of Earth could only see and hear what I'm experiencing, they would turn from the wickedness of the world and run to Jesus.

"Hey Daddy, after I got killed, you and mom were in mourning. Do you remember having certain dreams?"

"Yeah, as a matter of fact I had quite a few dreams. Why do you ask?"

"Well, God allowed me to visit you and mom several times through dreams."

"Really, so they were real?"

"Yes, I don't know why but I could only come as a younger me, well I mean as a little girl."

"I know, each time I dreamed about you, you were around four or five years old."

"Daddy do you remember the hugs I gave you?"

"Oh yeah, the dreams were so real. I can even remember smelling your hair and feeling it on my face. But when I would suddenly wake up, the reality of you being gone would hit me hard. The pain and sickness would overtake me to a point that I would wail and cry out like I was dying. I guess I was really dying, or at least a part of me died with you when you were gone. You know Sweetie, as a dad I've always been a fixer. Something breaks, I would fix it. Any kind of problem that would come up, I could figure out how to make it better or fix it. When you died, I was helpless, I wanted so badly to fix it, but I couldn't. That was beyond anything I had ever dealt with. Through your death I was drawn closer to the Lord than I'd ever been and that's how I continued on through life. Summer, it took me a couple years before I could even look at your pictures without falling to pieces. Videos were out of the question; I would refuse to watch. I just couldn't bear the pain, it was too great. If I had only known for sure you were saved and were living here in Heaven, it would have made it a lot easier to deal with when we lost you."

"I'm so sorry Daddy; I know I put you and Mom through a lot."

"Hey that's okay Sweetie, just look at us now. We're laid back against a three thousand pound bear listening to a concert on a beach in Heaven!"

"I know, it's so awesome, and I can't wait for Mom to get here."

"Yes, she misses you really bad kiddo."

Daddy, the reason I brought up the dreams, is I feel God urging me, to remind you of one particular vision you had. I believe it's got something to do with the mission that God has you on."

"Okay Sweetie, you've got my attention."

"Well Dad, in your vision, you were standing in a national park, and I was riding on a school bus loaded with kids. As we were getting off the bus, I saw a small demon disguised as a kid throwing tiny spears over in the crowd. You turned from trying to find me and chased the demon away, throwing spears back at him.

Then a table was lowered from the sky and it had gold coins and large black ink pens lying on it. Several people stood around the table, and were to choose between taking the gold coins or the pens. Everyone else chose the coins, and you couldn't seem to make your mind up. Suddenly the table started to rise back up, and just before it was too late you jumped up and grabbed two pens. Then you were walking through the crowd crying out my name; that's when I ran up to you and in the middle of our hug, I had to suddenly vanish. At that very second, you saw a white flash that reminded you of an ole-timey black and white camera flash. During the brief blinding light you had a vision of a city laid waste from a nuclear blast.

Then the other vision in your dream, was about the old lady in a wheelchair. Her husband wheeled her up to you at her request. She held your hand and told you how much she enjoyed your songs. You suddenly fell to your knees and placed your head in her lap. As she started caressing your hair, you felt the Holy Spirit flood over you. Not realizing; that you were now laying your head in the lap of Jesus. Daddy, I don't know what these visions meant, but God wanted me to remind you of it right now."

"Well Sweetie, if God's been urging you to share that with me, it has to be something pretty significant. Summer, I'm hoping I'll find out soon what this whole mission is about. Maybe you're right, and the visions are somehow tied to all of this."

After enjoying several more beautiful songs, Rosie heads straight for Summer. As they embrace, she curls up in her arms and quickly falls asleep.

I look over at Uriel, "Hey bud, those kids are something really special, don't you think?"

"Yes they are, Little Soul. Yes they are."

The gentle wind continues to play a sweet lullaby, blowing through the seashells, and my eyelids begin to feel so heavy. I look around and everyone is fast asleep except for Uriel. He stands just a few feet away as if watching over us like a Sentinel, guarding a precious treasure. As I stare into the small campfire just before falling asleep, the visions Summer reminded me of, are now replaying in my mind.

Why was the table being lowered from the sky? Having to choose between the gold coins and pens, was this a test? Did I choose wisely? The demon disguised as a child throwing spears, is there a hidden message there? The blinding flash from the old camera and seeing the city laid waste, could this represent a nuclear war in the future of the Earth? I remember dark red blood covering skulls and piles of bones, and the sky behind the burned out and crumbling buildings had turned to a dark orange glow.

"Hey Chado, wake up. You were talking in your sleep. Hey get up, you need to see this!"

"Okay, okay, I'm up! What do you want me to see?"

Uriel whispers, "Follow me, Chado."

29

When Angels Sing

We walk away from the campfire a few feet, just enough to see clearly, while standing in the darkness under a canopy of stars and twin moons. I look up at this strange galaxy and I am awestruck by its beauty. The stars almost look close enough to reach out and touch.

"Uriel, this is beautiful."

"Yes it is something to behold, but viewing the stars wasn't why I woke you."

He suddenly bumps me in the ribs, points to our left down the beach and then to our right.

"Oh my goodness! What the heck Uriel?"

I see several hundred Angels pouring out of the sky from both directions. The roaring sound of their wings as they slow down to land reminds me of a distant rolling thunder. Their bright white and silver colored wings are glowing as they're reflecting the rays of light from the stars and moons.

I am totally speechless while watching the Host of Heaven as they all start to line up behind the conch seashells.

"Uriel, what's happening? Is this another concert? They're standing exactly where the children's choir was when they sang!"

Suddenly the voices of these Angels come together like nothing I've ever heard, "Holy Holy is the Lamb, the Lamb of God, Holy is He that sits on the Throne, Holy is the Lamb..."

I whisper. "Hey Uriel, I thought the kids were good, but this is unbelievable!"

He smiles as we both stand facing the choir, feeling the presence of the Holy Spirit getting stronger as it pours over us.

Just as I have the thought of waking Summer, I feel a gentle touch on my shoulder, and without looking back, I place my hand over the hand that's touching me. This doesn't feel like Summer's hand.

Without looking behind me, out of the corner of my eye, I now see the hand that's on my shoulder. It's the nail-scarred hand of Jesus! My Savior is here, and He's touching me!

At first, I'm shocked, frozen in my tracks. I'm not worthy to touch the strap of His sandal, and He has His hand on my shoulder. I want to turn around but I can't seem to move.

"Welcome, Little Soul."

As I hear His soft still voice, I fall to my knees, and slowly spin around in the sand. Being overwhelmed with His presence and my humility, I embrace my Lord around His legs. As I feel the soft cotton garment on my face and the presence of the Holy Spirit, tears of joy fill my eyes.

He kneels down and with a whisper, "Stand up friend; let your heart not be troubled, but rejoice and rest in my Father's love."

Reaching down with His nail-scarred hands, I take hold. My Savior helps me to my feet. I'm now staring into the eyes of Jesus.

"Little Soul, how about we three break bread, I'm sure you desire to know the mystery behind your journey." He smiles as he turns and heads for a bench and table made of palm wood near the camp fire.

Jesus reaches over in a wicker basket and retrieves one sand shroon. He lays it down on the table, grabs our hands, "Thank you Father for this blessing." While smiling he breaks

333

the shroon into three pieces, handing Uriel and me each a portion. After Jesus takes a couple bites, "I thirst for new wine."

Without having to call or chase Bennie the spider monkey to fetch the wine, the little furry wine bearer suddenly drops down out of a coconut tree, dragging Sampson's wine pouch straight over to Jesus.

After having a late night snack and a few sips of new wine while enjoying another concert, I have the thought, *I wish Summer, Lori, Dad, Uncle Spike and the kids were awake. They are missing out.*

"Hey Jesus, can I wake Summer and the children?"

"Not yet Little Soul, we have a journey that needs to be discussed."

"Okay, I understand."

"As you know, my Father has chosen you to take part in drawing millions away from the clutches of Lucifer. He has blinded God's very elect and they have drifted away from the truth. Satan's cleverness throughout history, and now in modern times, has explained away my love and replaced it with science and the theories of men. As we near the tribulation, this great falling away has to be stopped."

"Lord, I have always loved you, but I've walked the earth a sinful man, undeserving of anything. Why has God chosen me for this journey?"

Jesus smiles while placing His hand on my face. "Little Soul, my Father saw in you a pure heart and a strong desire for righteousness. Under the conviction of the Holy Spirit, you always humbled yourself before God and He was true to forgive your sins.

Little Soul, I ask you this; why did He choose Adam as the first man, Noah to build an Ark, Jonah to be swallowed by

334

the fish, or Moses to free the slaves? They were men that He chose to fulfill His purpose. He saw them as willing vessels with pure hearts."

"I am yours Lord, tell me what to do."

Suddenly a blinding bright light flashes behind us. I ask, "What was that?"

* * *

"Fear not Little Soul, we have company."

With my back to the campfire, I slide around in my seat looking in the direction of the fading flash.

Out of the darkness a mighty Lion appears. As he stands just on the other side of the fire, overwhelming fear and trembling washes over me. I fall to my knees as a man dying and began to cry. Again I feel the hand of Jesus on my shoulder as He whispers, "Weep not Little Soul. Behold! The Lion, King of Kings and Lord of Lords!"

As I look up wiping the tears from my eyes, the Lion is now standing only a couple feet away. In His mouth He's holding two scrolls. He takes another step closer and I suddenly remember my dream. The dream of the lion and the scroll is now unfolding before me. I reach out with my hands still trembling and the mighty Lion releases the scrolls, dropping them into the palms of my hands.

To my surprise he reaches down taking hold of my shirt with his giant teeth, and gently lifts me up from my knees. As I stand, He rubs His thick mane against my face and just as I reach out to touch His fur, He quickly turns and walks away. We all watch as He walked over and lies down in front of Summer and the kids.

"Little Soul, My Father wants you to go back to Earth and spend twenty-one days on God's Mountain where the Ark of Covenant rests. There you will write down everything you've seen and heard on your journey here. The Holy Spirit will overcome you and help you with His final message. Then you will duplicate the second scroll with the same message as the first. When the scrolls are complete at the end of the twenty-first day, you will follow Uriel and witness several events that will unfold on Earth.

Shortly after you'll be led on two different journeys. At the end of each, you will give the scrolls to two different people who are each caught between death and life.

Then you will walk through the portal of the damned. At the gates of Hell you will recognize the one that cheats death. He was one of your close friends back on Earth. He is an unbeliever but has been chosen to receive one of the scrolls.

You will meet a second person at the eleventh gate of Heaven. This believer that also cheats death will receive the other scroll. You will give the scrolls to these two chosen vessels with instructions.

As they rejoin the living on earth, they will both fall under great condemnation as they stand as My witnesses before a perverse world; many of which have ears but cannot hear, eyes but refuse to see, and hearts that have grown cold, without feeling.

Most assuredly, I say to you, this wicked and perverse generation shall not pass away before they see Heaven open up and the Angels of God ascending and descending upon the Son of man. The final days are at hand and there will be no hiding place from the wrath of my Father.

These two chosen vessels will be used to show the world through the Bloodline of the Scrolls. It's my Father's last offer before His coming."

As soon as Jesus finished telling me what was to take place, I see the Lion stand and slowly walk away. Before He is almost out of sight He turns, looks back and His left eye sparkled. It was like the Lion had just winked at me! I suddenly have a funny thought, *In the tunnel when Tizzy the sea monster winked at me, was that the Spirit of God in the Leviathan and now the Lion?*

I'm trying to stare through the darkness just to catch another glimpse. I notice a growing bright light coming from His direction. I hold my hand up trying to protect my eyes from the brilliance; it's becoming unbearable.

Just before the peak of a blinding flash, Jesus quickly steps in front of me, sheltering me from the light. His action reminds me of scripture, *"So it shall be, while My glory passes by, I will put you in the cleft of the rock and will cover you with My hand while I pass by."*

Jesus whispers, "My Father took the form of this great lion so He could walk among His children."

I suddenly realize this was the only way we could look into the eyes of God and live.

Jesus takes my hand, "Walk with me Little Soul, let us go to the water's edge and watch the rising sun."

As I stand beside the Savior of the world watching my first sunrise on the beach of Heaven, I'm overwhelmed with joy and thanksgiving.

I look over at Jesus as the first rays of sun peep over this crystal sea. His face seems to be glowing.

"Little Soul, are you staring?"

"Sorry Lord, I couldn't help myself."

Jesus starts laughing, "Hey, it's okay Chado. I get that a lot."

"Lord, you're too funny!"

As we stand watching the sunrise, I hear a familiar voice. It's Rosie; she has awakened and had already joined in with the Angel choir.

"Lord, that Angel choir is so awesome, and little Rosie, she can sure enough sing."

"Chado, do you recognize that song?"

"Yes, that's Living Water. That's a song I wrote! Well a song You gave me to write."

"We thought you might like hearing it performed by an Angel band, and it's a nice going away present. Speaking of going away presents, look down the beach."

I turn, and a couple hundred yards out, I see a huge dog running full speed along the water's edge, with the occasional splash as the dog edges over hitting the shallows. "Lord is that your dog?"

"No Little Soul, that's *your* dog. You do remember Buck don't you?"

"Buck, my faithful old dog Buck from Earth! Lord, you let Buck come to Heaven?"

Jesus starts laughing, why wouldn't I let that ole warrior come to Heaven, he is a good dog!"

A few feet before Buck got to me, he stops and does his old trick of crawling on his belly and grinning, yep grinning. After a bit of rolling around in the sand and a bunch of dog licks, Jesus taps me on the shoulder.

"Chado, I want you to bring Buck with you on your mission, he will play a big part in protecting you from the hell hounds when you and Uriel pass through the gates of Hell."

"Okay Lord, we've got fallen angels, demons and now we have to deal with hell hounds?"

Jesus chuckles, "You will be fine, just remember Who has your back."

"I understand, Oh yeah, one other thing Lord..."

"Name it, Little Soul."

"I just want to thank you, Jesus."

"What would you be thanking me for, Chado?"

"Well Lord, through the years in my prayers, I have thanked You for so many different things. The main one was thanking You for what you did on Calvary. But anyway Lord, I never thought I would be standing beside You, I mean in person, here and now. So I would like to thank You for it all!"

Jesus reaches over, wraps His arms around me giving me a great big hug. "Little Soul, you have a journey ahead of you. Go say your goodbyes to everyone and be about My Father's work."

I turn and head back to the camp, shaking hands and hugging necks, until I get to Summer.

"When will you come back, Daddy?"

"I'm not real sure Sweetie; I won't be long if I can help it."

"Is it dangerous?"

"Well I'm not real sure about that either. I have to write some stuff down on these two scrolls and then deliver one to someone at Hell's gates and the other one to another person at the eleventh gate of Heaven. Hey don't worry; I'll have Uriel and Buck with me. By the way, have you seen Uriel?"

She points down the beach. "Yeah Pop, there he is standing in front of that portal."

As I turn around, to my surprise Uriel has lost the street garment and has gained his body armor, shield, sword and his huge wings.

"Summer, it looks like it's that time. I believe Uriel is ready to go. Give me a hug, Sweetie."

"Come on Daddy, I'll walk you to the portal."

Just before we get to the threshold I hear the pitter pats of bare feet. "Wait my Pawpaw! Wait!"

Little Rosie jumps up, hugging me as though I was leaving forever.

"Hey little one, you were really making Pawpaw proud when I heard you singing with the Angel choir this morning."

"Thank you my Pawpaw!"

"Rosie, I want you to watch over Summer while I'm gone, and as soon as I can, I'll be back."

"Okay my Pawpaw. I will."

Uriel nudges me with one of his wings, "Let's go Chado."

As we step through the portal I hear the fading voices of Summer and Rosie, "We Love You..."

The End of the Beginning...

Russell L. Martin, Biography

Russell L. Martin, known to his family and friends as Rusty, was born and raised in Grant Parish, located in central Louisiana. His family lived near the poverty level throughout his childhood. With a limited education and a strong desire for a better life, he hired out with a traveling construction company that installed oil and gas pipelines all across the U.S.A. Starting out at the bottom of the food chain, working as a laborer with little to no money, he would camp out near creeks and rivers to survive the high cost of living away from home. When his strong work ethics became noticed by his supervisors, he was allowed to advance and work in all phases of the oil and gas industry.

After several years of working on land, Rusty decided that it was time to get a taste of installing pipelines in the Gulf of Mexico. To further his education in this part of the industry, he received commercial diving degrees at The Ocean Corporation in Houston, TX. After only a couple years working in the Gulf as a diver he went back to land-lay operations, due to a family crisis. He continued working freelance for multiple pipeline companies, until finally retiring after 34 years in the oil and gas industry.

It was not until he decided to settle back down where his roots of life started in central Louisiana, that he finally surrendered to becoming an author. His love for God, paired with many strange events throughout his life, left him with a gift of telling amazing stories. He has stated, and truly believes, God led him to the keyboard of his old work laptop. Surprising his family and friends, he unveiled a hidden talent that no one realized he possessed, including himself.

After writing the Christian novel, "*Scars of My Guardian Angel*", several proof readers were asked to give an unbiased opinion of the book. Their incredible reaction and positive reviews inspired this new author to continue writing, what is now called "The Portal Series". The second book, "*Bloodline of the Scrolls*", was self-published in December of 2018. Russell is now writing a third book of the series, "*Revelation of the Scrolls*", with intention of publishing in 2019.

Thirteen wonderful Christian songs are among the collection of Russell's writing. He and his wife enjoy sharing them in local churches around their community. Playing his Taylor guitar and singing Christian music is truly a deep passion of his heart.

Rusty and his wife, Laura, live a humble and quiet life on a few acres nestled in the middle of Kisatchie National Forest. They enjoy spending time with their two beautiful horses, Ellie Mae and Hollywood. This couple also loves three stray dogs they rescued out of the deep woods. The one they call Daisy Lou, looks like she might be a Redbone Coonhound. Another, Moushie, the most recent addition, looks very much like a Mountain Cur. Lastly is Benji-faced Nibbles, well he's just a dog with a cute little underbite.

Feel free to join us and continue your experience throughout "The Portal Series"

Our website:
www.russellmartinauthor.com
has links to several Social Media platforms,
including Facebook and Twitter.

- Please share your thoughts and feelings with friends and love ones after reading: *Scars of My Guardian Angel*

- Your honest review on Amazon, or the platform where you purchased the book, is greatly helpful to our ministry.

- We welcome any communication with the author. Read blogs and updates, and stay up on the release of book two.

- Any request for the author to speak with your organization, feel free to make contact through the above web site.

Available Now, Book Two of "The Portal Series"
Bloodline of the Scrolls

Coming in 2019, Book Three of "The Portal Series"
Revelation of the Scrolls

Made in the USA
Lexington, KY
09 March 2019